SONG OF THE
MEADOWLARK

Treasured Romances
by Sherri Wilson Johnson

* * *

To Dance Once More

Song of the Meadowlark

Coming Soon...
To Laugh Once More

SONG OF THE
MEADOWLARK

SHERRI WILSON JOHNSON

OAKTARA

Waterford, Virginia

Song of the Meadowlark

Published in the U.S. by:
OakTara Publishers, P.O. Box 8, Waterford, VA 20197
www.oaktara.com

Cover design by Yvonne Parks at www.pearcreative.ca
Cover images © shutterstock.com: closeup of gorgeous young female/Yuri
Arcurs; meadowlark sings in the morning sunrise/Dustie
Author photo © 2012 by Kayla Johnson Photography

ISBN: 978-1-60290-327-2

Printed in the U.S.A.

* * *

In loving memory of my dad,
REV. WILLIAM (BILL) ARTHUR WILSON,
who passed away while I was writing this novel.
His love (expressed by pinching my nose or poking me in the side)
and his knowledge of the Word of God challenged me
to be the best person I could be.

Acknowledgments

To my Lord and Savior, Jesus Christ—thank you for giving your life for me and for answering the Prayer of Jabez (1 Chronicles 4:9-10) I've been praying regularly.

To my husband, Dan, who keeps on believing that I can write more stories, for always being my hero.

To Kayla and Seth, for putting up with my romantic silliness and for helping me choose the artwork for my book covers. May you see that perseverance always brings rewards.

To all of my family and friends, for your love and support.

To Ramona Tucker (OakTara), for being so amazing!

To Norm Rohrer, my writing instructor with the Christian Writers Guild, for teaching me how to write, for telling me the truth, and for prompting me to show (not tell) my story.

To my social media friends, for your support through sharing about my books.

1

June
Lake Murray, South Carolina

Cora Buchanan stared out the paned window of her bedroom at Lake Murray through a mist of rain and sighed, her olive green eyes filling with salty tears. This picturesque place had become a prison to her.

Tossing her dark hair over one shoulder, she moved across the room to her bed. Lying on her stomach on her flowery comforter, she remembered how it had all happened. For the first time since then, she scanned the tattered pages of her scrapbook, memories flooding her with weariness. It had been such an innocent time.

On the next page, she saw the pictures from her twenty-first birthday party. Twenty-one had seemed so old and wise at the time, and Panama City, Florida, like the big city. She'd worked awhile in college and considered herself a perceptive woman. But her middle name should have been Naïve, since she didn't see some people for who they really were.

Cora rolled over onto her back, propping herself up on her pillows. She raised her knees and placed the scrapbook on her legs. Her eyes found the picture of her running in the town relay race with *him,* and she remembered the pulled calf muscle that still hurt on cold winter days. As she turned the page, she saw her engagement pictures and the newspaper clipping from the wedding announcement. She remembered that day like yesterday, her parents' disapproval forever seared into her mind.

She closed the scrapbook, and it fell to the floor with a thud, another chapter now over in her life. Three years had passed since Cora's marriage to *him,* and she now lived, as a twenty-five-year-old woman, with her in-laws. As she sat up on the edge of her bed, she wondered where to go from here. She couldn't wait any longer to move on.

Cora left her room and entered the earth-toned den. The Buchanans were watching *Wheel of Fortune* on the television.

"It's been a year tonight." Cora knew she didn't have to explain what she meant. She plopped on the couch next to Judy. "I think it's time I finally do something."

"What do you plan to do?" Judy looked up from the television and patted Cora's knee.

Cora pushed her hair behind her ears. "A good place to start would be to go home and take time to figure out what to do and how to make amends with Mom and Dad. I want them to forgive me."

"I hope they're ready. You could not have predicted the future," Ben said tenderly.

"I'm tired of this wedge between us. Three years is a long time, but I've feared the arguments that will, without a doubt, occur."

Judy nodded. "That's the mature thing to do."

"I hope so, Mom."

With her mind made up, Cora felt a load lifted off her shoulders, like at the end of a tornado warning. Though she still hoped deep inside things would change before she left for Florida, she doubted they would.

* * *

"Hey, Anne."

"Cora. I'm glad you called. What's going on?"

"I'm coming home." Cora folded her pajamas and stuffed them into her suitcase.

"You are?" The voice of her best friend was incredulous.

"Yep. Clark's been gone a year, and I can't wait around here any longer." She opened another drawer, took out her socks and pantyhose, and stashed them in the side pocket of the suitcase.

"Are you going to file for divorce?"

"No. I don't want to make such a drastic move. I figure I can come home and try to patch things up with Mom and Dad. If Clark returns, he'll know where to find me." Cora went into her bathroom and started packing her skin-care products and extra makeup into her duffle bag.

"I'm so sorry you have to go through all of this. I know it's driving you crazy with him missing."

"That's the hardest part. I don't know if he's dead somewhere or living in another country with a new woman." She examined her reflection in the mirror. Not even the flecks of gold in her eyes could disguise the bags underneath them. *I look like a ninety-year-old woman.*

"No, don't think that way. I'm sure he's fine....but I guess that doesn't make you feel any better."

"Not really." Cora laughed.

"When are you going to be here?"

"I'm leaving in the morning. I should be home sometime tomorrow night."

"Okay. Call when you get into town. Or from the road if you need someone to chat with while you're driving."

"I will." Cora hung up the phone. She picked up the cardboard box by her bed, added the books off her bookshelf, and the scrapbook from the floor. Then she sat on the bed, looking through her too-often-forgotten Bible, and cried.

* * *

"That looks like everything." Cora shut the trunk of her '68 candy-apple red Camaro and glimpsed the pain in her in-laws' eyes. "Don't look at me that way. I told you I plan to be back soon."

"We hate to see you go. It worries us that you're driving by yourself. The big rigs own the road. The highway can be very dangerous, and your car is old." Judy brushed a hair from Cora's misty eyes.

"Mom, my car will be fine. I promise to drink plenty of coffee if I get sleepy. I'll call you when I stop to eat and rest. I plan to drive until Atlanta, just four hours or so. Then to Columbus—five-and-a-half hours—and stay the night."

"We know you'll be careful, dear. Here, take this. You may need it." Ben handed something to Cora.

"What's this?"

"Some money," Judy answered. "It isn't much, but we hated to send you off without something."

"You can't give me money. I'm fine. I have all I need, really. Please, take this back." Cora tried to return the gift.

"No, you keep it. If you don't use it on your way to Panama City, you may need it on your way back." Ben pushed against Cora's hand.

"Okay, but I hate taking it from you." Cora's heart ripped from her chest as she looked at Ben and Judy. "Guess I'd better go. Thanks again for everything you've done for me."

"Don't you think for a moment we're upset with you for leaving. You've waited long enough. It's time for you to move on." Judy's eyes filled with tears.

"Even if I do decide to stay with my parents, I'll never stop loving you both. My heart will always be here with you. You've been a lifesaver."

"We wish you well, Cora." Ben squared his jaw.

Cora hugged both Ben and Judy tightly, then got in to the driver's side of her car. Careful not to tear the rip in her leather seat any further, she shut the door, cranked up, and drove away without looking back. She had to do this, though it could very well prove to be the hardest thing she'd ever done. Tears cascaded from her eyes like waterfalls.

Cora drove through town—down Columbia Avenue, glancing at the places she'd become accustomed to as she headed toward I-26 East. Merging onto the highway symbolized the launching of her new life—slow, cautious at first, and then no looking back. Moving away from Lake Murray took more out of her than moving away from her childhood home in Florida had. She pondered Ben and Judy's faith. They seemed so sure God would work out her life. She wished her faith could be that strong. She still had so many doubts....

An hour and a half later, Cora entered Georgia and smiled at the welcome sign with the giant peach. As she drove through one small town after another, she listened to country music on her radio—not her music of choice, but definitely the most available. The steel guitar and fiddle tugged at her heart as she went over railroad tracks, past historic battlefields and glorious pastureland.

The temperature held at 85 degrees, and Cora enjoyed the sunshine beaming down on her car. She kept the windows rolled down and let the wind blow her cares away. White, fluffy clouds painted pictures across the blue Georgia sky. She hoped the weather would remain clear until she got to Florida. She hated driving in the rain.

Another two hours went by as Cora admired the beauty of the land—pine trees and crape myrtles, black-eyed Susans and old oak trees. She cracked up at the mailboxes along the way—a giant emerald green fish, a miniature mail truck, and a mailbox about the size of a washing machine box. She smiled when an old man in overalls climbed down out of his tractor to retrieve his mail from his cow mailbox. "Aww, he's so cute."

Outside of Athens, she took a second look at a teenage boy who rode a motorbike in the pasture of a farm while his pet Yorkie chased him. "I've seen it all now. Oh, I can't wait to tell…no one would believe me." She laughed.

Eventually the green grasses and golden hay made way for the city. Her stomach growled, and she decided to have lunch before getting into Atlanta. Stopping at Arby's, she ordered a roast-beef sandwich, fries, and a Coke. The cold drink almost burned the inside of her throat as it slid down. She added a cherry turnover for dessert, deciding to save it for later.

Rubbing her bleary eyes, she jumped back into the car again, stopped for gas and to check her tires, then headed toward I-75 South. She'd really have to pay attention to make sure she didn't miss I-85 South since there was no actual exit, just a certain lane heading south. It was so long since she'd driven through here.

Cora squinted in the afternoon sun and talked to herself. "Why did I forget my sunglasses?" Cars zipped by like something from a futuristic movie. "Good grief, where are they all in such a hurry to go?"

Once on I-85 and heading in the right direction, Cora battled construction along the highway. The roads were extra narrow with cement blocks along the shoulder to keep cars from veering into the construction zone. "Oh, I hate this!" She gripped the steering wheel until her knuckles whitened. If she could make it through this stretch of road and get to Columbus before having a nervous breakdown, she'd stay the night there and give her body a respite.

Cora passed rolling hills and tall spindly oak trees. Call boxes were every mile or so. Cora checked her cell phone and saw she had a signal but was thankful to know she could walk to a call box if the car broke down and her cell didn't work. Her mind wandered to the creepy movies she'd seen too many of. White crosses lining the roadway didn't help her relax, either.

"I didn't think I-85 was this remote." Cora dialed Anne and talked to her for a while to stay awake and to drive away her fears of being lost and alone.

It had been awhile since Cora had seen a road sign, a mileage marker, or an exit. By now she should be to Columbus. She started to have that sinking feeling she'd missed an exit and might be heading in the wrong direction. Up ahead she saw a sign and squinted to see what it said. "I-185? How did I get on I-185? What happened to I-85?" She hit the steering wheel with her hand and let out a scream. The late afternoon sun caused a glare on her windshield and she rubbed her tired eyes again, scratchier than sandpaper. "I'm going to have to stop and ask for directions."

The sign up ahead read *Lewistown*. "Mmm, I don't remember seeing that on my map, but it's worth a shot." As she pulled off the highway, looking for somewhere to get coffee and use the bathroom, her car started lunging forward and skipping. It was all she could do to keep it on the road. She drove down Main Street hoping for a service station, even though it was now late in the day. She passed a Piggly Wiggly grocery store, a Burger Hut, Mike's Barber Shop, and there, a block up the road, a service station.

Once at the station, Cora climbed out of her car and peered around, not knowing what type of people she'd encounter here. The red lettering on the white sign at the top of the building announced *Millburn Service Station*.

Sounds like a family business. Maybe there's someone nice inside. She walked into the office and found a young gentleman standing behind the counter locking up the cash register and the desk drawer. The smell of gasoline, new tires, and oil filled her nostrils, sending a wave of nausea to her stomach.

"Excuse me, sir." Cora scratched the back of her neck. "My car just died, and I hope you can help me." She fidgeted with her hands.

"Sure I can. Let's go take a look at it. You must be new in town." The gas station attendant wiped grease off his hands with a rag covered in oil and gas and pushed open the door, leading the way outside.

"Actually, I'm only passing through. I'm from Lake Murray, South Carolina. I'm headed for Florida." Cora was relieved at man's pleasant spirit.

"You got you a long way to travel. We're glad to have ya here, even if it's only for a short time and under a bad circumstance. My name's Bobby Millburn. I own the place." He regarded the station with a prideful grin.

"How wonderful. Now I know I'm in good hands. I'm Cora."

Bobby lifted the hood, looked around, and wiggled some wires. He got down on the ground on his back and slid his body up underneath the car. He pushed himself out from underneath and stood, wiping his hands on his rag, then adjusted his cap.

"Do you think you can repair it?"

"From the looks of things, it's your transmission. I can repair it, but I ain't so sure if we can get the parts for ya right away." Bobby considered her with a slight frown on his grease-smeared face, his plain blue eyes full of regret.

"I was afraid the transmission had gone out. It has been slipping a bit lately. How long?"

"A week, probably. We don't get many cars like this in here." He took a long admiring look at the classic automobile.

"Is there anyone else around who could get me out of here by tomorrow?"

"I don't think so. I'm pert near the only repair place for miles. I'll tell ya what, though. I'll try to find someone for ya—maybe someone a town or two away. Do ya know where ya'll be staying tonight?"

"Not yet. I got off the exit and came straight here."

"I could check around for ya in the mornin', and let ya know if anyone has the parts or if the repairs can be done sooner than a week."

"That would be great. Do you know of an inexpensive place to stay?"

"Shore do. Go up this street and over two blocks. There's a bed-and-breakfast, Apple Springs Inn, on the corner. Ms. Lottie McCallister runs the place. You can get a wonderful meal and a comfortable room. She won't charge ya much. Tell her I sent ya."

"Thanks so much. I really appreciate your kindness."

"Would ya like me to drive ya up there?" Bobby shut the hood.

"Oh, no, that would be asking too much of you."

"But you have your luggage with ya. You can't carry all of it."

"I guess you're right. I'm pretty tired. I've been driving all day." Cora hoped he'd do this favor without expecting payment of some kind. She'd also never gotten into the car with a stranger before, and she hoped she'd be safe.

"Give me a few minutes, and I'll lock up."

"Thanks."

* * *

No more than fifteen minutes passed before Cora stood in front of the Apple Springs Bed-and-Breakfast inn. This historic home had elegant country charm with its porches, ferns, and swings. The oak trees towering above the house had to be more than a hundred years old. At first sight, Cora's nerves settled, and she relaxed her tense shoulders. Bobby helped her with her bags as they entered the inn. Cora's nose filled with a mixture of potpourri and lemon polish on antique furniture.

Ms. Lottie, standing only an inch or so taller than five feet and round, with her gray hair gathered into a knot on top of her head, wasn't a quiet woman. Her voice demanded attention as she led Cora up creaking stairs to her room. "Supper is at six o'clock. I like my guests to be on time."

"Okay." Cora closed the door behind her and surveyed the room's antique furnishings. More lemon and potpourri scent wafted over her. Opening a door, she found an ample closet. The next door was a bathroom. She let out a gasp of excitement. She'd assumed she'd have to share a bath with the other guests. Stashing her bags in one corner of her room, she opened only the suitcase with her traveling clothes and toiletries. After freshening up in the bathroom, she changed into a pair of blue jeans and a cotton button-down blouse.

Cora turned on the television and lay down on the soft antique bed. The room reminded her of her grandmother's cozy guest room; vermilion walls made it dark in there. She had thirty minutes until dinner. She knew she should go help Ms. Lottie, but her legs felt cramped from riding all day, and her head was pounding. And, after all, she was a guest.

She debated what to say when she phoned Ben and Judy. Should she tell them her car had broken down, or not? She was afraid they'd want to come get her. Swallowing her pride and inhibitions, she picked up the telephone and dialed the operator since her cell phone battery was dead. She called the Buchanans collect, knowing they wouldn't mind. As she'd suspected, they did want to come get her, but she insisted she'd be fine and that she was enjoying the adventure.

Next Cora called her parents simply to say she'd stopped in Lewistown for the night and would be on her way soon. She knew if she told them about her car breaking down, her father would be on the next plane to get her. She also phoned Anne.

As she left her room for dinner, she wondered how she was going to pay for her car repairs. She had no idea how much it would cost—or how much the expenses of staying at the inn would be. Would she run out of money before she even left Lewistown?

Cora prayed that all would work out and thanked God for a safe place to stay the night.

2

"Oh, please tell me it isn't time to get up. Please." The alarm clock on the nightstand rang in Cora's ear. "Eight o'clock. Ugh." She rolled unwillingly out of bed on this Friday morning and headed for the bathroom. Her neck still felt stiff from driving.

As she showered, she slowly began to wake. She had to hurry and get ready so she'd be on time for the savory breakfast downstairs. Ms. Lottie was indeed strict about being on time for meals. Cora couldn't help laughing, remembering how the sweet little woman had bossed everyone around at dinner the night before. Her customers all loved her, though...obviously, or they wouldn't keep coming back.

Cora emerged from the shower refreshed and began to dry her lengthy hair. If breakfast tasted half as good as dinner, she'd never want to leave.

After slipping on her jeans and shirt, she headed down the stairs of the old mansion, allowing her nose to lead her to the much-coveted food. Guests already crowded the dining room. She saw quite a few new faces this morning, so assumed people other than guests came in to eat at the inn on their way to work. Ms. Lottie had to be a popular cook.

Cora found a stool at the bar. She didn't want to take up a whole table by herself and didn't feel comfortable eating with others. Only a few minutes passed before Ms. Lottie stepped up and asked her what she wanted for breakfast. Cora ordered scrambled eggs and crispy bacon, a fruit salad, and a biscuit with butter and preserves on the side.

It wasn't long before the food was joyfully filling her stomach. She drank two cups of Ms. Lottie's extraordinary coffee, which warmed her soul as much as her body and would help her stay awake as she drove. Then she remembered her car temporarily called Millburn's Station home and groaned. Finishing her feast, she left the money on the bar and headed toward the exit.

At that moment, Bobby stepped in. "Ms. Buchanan? I'm glad I caught ya." He removed his cap, his hair sweaty and stuck to his head.

"Oh, Bobby, I was just coming to see you." Cora smiled at the odd, grease-covered man.

"About your car...I checked around everywhere, and nobody has the parts. I'm afraid you need a lot of work done on your transmission. I don't have

9

to replace it, though, so that's good. But it'll take a week to get the parts here. Sorry."

"It isn't your fault." She sat back down on the barstool. "I shouldn't have driven the old piece of junk."

"Hey, now, don't talk that way. It's a great car." He smiled. "You couldn't have known this would happen. Do ya want me to repair it, or have it towed somewhere?"

"Gracious, no, I couldn't afford that. I want you to repair it. But do you have any idea how much it will cost?" She hoped it wouldn't wipe her out.

"About three hundred bucks. I need to repair a few other things, or ya won't make it to Florida. I'd hate for ya to get stranded again."

"You're right. The repairs are necessary. I should've had everything checked out before I got out on the road. Go ahead and order the parts. But let me know if it'll be more than three hundred, okay?"

"Yes, ma'am, I will." He grinned. "At least you have a nice place to stay."

"You're right about that, too." She smiled at her lovely surroundings.

After Bobby left the inn, Cora headed back to her room in frustration. She'd wanted so badly to start her life over without anyone's help. Now it looked like she'd have to return to South Carolina. Her only other option was to call her father and ask for some money to get her to Panama City.

She counted her money and added the cost of the repairs with the cost of staying at the inn. Clearly she didn't have enough to stay with Ms. Lottie. She exhaled in exasperation before flinging herself down on the feathery bed. The June sunlight from her window played across the room as she wondered what to do. She didn't have a credit card to charge the repairs, so she'd have to find a job. Maybe someone would let her work just for the week.

Her determination grew. Instead of sinking into the bottomless pit she felt destined for, she'd walk the streets of Lewistown and find someone who would hire her. She jumped up off her bed, freshened up in the bathroom, and headed down to see Ms. Lottie. "Ms. Lottie, may I have a word with you?"

"Sure, child. I'm just clearin' away the last of the breakfast dishes." Ms. Lottie bustled about.

"I wanted to ask you if it would be okay for me to stay through next Friday. I hope you have room for me."

"Of course I do. What's the matter?"

"My car won't be ready until the end of the week, so I can't go on to Florida." She followed Ms. Lottie to the kitchen.

"I'm sorry to hear that. I know ya wanted to get home. You're welcome to stay here. Is your room okay?"

"Oh, yes. It's great. The bed sleeps so snuggly." She paused. "Ms. Lottie, may I ask you another question?"

"Sure."

"Do you know anyone who would hire me for the week? I'm going to need some extra money to pay for the repairs and for my room and board here."

Setting down a serving tray and throwing her towel over her shoulder, Ms. Lottie turned and gazed straight up into Cora's eyes. "Do ya know anything about serving food? Cookin'? Or runnin' a cash register?"

"Not really. Well, I can cook. Also, I love people; I used to be a receptionist in Columbia. Why?"

"Well, next Wednesday is July the Fourth, and I always have lots of lunch and dinner guests. We get lots of people on their way to the beach. I could use some help servin' customers." Ms. Lottie wiped the counter with a dishcloth.

"Really? You're not creating a job, are you?" Cora bit her bottom lip.

"No, child, I couldn't afford to do that," Ms. Lottie said earnestly.

"I'd love to stay and help. I feel so content here." Cora surveyed the kitchen.

"Great. Then here's what we'll do. Your room and meals will be of no charge to ya. In return, you'll help me at all three meal times. During the week, we don't have many customers, but Friday through Sunday, we can hardly fit everyone in. Wednesday will be an exception, though, because of the holiday."

"That sounds great, but I still wouldn't be earning any money for the repairs on my car."

"You keep all tips customers leave for ya. Since you have the weekend comin' up and the holiday, you'll do fine. How much does Bobby think your bill will be?" Ms. Lottie washed the gravy off one of the dishes.

"Three hundred dollars."

"No problem. Now, do ya want to start workin' the lunch hour today?"

"That would be great."

"Okay, go get an apron out of the closet and start slicin' the cold-cuts and raw veggies. We have club sandwiches and munchies for lunch around here on the weekdays. Dinner is our big meal." Ms. Lottie grinned at her new helper.

"Thanks, Ms. Lottie. I could never repay your kindness."

"Wait until the end of the week, and then we'll see who's thankin' who." Ms. Lottie laughed.

Cora giggled too, knowing this would definitely be a new experience and challenge for her. She couldn't stop grinning at the thought of this big step toward becoming self-reliant.

* * *

Cora stood in the tiled kitchen of the inn, preparing a dinner plate for a customer. She'd worked during the afternoon meal, getting to know the people and the facilities. Ms. Lottie proved to be phenomenal to work for, very patient and always praising.

Dinner seemed different, though. During lunch, the customers had been taking a break from work and talked to Cora. However, the dinner guests consisted mainly of families or couples who talked amongst themselves instead of being neighborly to a stranger. She thought little of it, though, for she'd only be here a week and didn't long for new friendships.

As she carefully carried the steaming plate of country-fried steak, corn, green beans, biscuits, and gravy to a customer, she noticed a new customer with a downtrodden appearance at the counter. "I'll be right with you, sir."

A minute later, she was back. "What can I get for you today, sir?" She clicked her pen and turned to a new page in her order booklet.

"Where's Ms. Lottie?" he growled like a bear, scowling with distrusting dark eyes.

"She's in the kitchen." She pointed with her pen. "I'm helping her out until next weekend." Cora lifted her brow, hoping she'd answered to his satisfaction.

"Hmm, she's not sick or anything, is she?" He looked into Cora's eyes, revealing no emotion.

Cora bristled at the rude man's intimidation. "No, she's fine. I needed some extra cash. She offered me a temporary job." She smiled at the man who seemed to have a chip on his shoulder and who must receive special treatment quite often from Ms. Lottie. But why did she feel like she had to defend herself? *Who is this guy?*

"Nice lady, that Ms. Lottie. You'll find no other like her."

"I'm sure." Cora returned his stare until he looked down at the menu.

He sat quietly for a minute, then said, "Tell her Rex sends his best. Oh, and I'll take today's special." The corners of his mouth turned up ever so slightly and revealed the laugh lines around his haunting eyes.

"I sure will. And I'll get that order placed for you. Let me know if you need anything else, okay?"

Rex tipped his hat and nodded.

Returning to the kitchen, she pushed the swinging doors open with her back and found Ms. Lottie in front of the stove cooking an order. "Ms. Lottie, a gentleman named Rex says hello."

"Rex is here? Well, I'll be. I need to go see him." She wiped her hands on her apron. "Watch this for me, would ya?"

"Sure, Ms. Lottie. By the way, who is he?"

"One of my babies. He's like a son to me, dear. Lives on a ranch outside the city. Biggest, prettiest ranch you'll ever see in your life. He comes in once or twice a week to eat." Ms. Lottie rushed out of the kitchen.

He sure does seem peculiar. I wonder what Ms. Lottie sees in him. Cora walked over to the swinging doors and peeked out over them at Ms. Lottie and Rex. The two hugged like best friends. When she saw his broad smile, Cora's breath caught in her throat, and her heart fluttered.

* * *

Later that evening, after the overnight guests went to their rooms and the dinner guests left, Cora cleared and washed the dishes before retiring. She skipped Ms. Lottie's offer of cold lemonade on the screened porch. She only had enough energy to climb the stairs, pull on a loose-fitting cotton gown, and crawl into bed. Closing her eyes, she began to say thanks for her job and the safe place to stay.

But she never finished those prayers. Within minutes, she'd melted into her pillow and slumbered like a baby.

* * *

July the Fourth came quicker than lightning. By then Cora talked to the townsfolk as if she'd known them her entire life. Most of Ms. Lottie's customers had gotten used to seeing her around and acted very friendly. She'd even learned to be a moderately good waitress, and she didn't mind the tips either.

Everyone had been planning for months for the big Fourth of July parade and BBQ. Cora had never been part of a celebration like this one and the thought of it sent tingles up her spine. Folks from miles around came into town, and most stopped in to see Ms. Lottie.

A middle-aged couple sat at a table near the front of the sun-drenched dining room. Cora clicked her pen to an open position.

"Good morning. May I take your order?"

"Yes, thank you," the lovely dark-haired woman said in a Southern drawl. "Wait, you must be the new girl."

"Pearl, don't make this pretty young lady feel like she sticks out like a sore thumb," the handsome gray-haired gentleman spoke. "You'll have to excuse my wife. She never meets a stranger."

"Oh, that's okay. I don't mind. My name is Cora. I'm only here for a little while—just passing through."

"I didn't mean to embarrass you." Pearl touched Cora's hand lightly. "We had heard about the lovely young lady here at Ms. Lottie's. But I didn't expect her to look so beautiful."

"Oh, please, you're too kind. What can I get for you two?" She wondered how these people had heard of her. Who would have paid her such a high compliment?

The two ordered their breakfast, and introduced themselves as R.L. and Pearl O'Reilly. Cora instantly took to them, and not only because they had complimented her. Their sweet, calm nature made her miss Ben and Judy.

After the breakfast crowd left Ms. Lottie's place and the dishes were cleared, Cora went out onto the front porch to wait for the parade to begin. The O'Reillys sat on the porch swing, enjoying the morning breeze.

"Come over here and sit by us, Cora," Pearl called out.

Cora rested her weary bones in a rocking chair next to the swing. Her feet throbbed from standing in her flat tennis shoes all morning. She wished she'd brought some shoes with arch support.

"Have you ever been to a parade like this one?" R.L. asked curiously.

"No, I sure haven't. I grew up in Panama City and then moved to South Carolina a few years ago. Neither place had 'hometown' celebrations like this."

"How did you get to Lewistown, if you don't mind my asking?" Pearl questioned as Ms. Lottie joined them.

"Oh, I don't mind. I was going to my parents' in Florida and somehow got lost on I-85. I ended up on I-185."

"That happens so easily," R.L. chimed in.

"My car broke down as I was getting off the exit to ask for directions. Perfect timing, I suppose. Anyway, Bobby is repairing it. It won't be ready until Friday. I needed a place to stay and some money for the repairs. So Ms. Lottie graciously let me stay here with her and work."

"It was a blessin' in disguise, believe me. I would have died tryin' to serve all these customers this mornin'. Lunch'll be busy too. I'm not quite up to these celebrations like I used to be."

"I haven't helped that much," Cora said. "I probably get more orders wrong than right."

"Now who's tellin' the story? You're marvelous. And the people love you." She patted Cora's leg.

"She's right. You're great with people. I wish you'd come work for us at

14

the ranch." Pearl looked to her husband for support.

"You're absolutely right, dear. She would be wonderful!" R.L. agreed.

Ms. Lottie frowned. "You can't take her away from me."

"I'm only staying here until Friday," Cora said quickly. "As soon as Bobby gets my car ready, I'll be heading on to Florida. But thank you for thinking of me." But an instant later, she added, "What exactly did you have in mind, anyway?" *Cora, why do you care?*

"Our grandchild lives with us at the ranch just outside of Lewistown. We need a nanny for her. Her mother passed away last year, and we can't seem to do for her what her mother would do. She's only three years old. She's such an angel, but we grandparents don't have near the spunk it takes to raise a little one. Our oldest son, her father, is busy with the ranch. We have a daughter, but she's more interested in her friends right now than helping with a niece. Our other son is too busy chasing girls."

"She sounds precious. I can tell you love her deeply. It's a shame your kids don't want to help you with her. If I weren't going home, it would be an ideal job for me. I don't know that much about little ones, but I'm sure I could learn." She almost considered the position.

"You let us know if you change your mind. We'd love to have you at the Southern Hope." R.L. winked at her.

Soon the parade started, and the people-lined streets roared with activity. Everyone screamed and whistled, throwing confetti and streamers. The bands played, and cars honked their horns. Cora smiled until she thought her face would crack.

However, in the back of her mind, she couldn't forget the O'Reillys' offer.

3

That night and all the next day, Cora thought about the O'Reillys. *Lord, do you want me to stay here for a while? Am I not supposed to go home yet? Are you opening a door I need to walk through? Why have you brought me this far off course?*

On Friday, she prepared to leave Lewistown, the temporary home she fit into like a hand in a tight leather glove. Ms. Lottie told her she didn't have to work the breakfast hour, so she packed her bags instead. She'd already washed her dirty clothes that morning. While she was folding them and packing them into her suitcase, someone knocked on her door.

She opened her door, and there stood Bobby in his blue coveralls. "Hey, Bobby."

"Ms. Buchanan." He removed his grease-covered cap. "Could we talk for a minute?"

She walked out to the sitting area in the hallway with him. One look at his solemn face, and she knew something had gone wrong with her car. She sat down on the flowery Victorian-style couch in the hall. Her shoulders slumped.

"It's goin' to be Sunday before I'll have your car ready. And it's goin' to cost a little more than I thought. I had to get some parts shipped here overnight. I hope you're not mad."

"I'm not, Bobby. Just a little angry with myself for driving so far with an old car." Why hadn't she listened to her in-laws—and her parents? They seemed to know the car would not make the trip. *Why do I have to be so bullheaded?*

Back in her room, she plopped on her bed and flipped on the television. Nothing to watch but the news, and it all seemed bad—another missing girl report and a drug bust. She turned off the set and tossed the remote aside, disgusted. *Guess I'll call Mom and Dad and ask for some money to get me home.* At that thought, she burst into tears. *I can't call them. But I can't call Ben and Judy either, because they don't have the money. Lord, give me strength to swallow this big dose of pride.*

She rolled over onto her stomach. Pulling the telephone to the bed, she dialed the operator, then called home. She could hear her mother's voice talking to the operator. She seemed so far away.

16

"Mom?" She held back the tears to keep her voice steady.

"Cora? Where are you? I thought you'd be home by now."

"I'm in Lewistown. My car broke down, and they couldn't get it finished today. He says it will be ready tomorrow evening. I'll have to wait and leave Sunday."

"Well, if you had let your father fly you home, you wouldn't be stuck in some little roadside town alone!"

"Mom, it isn't a roadside town. It's Lewistown, Georgia. It's right outside Columbus." She stretched the truth a bit.

"Don't be smart with me, young lady. Tell me where you are, and I'll have your father come get you."

"I don't need him to come get me, Mother. I just need him...to send me...some...money." She did not want to be needy. She bit her lip.

"He will do no such thing. He'll come get you. Now tell me where you are, and I'll have him call you back. If you'd only listen to your parents, you wouldn't get into trouble!" Her mother was on her usual high-horse.

"I'm not in trouble. I had a problem with my car, and I don't have enough to pay for the repairs. That is an unfortunate incident. Not trouble."

"Give me the number there. Your dad will call you in a few minutes."

Cora gave her the telephone number and hung up. *I'm a married woman, twenty-five years old. Why do they still treat me like a child?*

Within a few minutes, Walt Sinclair did call her.

"Hello, Dad."

"Cora, your mother said you called. She said you need some money."

"Yes, sir." She squeezed her eyes shut, expecting an eruption.

"How much?" Walt calmly asked.

"One hundred dollars. Enough to pay for my room and food until Sunday."

"What about the rest of the trip home? Have you thought about that? What if something else happens to your car?"

"I don't know. I hope nothing else will happen. Bobby is checking to make sure everything works right."

"Cora, you've got to learn to be more responsible. It will take you another day on the road to get home; you'll need food and gas money. You should have thought ahead. Why didn't you let me fly you home? It would have saved everyone a lot of inconvenience."

"Daddy." Anger rose in her throat like a volcano. "I wanted to get home on my own. I had to prove to myself that I could make it without anyone's help."

"I guess you see now that you can't," her father shot back. "You've never been able to do anything. If you had never married Clark, and stayed in college instead, you could have met a nice young doctor or lawyer. You could be happily married with several children by now. But you had to do things your way. What has that gotten you? Deserted! Now, I'm coming to get you, and I don't want to hear another word about it!"

Her hair stood up at the roots, and she made her decision. "You are *not* coming to get me," she said calmly. "What's the difference between sending me a hundred dollars and you spending the money flying out here to get me? It's cheaper to send me the money."

Silence rang on the line.

"You know what, Daddy? A very nice family offered me a job here. They think I'm an outstanding person. I feel good about myself when I'm around them. That's more than I can say for you and Mother. You want me to be more responsible? Then I'm going to stay here for a while. I think coming home right now would be the wrong thing to do." She was proud of herself for never raising her voice even while she released her fury on her father. She still loved and respected him very much.

"If that's how you want it, then so be it," he said, his tone an icy steel. "But do not ask for my help again. I will not come looking for you. If you're ready to come home, you can find your way. The door is always open." The telephone went dead.

Cora looked at the telephone in disbelief. Had her father really hung up on her? Had he really released her? She did not want that. Or did she? No, she wanted her daddy. She wanted him to be proud of her. What had she done? Maybe she should have gone home the way he had demanded.

If she had, however, she would have lost herself again. She could not bear the thought of her parents being angry with her, but she had to find herself. Which was more important?

* * *

Evening came, and Cora finally stopped crying. She had stayed in her room all day long. Ms. Lottie came up to check on her and asked if she wanted to work, but she declined. She felt like a truck had run her over...like the bits of roadway those bulldozers were scraping up back in Atlanta. Eventually she gathered her strength to clean herself up a bit and go down for dinner. She hadn't eaten since breakfast, and her stomach rumbled its disapproval.

When she entered the aromatic dining room, there sat R.L. and Pearl, with two of the biggest smiles she'd ever seen. She tried to reciprocate, but their smiles faded when they saw her. *I must really look a mess.*

18

"Cora? Are you feeling okay?" Pearl asked. "I thought you'd be headed for home by now."

"I should be headed that way. But I'm not going home yet." She sat at the table with the O'Reillys.

"Why not?" Pearl asked.

"My car isn't going to be ready until Sunday. It's going to cost a bit more than I'd hoped. So I'll be staying a little longer than planned." The words crawled out of her mouth. Here she was, confiding in people she hardly knew. Yet she felt more comfortable talking to them than her own parents.

"What are you going to do for money? Do you need to borrow some? Or are you planning on staying here and working with Ms. Lottie?" R.L. inquired.

"That all depends on you two." Cora smiled.

"Us? Why us?" Pearl questioned.

"Were you serious when you said you'd like to have me out at the ranch?"

"Oh, yes!" Pearl exclaimed.

"Then I'll come. I don't know how long I can stay, but I'd love to help you out with your granddaughter, and I could use the money."

"It's settled then. You eat dinner with us, and we'll get your things and take you home tonight." R.L. clapped his hands together.

"Don't you need to clear it with your son first?"

"No. He's so busy with the ranch, he'll hardly notice you're there."

Pearl clarified, "What R.L. means is he's swamped with trying to keep the ranch going. It's hard to make a living these days like we did in the old days. And it's a passion of his. He doesn't like change. Please know R.L. didn't mean to imply you wouldn't catch our son's eye."

"Of course, I understood what you meant." *Catch his eye? What exactly do they have in mind?*

But as Cora ate with her new friends, her heart felt lighter. She tried to forget about her parents for the time being.

* * *

A thirty-minute drive out of town led to a quiet region with nothing but flat farmland sprinkled with green hills and valleys. Cora's mouth flew open when they pulled under the archway and drove down the long, curving drive toward the Southern Hope cattle ranch. Bradford pear trees lined the gravel drive leading the way to the home she would call her own for a few days. The plantation-style home reminded Cora of something out of a movie where the rich landowner dominated the society around him.

Climbing out of the car, she marveled at the turnaround drive, the brick-paved parking area, and the grandiose porch with the swing at the end near the pasture. Flowers bloomed in the numerous flower beds surrounding the walkway to the front door.

"I hope you'll find the house to your liking. Please know that whatever we have is yours. And feel free to ask for anything you can't find." Pearl opened the front door, and they walked inside.

"Thank you." Cora was overwhelmed.

"It looks like our oldest son has retired to his office and our other two children are out for the evening. Our granddaughter is in bed already, too. Let me show you to your room." Pearl led the way up the winding staircase.

"Is it okay if I make a long-distance call to my friends in South Carolina to let them know where I am?"

"Yes, and talk as long as you wish," Pearl added.

Once settled in her room, Cora called Ben and Judy and told them what had happened with her parents. Her cell still had no signal, so she gave them her new telephone number, then hung up before giving herself a chance to get emotional. Snuggling against her plush pillow, her body underneath cool cotton sheets that smelled like summer flowers, soon she was fast asleep.

* * *

Cora awoke to birds chirping, dogs barking, horses neighing, and cows mooing. She yawned and moved her legs, but the covers barely budged. She opened her eyes to a young child sitting at the foot of her bed. With eyes like those of a fawn and hair much like golden silk, this tiny princess said not a word. She only stared at Cora.

Cora sat up in her bed, fluffing her pillows so she could lean back. She pushed her hair out of her face and smiled at the angel. "Hello," she murmured.

"Hi," the girl responded, looking down at her hands.

"What is your name?"

"Susie." She rubbed her hands together nervously.

"My name is Cora. How are you?"

"Good." She smiled.

"How old are you?"

"Free." Susie held up three fingers.

Cora smiled.

"Knock, knock. Cora, are you awake?" Pearl asked from the hallway.

"Yes, come on in."

"I'm sorry to bother you, but Susie seems to be miss—" At that instant Pearl must have spotted her granddaughter at the foot of Cora's bed. "I'm so sorry. Susie, you should have asked Gramma before coming in here. Cora is new to the ranch. You might have startled her."

"She's fine." Cora winked at Susie. "She's so lovely, I could squeeze her."

"Then you don't mind her coming in here unannounced?" Pearl asked.

"Gracious no. She's welcome in here anytime, especially if I'm going to be helping out with her." But she felt a bit uncomfortable in her nightgown.

"Let me take Susie downstairs. You get dressed. Breakfast is almost ready. Cook likes us to eat by eight."

"Yes, ma'am. I'm used to being ready for Ms. Lottie. I'll be right down. I'll see you in a minute, Susie." Cora waved to the little tot, and the child giggled. "Oh, by the way, Mrs. O'Reilly, will I get to meet your son?"

"Rex? Oh, yes, he'll be at breakfast. He usually works with the ranch hands before coming in for breakfast. I can't wait for you two to get to know each other. I forgot to mention, he's the one who told us you worked for Ms. Lottie." Pearl took the child's hand and left the room.

When the door clicked shut, Cora gasped and threw her head back onto the headboard. "Rex? It couldn't be the same Rex that Ms. Lottie loves so much. She never let on that the O'Reillys were his parents. Oh, no. I don't think I can work for him. He seems so...so...temperamental."

Cora showered and dressed. She touched up her face, trying to cover the dark circles that never seemed to disappear, and then followed her nose to the room where the family sat around the table. When she saw the dark-haired man, she recognized him: the very same Rex she'd served several days earlier.

"Morning."

"Good morning." R.L. welcomed her into the room. "Cora, this is Matt, Clarice, and Rex." He waved his hand in their direction. "And this is Cora Buchanan." He motioned toward her. "She's going to help us with Susie for a little while. I trust you slept well."

"Like a baby. I haven't had a night's sleep like that in quite a while." She recalled the long sleepless nights she'd endured since Clark's disappearance. As she walked over to the chair pulled out for her by R.L., Susie yelled out for her to sit beside her. Everyone laughed, but Rex showed no emotion.

As she sat down, she darted her eyes at Rex with the speed of a hummingbird feeding on nectar, quick enough so he wouldn't see her looking. When she'd seen him at Ms. Lottie's, covered in dust from working, he appealed to her some, but less than at this moment. She glanced at him again—this time a little bit longer. Her breath caught in her throat as she watched this man who seemed to define masculinity. She hardly noticed his younger brother—*Was his name Matt?*—who seemed closer to her age.

Rex's skin featured a tan from the sun, and his wavy hair and eyes possessed a darkness that caught Cora off guard. A thick mustache rested lazily on his upper lip and a dark beard covered his face. She felt her neck turning red. Her heart beat like a flame flickering in a breeze. Guilt twinged through her for taking a second look at him—the first man since Clark to get her attention.

Rex looked up as she was staring at him. "So you're the woman Mom and Dad hired to watch after Susie?" He gnawed on a piece of bacon.

"Yes, I'm going to try things out." She swallowed a piece of fried egg whole.

"I saw you at Ms. Lottie's." Rex glanced at her.

"Yes. I worked there all of last week." The lump in her throat built, threatening to choke her.

"Nice to meet you again. I told Mom and Dad about you, and that you seemed pretty nice. Do you plan to stay long?" Rex swigged his coffee.

"I'm not exactly sure yet. I originally planned to return to Florida to be with my parents. My car broke down, and I found myself needing money. That's why I worked for Ms. Lottie. Then your parents asked me to come here."

Rex studied her face for a minute, gulping the coffee in his cup. Then he set his cup down with a bang on the table. "Well, if you don't think you'll be here long, don't bother staying at all." Rex pushed his chair back and stood. He wiped his mouth and tossed his napkin onto the table.

"Rex! You apologize to her." Pearl glared at him.

Ignoring his mother, Rex continued, "I don't want Susie to get attached to you, if you're going to turn around and leave her. She's already lost her mother. She doesn't need to lose anyone else." Rex swiveled and stalked from the room, grabbed his Stetson hat from the hall tree, and exited the front door.

Her face burning, a motionless Cora stared at the doorway where Rex had only moments before stood. "What did I do?" Tears leaped to her eyes.

R.L. shook his head. "You did nothing. Rex is a tough one. He's had a hard time getting over Patricia's death. He doesn't mean any harm."

"Cora, I'm so sorry. Rex hasn't been himself since he lost her. He hardly ever smiles. Patricia died last year. That's why we wanted you to come out here and work with Susie. She needs someone so badly." Pearl frowned.

"I'll try to do all I can, but I'm not sure I can work with him. I can't promise I'll be here forever." She looked at Susie. *Should I leave now, before Susie grows attached to me? Or should I stay awhile and give her the love she needs? I want to stay because I need love, too. We could be good for each other.*

Susie hardly let Cora out of her sight the whole day. She smiled with her dark eyes in a way that made Cora grin. Her ideas for fun never ran out, and she insisted on holding Cora's hand everywhere they went. She showed Cora every toy in her princess room and invited her to a tea party.

Cora finally felt like she belonged to someone, like she did when she was little and would climb into her grandmother's lap. Except this time she was the adult and not the child. Unconditional love flowed as freely as a river.

At dinner, Matt and Clarice filled her ears with details of their lives, but Rex did not dine with them. Matt, obviously a girl-chaser judging by his description of his day, tried a few moves on Cora during dinner. Twenty-five, her same age, he worked with R.L. at their offices in the city. Matt dressed in Calvin Klein suits, with vests and ties, and bold colored shirts, contrasting Rex's rugged style. He wore arrogance like a medal and boasted a smirk on his face and a glimmer of trouble in his blue eyes.

Clarice, twenty years old and overly tanned and finely manicured, had plenty of friends and wrapped herself up in their lives. She concerned herself more with the latest fashions and gossip than with anything else. Her glossy dark hair, like that of her siblings, fell right above the collar. Her dark eyes, covered in frosty blue eyeshadow and lined with thick lashes and dark liner, could knock a man off his feet. They held the same sparkle as Matt's, although of a different color.

Cora laughed inside as Clarice tried to prove she knew more about life than her mother did and tried to worm her way into her daddy's heart. Matt and Clarice were pleasant but very spoiled like the young adults at the Country Club back in South Carolina and were in great need of a reality check...in Cora's opinion.

After dinner, she read a story to Susie, bathed her, and put her to bed. Susie wrapped her arms around Cora's neck and squeezed her tightly. She told her she loved her, and Cora's heart filled with joy she never knew was possible.

Cora's back ached after the long day of caretaking. *I'm getting so old.* She rubbed her side. Realizing her need for quiet, she poured a cup of coffee in the kitchen, then stepped onto the porch to rest her weary body on the swing. The porch light glowed dim, and she enjoyed the privacy. As she sipped her coffee, a bird sang melodiously. The song helped her to relax. She wondered what kind of bird chirped such a peaceful song at dusk.

Suddenly, from the shadows, she heard the shuffle of boots and jumped, thinking it might be a ranch hand. "Who's there?" she called, already getting up from the swing.

"Keep your seat. It's just me, Rex."

"You startled me. I didn't know anyone else was out here."

"I come out here almost every evenin' at dusk. I like hearin' the birds sing."

Cora stared at Rex, surprised that a rough-hewn man would appreciate the gentle sound of a bird, especially after the way he'd acted earlier. "What kind of bird is that?"

He moved out of the shadows and sat down in a wicker rocking chair near the swing. "It's a meadowlark. Whenever I feel outta sorts, I come out here and listen to it sing, and I feel better." A gentle breeze blew across him, whipping his curls across his forehead.

His tenderness struck Cora speechless. "Oh."

As she gazed at him, his face showered with muted light, she couldn't help smelling his earthy scent as the wind blew in her direction. His bronze skin accented his deep brown hair and coal black eyes. She felt sorry for him. She, too, knew the pain of loss. She thought about sharing her past with him, wanting to reach out to him.

But as soon as she opened her mouth to tell him about Clark, he spoke. "Well, I'll see ya tomorrow. I've gotta get to bed." He stood from the rocker.

"Okay. It was nice talking to you. Good night," she said softly.

"By the way, I'm sorry I came on so strongly this mornin'. I just want the best for my girl." Rex walked away.

"I..."

Rex disappeared back into the shadows before she could think of what to say to this mysterious man. She finished her coffee, scolding herself for letting her thoughts stray toward him in the first place. She'd briefly forgotten about Clark. She was, after all, still a married woman.

4

Cora came through the dining-room doorway, heading up the giant staircase, when Pearl called out to her from the family room. She turned and walked through the foyer into the room.

"Yes, ma'am?" Cora answered.

"We wanted to know if you would like to ride into town with us in the morning for church. We always take Susie. You're welcome to go with us."

"Oh, I'd love to come along." She smiled. "What time do you leave?"

"About nine-thirty."

"I'll get up and get Susie ready, and go with you. Thanks for asking me." Cora swiveled toward the stairs and missed landing in Rex's arms by only a few inches. "Oh, excuse me. I didn't know you were behind me." Cora gazed up at this towering man, his warm hands on her shoulders, and felt herself blush.

"I just walked up. No harm done. G'night."

"Good night." As Cora climbed the stairs, she couldn't help overhearing Rex talking to his parents.

"Mom, I'm going to Wild Bill's."

"At this hour? Rex, it's after ten."

"Mom, I'm twenty-seven years old. I can go out past ten." Rex shuffled his snakeskin boots across the pine floor.

"Son, your mother is only concerned about you. Do you really think you need to be going there? Regardless of what time it is, it's hardly the place for you," R.L. pleaded.

"Pop, I can take care of myself. I need to get away for a little while. That's all. I'll be back later. Don't wait up." Rex turned to leave.

Cora crept quietly up the stairs, hiding in the shadows but not getting out of earshot. She wondered why he had told her he planned to go to bed, if he intended to go out.

"We've got so much to work on with the ranch, son. You don't need to be out at all hours of the night."

"What about church, Rex?"

"Mom!" Rex shut the front door.

Cora went to her room, thinking about what Rex had said. What was Wild Bill's? A bar, probably. She sighed heavily, sad that a little girl lay in her bed needing her father while he found solace elsewhere. What kind of example would he set for his daughter? He didn't even attend church with her. *I shouldn't be so judgmental of him. He still hurts over losing his wife. How would I be in that situation? Wait—I am in that situation.*

Cora said her prayers, then fell asleep peacefully. She found it hard to stay asleep though, tossing and turning, wrestling with the covers. She couldn't seem to get Rex off her mind. At three in the morning, she heard his truck pull into the drive and wondered if he had been drinking. The thought of him driving home drunk made her sick. She couldn't imagine why he would put his life at risk like that. Cora fought the desire to go downstairs and check on him. Instead, rolling over in her bed, she forced herself to go back to sleep.

* * *

Seven a.m. on the alarm clock rang all too early for Cora. Once she was dressed, she headed down the hall to wake Susie. After breakfast, they left for church. Church was exactly the thing Cora needed to make her feel a part of the community. Everyone she met treated her as if she belonged. Susie introduced her to her Sunday school teacher and to all of her friends.

After they returned home from lunch at Ms. Lottie's, Cora and Susie went for a swim in the pool. Cora laughed at Susie's charismatic way of running and jumping in the pool with her water wings and nose plug. Her potbelly kept her from staying under the water for too long.

After swimming, they walked around the ranch, meeting the ranch hands and petting every animal they saw. The pigs were Cora's favorites, although she guessed they would all eventually end up on the breakfast plates.

When Susie's bedtime finally came Sunday night, Cora felt more exhausted than her tag-along. Pouring a glass of lemonade, she headed through the double French doors onto the porch and toward the back porch swing, hoping to see Rex there. Only a minute had passed when she heard splashing and voices coming from the pool. She assumed it might be Matt or Clarice with a friend. Cora couldn't help overhearing the voices.

"Rex, swim over here. I bet you can't catch me," a husky voice purred.

"Shhh, you'll wake up the whole house. Besides, I can too catch you."

A trellis of roses prevented Cora from seeing the pool and shielded them from seeing her, as long as she remained seated. She wondered who the woman in the pool was. She couldn't look because Rex might see her, and he'd surely be furious with her. So instead she eavesdropped, craning her neck.

"Come on, let's go in the house," the woman begged.

"Are you crazy? My parents are in there," Rex stalled.

"Then let's go in the barn or the pool house." The woman splashed in the water.

"We can't. Not here."

"Take me to your cabin, then."

"No!"

"Rex, when are you going to give in to me? Every time I ask, you find an excuse."

"I'm not comfortable being with you…here, I mean."

"Why?"

"Veronica, drop the subject. Let's get out of the pool." Rex's mood had changed unexpectedly, like the weather in March.

"Don't get out of the pool. We could stay here. No one would know."

As the woman tried to convince Rex that they could have a secret liaison in the pool, Cora struggled with how best to get up from the swing and silently head back into the house. She didn't want to be present for what might happen.

Once inside, Cora put her glass in the kitchen sink and hurried through the kitchen to the foyer and up the stairs toward her room. Her face felt hot with embarrassment over what she had overheard. Anger rose in her chest at Rex for being so open with his love life, and resentment ran a close second. She had hoped Rex held his wife's memory close to his heart. Evidently she'd been mistaken.

An hour later, Cora heard Rex's truck crank up and pull out of the drive. She fell asleep in a huff.

* * *

A week later, Cora was still as perplexed by Rex O'Reilly as she'd been the first day she had met him. She tried not to think about him, especially since she still had a husband. She'd constantly reminded herself that Clark could appear as easily as he had vanished. *God, why did you allow me to meet Rex at this time in my life? Why am I here?*

Cora filled her days with creating beautiful memories with Rex's precious child, finding it hard to believe that a child could be so sweet. Susie clung to Cora every waking hour. Cora had to peel the child off just to take restroom breaks. Susie usually sat out in the hallway, waiting for Cora to come out.

Pearl was kind enough to relieve Cora of her duties every afternoon for an hour or two. Cora relaxed while walking around the ranch or simply sitting on the porch. She spent this time in reflection. She thought often of Clark, his parents, and her parents, too. She hated that she'd left her relationship with her parents in such an uproar, no matter who was right or wrong.

Living at the Southern Hope ranch fit Cora at this time in her life. She wasn't sure if she'd ever want to leave. She knew she'd need to make plans someday, but she wasn't ready yet. She now had more than enough money to travel home on, but she couldn't bring herself to leave this haven. The O'Reillys wanted her to stay, as did Susie.

* * *

During Cora's second week at the ranch, she had the misfortune of meeting Veronica Ludlowe.

"Hello," the woman hissed, holding out a lotion-slathered hand, leering at her with eyes of ice. "I'm Veronica, Rex's girlfriend. You must be the new nanny."

Cora shivered at the coldness and held her breath so Veronica's department-store perfume wouldn't suffocate her. The two women exchanged a handshake. "Hi. I'm Cora. I don't know if you could call me a nan—"

"Well, whatever. It's good to know Rex's time will be freed up to be with me." She smiled and hung all over Rex, as if she were afraid he'd get away from her if she let go.

Cora grimaced, dropping her hand to her side and wiping it on her jeans. She disliked this woman instantly, and it was obvious the feeling was mutual. This blond-haired, blue-eyed viper was only out for Rex's money and Cora knew just how she was keeping him. That had been obvious the night she'd overheard them at the pool.

Later that day, while taking a walk around the ranch and listening to her MP3 player, Cora overheard Rex and Matt arguing about the ranch and its future. She tried not to eavesdrop, but the daggers the two brothers shot at each other shot right past her ears. She couldn't understand completely what the argument pertained to, but from what she could tell, it was intense. The O'Reilly brothers scratched and kicked in the sawdust of the barn and snorted like the steer in the pasture. Cora quickly headed back toward the house. The hair on the back of her neck remained standing for several minutes.

* * *

The day Bobby Millburn called to tell Cora her car was ready was bittersweet. Nothing held her back from leaving now. She wanted to go home to see her parents to resolve their issues and having her car meant she was free to leave any time she wished. But she still wanted to spend more time with Susie. The attention Pearl and R.L. gave her filled a hole in her heart left by years of familial disharmony. On the other hand, Rex and his lifestyle got under Cora's skin like a splinter. Now was the time to make a decision.

"Hello, Ms. Buchanan," a man's voice said as she reached into the refrigerator to retrieve the orange juice.

"Please, call me Cora. Everyone else does."

"No, no, I couldn't. That's not respectful."

"Cook, I'm hardly someone worthy of respect. I'm a temporary employee. Please, I insist. Call me Cora." She grabbed a juice glass from the cabinet above the dishwasher.

"Okay, Cora, I will."

"What is your name?" Cora put the juice back in the refrigerator and shut the door. She studied Susie's drawings held in place by various magnets.

"Cook."

"No, your real name?" She pivoted to look at him.

"Jimmy." He smiled, as if saying his name for the first time in a long time.

"I like that, Jimmy. I hope you don't mind if I call you by your first name."

"Not at all. I prefer it." He gave her a knowing look.

"Good. Jimmy, when do you go to town next?"

"I'm going later today to the grocery store. Why?"

"My car is ready at Millburn's, and I need a ride to go pick it up."

"I'll take you. How about after lunch?"

"That sounds good. Thanks." Cora rinsed her glass out and put it in the dishwasher. "See you later."

* * *

The ride to Bobby's shop passed quickly. Cora and Jimmy laughed a lot as they shared stories of their pasts. She bounced her ideas off him about going home. His only advice was to stay away from home until she was ready to deal with whatever baggage she had left behind.

"Thanks for dropping me off."

"No problem. Do ya want me to wait?"

"No, I've got some errands to run. I'll see you back at the ranch."

"Okay. I'll see ya later then."

"Bye, Jimmy. And thanks again."

* * *

As Cora headed for the ranch in her Camaro, she reflected on the events of the past few weeks—the people she'd met, the new and challenging tasks she'd accomplished, the decisions she still needed to make. Her stomach churned at the thought of Veronica Ludlowe. Rex had brought her to the ranch with him eight or nine times since that first meeting, and each time Cora saw her, she disliked her more.

Lord, I know my feelings aren't right, but I don't like her ways. I can't imagine her being Susie's stepmother. It's obvious she doesn't like children. She never even talks to Susie. She'd be the type to send her to boarding school. And Susie doesn't like Veronica. When she comes to the ranch, Susie clings to me even more than usual. Lord, I know Rex may not even be thinking of marriage, but please protect Susie. She needs a much better stepmother than Veronica.

It didn't take long before Cora found herself meandering through unfamiliar areas of town on back roads. She turned left onto a street she suspected headed back toward the ranch, an unpaved road. *This is the one Bobby told me to turn onto.* As she drove, her heart beat a little faster because of her unfamiliar surroundings. The trees were tall and made the road dark and shadowy. She felt as though she was on someone's private property, and someone was closing in on her. She wanted to turn her car around, but the road was too narrow and there were ditches on both sides. *Stay calm. You're freaking out over nothing. Just find a place to turn around.*

She finally came upon a small driveway and pulled in to turn around so she could get back out to the main road as swiftly as possible. When her tires started to spin on the gravel, she slowed down. Suddenly, the car fishtailed as she felt a tire blow out. She slammed the brakes to the floorboard and stopped at a T made by the road she was on and another road entering it.

Of all days to have a flat! This car! And I don't even have my phone with me. Why didn't I wait for Jimmy to finish up in town? Okay, think. Where am I? Cora glanced out her driver's side window just in time to see a gray Ford F350 pickup heading right for her. Before she could reach for the door handle, the truck slammed into her, spinning the car and knocking Cora over almost into the passenger seat. A cry escaped her throat; blood dripped onto her pants. In shock, she reached up and touched her forehead. There was a gash in it, and it was wet from her blood. She looked around for the truck, but it was nowhere.

For several minutes she sat in the car, her hands cemented to the steering wheel. Maybe her circumstances had nothing to do with her car. Maybe the bad things were connected to this town instead. *I have to get out of this car and then out of this town! I only hope there aren't any wild dogs running loose or gun-toting backwoods people around here. Lord, after everything I've been through, why do I have to go through this? I'm sorry I took the back roads. Help me not to panic. Please protect me.*

Cora took the keys out of the ignition and grabbed her purse. Getting out of the car, she looked both directions and then chose to walk back toward the main road, instead of deeper into the woods. When she twisted her ankle, she cursed her decision to wear her new sandals. She dabbed at the place on her forehead and winced.

A stick popped in the distance, and her hair stood up on the back of her neck. She tried not to think about the sound. She didn't hear the truck coming, so she felt safe.

Then, without warning, she heard something running up behind her. Before she could react, she felt pain on the back of her head and then nothing....

5

Cora wasn't sure how much time had passed, but when she woke, she was alone in a dark, musty shack. Her bare feet were tied to a burlap-covered cot that smelled of cigars and sweat. Her hands were tied behind her back and her mouth gagged. Her arms were numb, and her shoulders ached from the weight of her body on them. Her head throbbed from the blow. Her stomach growled, and nausea crept up her esophagus. Very little sunlight came through the cracks in the shack. She guessed it was near dinnertime.

Maybe if I try hard enough, I can get myself free.

Cora tried, to no avail. She wiggled, squirmed, and pulled, but nothing worked. She broke out in a sweat from trying so hard. The gag prevented her from screaming. Who could hear her out here, anyway? She finally gave up.

Then Cora winced at the loud sound of a vehicle outside the shack and immediately thought of the pickup. Relief flooded her body at the thought of not being abandoned, yet she feared the unknown.

When the door opened, light burst in. Cora squinted her eyes at the brightness before her and then closed them briefly, allowing them to adjust. When she reopened them, a man stood in the room, his face shadowed by the hood of his jacket.

Reacting with the instinct of a fawn, Cora quickly stilled her body and reclosed her eyes. *Maybe he'll leave me alone if I lay still.* She wanted so badly to know who was under that hood. Who would want to kidnap her? Was this a stranger or someone she knew? Could it be Veronica? Maybe she wanted her to stay away from Rex. Could it be Clark? Maybe he was so angry she'd left home that he'd followed her. Or maybe it was someone affiliated with Clark who thought she knew where he was....

Cora could hear the person rummaging around in the shack, but she didn't dare to look. She had to carry out her charade.

Suddenly she was poked and pushed. "Wake up!" a harsh voice demanded.

She had no choice but to respond. When she opened her eyes, camping lanterns glowed across the room. The hood still rested over the person's head. She tried to talk, but it was impossible with her mouth gagged. Her assailant removed the cloth from around her head and the rag from her mouth.

Struggling to move her head away, Cora challenged, "Who are you? What do you want with me? Do I know you? Why won't you uncover your face?"

"Why all of the questions?" the voice grumbled.

"I'm trying to understand all of this. What is this all about? Why me?" Cora squirmed and tugged, trying to get loose.

"Don't worry. You'll figure everything out eventually. I'm just following orders." The attacker turned out all of the lanterns except one and opened the door, leaving as abruptly as he had come.

Cora could hear him securing the door as he left. She knew there was probably no way out for her, but she had to try. First, she had to find a way to free her hands and feet. She pulled and twisted, but she could not free herself.

I cannot give up. Think, think, think. How can I get out of here? She tugged a little more, and then rested. *I won't do myself any good if I'm worn out.*

Cora scanned the crude cabin to see what she could use to get free. Spotting a small chest of drawers across from her, she hoped she'd find a knife or scissors. She began to yank again to free herself from the cot. This time, she was able to pull herself loose from the bed and sit up. For a moment, she sat still, listening to the outside and gaining stamina. Then she swung her legs around, touching her feet to the floor. Hopping across the shack to the dresser, she turned her back to the drawers, squatting down. With her tied hands, she was barely able to open the top drawer. She stood again, turned around, and looked inside.

"Please let there be something in here I can use," she said aloud. "I need something sharp to cut these ropes." She searched but could not find anything. Shutting the top drawer with her knee, she again turned around, knelt, and tried to open the bottom drawer. She almost tipped over when the warped drawer finally flew open from the force of her pull. She sat on the floor and looked in the drawer. Nothing in there, either.

Cora struggled to her feet and surveyed the squalid place. The lantern made shadows across the room. Cora knew it was still daytime, since the daylight had streamed in the door when the attacker came to the cabin. She figured it was probably now about five or five-thirty. She knew she wouldn't make it home for dinner.

She remembered to shut the bottom drawer, in case the man came back before she was able to escape. Standing in the middle of the shack, she noticed a cable coming out of the wall and followed it with her eyes into a wall-mounted cabinet. Curious, she hopped over to the cabinet and used her chin to open it. When she finally got it open, she saw a telephone and let out a gasp. The captor had obviously hidden it so she couldn't find it. If she could only find a way to get herself loose, she could call for help.

Then she noticed a large tool chest, about two feet high, near the door. Hopping over to it, she knelt in front of the chest, which was unlocked. Turning around again, she pushed the lid open. It was metal and had a sharp edge.

"Ouch! Oh, boy, that's not good." The pain in her wrists proved she'd cut herself, and she could feel the blood trickling down her fingers. For a moment, she could taste bile in her throat. "Don't give up, Cora," she admonished herself aloud. "You cannot just let this happen to you. You have to fight to find a way out of here."

Cora peered in the chest, and although the corner of the room was shadowy, she saw a pair of branch trimmers. *If only I could get these behind my back and somehow cut the ropes off of my hands, I could get free. I could get out of here.* Cora tried to reach them but kept losing her balance. *I have to make this work!* If she could cut the ropes off with the same jagged edge of the toolbox she had cut her wrist on, she could get free.

She turned around, positioned her hands—one on either side of the edge of the chest—and began to saw back and forth. Sweat poured off her forehead, making it impossible to see. She could tell she was cutting herself, but it didn't matter. She had to do this. After about five minutes, she felt the rope tear, and she was free at last. She reached inside the tool chest, got the branch trimmers, and cut the ropes off her feet. Looking at her hands and wrists, she almost fainted. Blood covered her, and her hands throbbed. There was nothing clean enough that she could see to tie around her wrists to stop the bleeding.

She steadied herself for what she must now do. She had to call for help. *Who can I call? I don't know the O'Reillys' number by heart.* She weakly walked to the cabinet where the phone was. With blood dripping down her arms, she instinctively dialed the operator.

"9-1-1 operator. What's your emergency?"

"Please help me. Someone kidnapped me." Cora tried to remain calm.

"What is your location, ma'am?"

"I don't know. I was driving from Lewistown to the O'Reilly ranch in Southern Hope through some back roads, and I got lost. Then my tire blew out, and someone rammed me in a gray Ford F350 pickup. I was walking for help, and someone attacked me in the woods. I'm in a cabin. An old rundown shack." Cora's knees trembled.

"Okay, ma'am, help's on the way. Stay on the line as long as possible so we can trace the call. Okay?"

"Yes, ma'am."

Minutes later, Cora heard the rumble of the vehicle she had heard before. "I hear him coming back! What do I do? If he comes in here and sees me like this, he'll kill me!" Cora bit her bottom lip.

"Is there a back door or maybe a window you can crawl out of? The officers and medics will be there in a few minutes. Is there a way out of there?" the operator asked calmly.

"There's a window. I'm going to try to get out."

"Do not hang up this phone. Keep the line open."

"Okay." Cora laid the receiver down beside the phone and ran over to the window, which had no glass. There was nothing but some type of handmade wooden shutters covering the opening. She pushed and banged like an insane person until she got it open, blood splattering all over her and her clothes. With all of her strength, she threw herself out of the window and ran into the woods as fast as her bare feet would carry her. It was now almost completely dark, so it was difficult for her to see. She was thankful for the darkness, however, because it would be burdensome for the aggressor to see her.

Cora didn't know when to stop running, only that she wanted to get far enough away from the cabin, but not too far away from the help was coming. She tried to be as quiet as possible, to keep the captor from hearing her, and stayed focused on what she had to do. She didn't even think about her bleeding wrists, nor did she have the thought to cry aloud. She merely kept running, despite the pine needles that stuck into her feet.

She ran until she could run no more, then ducked behind a huge pine tree and sank to the ground. The ground was damp with evening dew, and the bark from the pine scratched her arms. There were pinecones and pine needles all over the ground. Exhausted, she tried to be silent with her breathing to keep herself undiscovered.

She waited nervously behind that tall tree for what seemed like a lifetime. Then she felt herself drifting away, off to sleep, and couldn't seem to stop herself.

* * *

Cora opened her eyes, instantly grimacing from the pain in her head, and focused on the first thing she saw—a sign, *Emergency Room.* Turquoise curtains made mock walls on both sides of her. Peering through the opening in the curtain at the people bustling about, she listened to the muffled sounds over an intercom system. She squinted in the bright lights, staring down at the IV in her arm. She frowned from the pain but also from confusion. The beeping of the machines by her side was irritating.

An instant later, a nurse came to her side and checked her pulse.

"Where am I?" Cora managed.

"You're at the hospital, honey. You've been through a terrible ordeal." The nurse pushed buttons and adjusted tubes.

"Am I okay?" Cora pulled her right hand out from under the heavy blankets and touched her forehead. Her entire body trembled.

"Oh, yes. You're just here for observation. You were found unconscious and you had some abrasions, so they brought you in."

"Is my family here?"

"The O'Reillys? Yes, I'll get them for you."

Immediately Cora remembered she was not at home with her parents nor was she with the Buchanans. She was with the O'Reillys.

The nurse returned promptly with Pearl and R.L. Pearl rushed to Cora's bedside. "Cora, I'm so glad you're okay." Her hands with their long fingers and manicured nails gently patted Cora's leg.

"Hey, dear." R.L. patted her leg also, but firmly, exhibiting his concern in a more urgent manner.

"What happened to me? All I remember is running in the woods and hiding behind a tree." Cora tried to sit up.

"Lay still, darlin'," R.L. said. "Your call saved your life. You evidently escaped the cabin just in time."

"I was so scared. All I could think about was getting home. I mean—back to the ranch. Am I really okay?"

"I believe so. The doctor said as soon as you regained consciousness you should be able to go home. He wanted to ask you a few questions and make sure you were not harmed in any way other than what's obvious."

"Pearl, I think I'm fine other than these cuts and the concussion. I don't—I didn't get attacked like *that*." *Thank you, Lord, that he didn't rape me!* "I remember getting lost. And then I blew a tire. But then I don't remember what happened. Wait! Someone crashed into my car!" She shook her head. "I don't understand. If only I hadn't decided to ride through those back roads, taking my time getting home, none of this would have happened. I didn't have my phone with me, so after my car got hit, I had to walk to get help. Out of nowhere, someone came up behind me and knocked me over the head. The next thing I knew, I was in that disgusting place all tied up."

"You poor dear." R.L. clasped her hand.

"I struggled to get free. I cut my hands on a metal tool chest in there. Then

I found the phone hidden in a cabinet. While I was on the phone with the operator, I heard the truck coming back. It was so loud, almost deafening. That's when the operator told me to get out of there. I knocked open the window and ran for the woods." Cora began to cry as she recounted her ordeal, shaking uncontrollably.

"Honey, don't think about it anymore. What's important is that you're safe now."

"I know. How did they know to call you?"

"A nurse recognized you from Ms. Lottie's, and they called her."

"Good evening, sir, ladies."

Everyone turned to see a mid-forties man in a dark suit standing in the opening of the curtains. His loosened tie languorously hung around his neck.

R.L. stood. The man shook his hand.

"How are you?" R.L. said.

"Fine, just fine. I'm Detective Ikeson, Ms. Buchanan. How are you doing?"

"I'm better, now that I'm safe." Cora still wiped tears from her eyes.

"I came to let you know we have a lead on the person involved in your kidnapping." He loosened his tie a little more.

"You do? Is it anyone I know?" Cora started crying.

"I don't think so. There's a gang of guys kidnapping and"—he met her eyes—"doing other things to women as some kind of initiation. We're pretty sure your incident had to do with them. Did you hear the reports on the news about the missing women?"

"I did hear something the other day. Oh, my gosh!" Cora threw her hands up to cover her mouth. "Why would they have wanted me?"

"Any number of reasons. Wrong place at the right time. Maybe you wandered into their territory. We're investigating the cabin where we found you, searching for any DNA we can find. We have a good lead on the other missing women. We've turned it over to the FBI."

"Wow, I can't believe it!"

"I have to get back to the office. Here's my card. Please call if you have any questions."

When the detective walked out through the opening in the curtains, Cora let out a sigh. "I can't believe this. I guess it was all worth it, though, if they have a lead on the criminals."

"You could have been killed. You're so lucky you got away." Pearl shuddered.

"Luck had nothing to do with it. God was guiding me the whole time."

"Praise the Lord," R.L. said.

"I bet you all were panicking when I didn't make it home for dinner."

"We were worried even before that. Cook got home hours before dinner and said you should have been home after your errands. We were about to send Rex out to look for you when the police called," Pearl said.

A nurse came to check on Cora, and then a doctor came in. The doctor reassured her she was okay to go home, but she needed to take it easy for several days. The bump on her head was bad, and the cuts on her wrists would take time to heal.

Cora was thankful to be going back to the ranch. "What about my car? Did they find my purse? What about all my boxes from home?"

"Don't worry. Everything has been retrieved," R.L. assured.

* * *

When Cora got home from the hospital, Rex was sitting on the front porch swing with Susie. "Hey."

"Hey, Rex."

"Cora! You're home!" Susie jumped down from Rex's lap, her face framed in ringlets from sweat.

Cora knelt down and received the child in a big hug.

Rex walked to the porch steps. "Are you feeling better?"

"I guess. But still weirded out a bit. I can't believe I was kidnapped."

"Yeah, that is weird. Well, I'm glad to see you're up and moving around. I thought maybe you'd decided to leave unexpectedly."

"No, I wouldn't do that." Cora searched Rex's eyes. There was something in the dark mirrors; she just didn't know what.

"I wouldn't blame you if you did. After the way I treated you." He looked away.

"Don't worry about it, Rex. We're good." She batted the thought away with her hand. "Listen, I'm pretty tired. I'm going to lay down for a while."

"Okay. I'll see ya after a while then."

* * *

It was now the first week in August, and Cora had been at the ranch for a month. Her physical wounds had almost healed. Her nights still included dreams of the cabin and her captor but were slowly improving. Rex had been cordial the few times she'd seen him. For that, she was grateful.

Pearl joined Cora in the playroom one afternoon.

"Susie and I've had a tea party," Cora reported, "and we played with blocks this afternoon."

"That sounds like great fun. Did you ever call your parents or your in-laws and tell them about the kidnapping?" Pearl sat in the chair by the window.

"No. I figure I can tell them about it when I go home to visit. Since my name wasn't on the news, I decided to keep it under wraps for now."

"I guess you're right. We're taking good care of you anyway." Pearl smiled, but there was a hint of sadness in her eyes.

"You sure are. How are you doing, Pearl?" Cora placed a book on the shelf.

"Oh, I'm fine." She sighed.

"You sure? Something seems to be bothering you." Cora studied Pearl.

"Gramma, do you want some tea?"

"Sure, Sweetie." Susie offered Pearl a tiny cup of imaginary tea, held carefully with her chubby fingers, and then ran to her dollhouse to play. "Thank you." A tear slid down Pearl's face.

"Pearl? What is it?" Cora sat beside her.

"I'm worried about Rex. He has so much on his mind with the ranch. And Susie. And I'm disappointed with his choice in women. I've prayed his relationship with Veronica wouldn't last long. But it seems they're getting serious." She sighed again.

"I'm sorry. He's a fortunate man to have parents who love him so much." It was all Cora could offer. She had her own opinions about Rex and his problems, and they were better kept to herself.

"I'm not so sure he feels that way these days. I think he resents our involvement in his life."

"I'm sure that's not the case, Pearl." Cora offered a smile.

"R.L. and I had so hoped once he began to date again, he would date someone like you."

"Like me? You mean a homeless woman who borrows trouble? I'm not so sure I'm a good catch right now, Pearl. I've got my own issues I'm dealing with." Cora laughed.

Pearl chuckled softly. "None of that matters. You've got a good heart. It's evident in the way you've taken so much care of Susie."

"She's an easy child to love, Pearl. You all are easy to love." But a twinge ran through Cora's heart at her untruth because she knew Rex was not as easy for her to love as the rest of the family.

6

Cora watched the late-night news in the family room with R.L. and Pearl after getting Susie to bed one evening. She snuggled up on the loveseat with a blanket and a cup of decaf coffee. Even though it was still summer, fall gently crept into Southern Hope, and the air conditioning kept the house too cool for her liking.

When the news anchor announced a report on another missing Columbus woman and the reporter on the scene alluded that the incident was tied in with Cora's kidnapping, she and Pearl exchanged a knowing look. Immediately following the missing woman story, the news anchor told of the death of a drug dealer who had been missing for a year. They said the name wouldn't be released until family members were notified. Cora needed no name. The details given described only one person—Clark Buchanan.

Cora swallowed hard and excused herself from the family room. She said nothing to Pearl or R.L., because they didn't even know she had a husband, let alone the details about him. She fled to the safety of her room and picked up the telephone to call Ben and Judy. She hated to wake them if they were asleep, but she had to know.

"Hello," called a weak voice.

"Judy? It's Cora."

"Hey." Her voice was sad.

"Did I wake you?" Cora feared her suspicions were accurate.

"No, Sweetie. We weren't asleep."

Silence hung heavily on the line.

"I called...because...I was watching the news..."

Judy interrupted, "Yes. It was Clark. We received the call an hour ago. We haven't been able to call you yet."

No longer able to hold back her feelings, Cora burst into tears. For a year, she had expected some kind of news, but this hurt worse than she'd imagined. "How did it happen?"

"Cora, it's Ben. Judy couldn't talk any more. Clark was hiding out somewhere in Nevada, and bounty hunters tracked him down. He wouldn't surrender, so they had to shoot him. They say he died instantly," Ben said softly.

"Thank you for telling me. I knew when I heard the report on the news it had to be him. I need to go. I need to be alone. I'll call you tomorrow." Cora hung up the telephone. She rushed out of her bedroom, down the stairs, and outside to the back porch.

When she sat in the swing, the floodgates opened, and she sobbed uncontrollably. She wanted to run, or hide, or lean on someone, or something. Oh, she didn't know what she wanted....

"Cora?" a familiar voice called from out of the darkness.

Cora jumped but could not stop crying. She couldn't even look up.

Rex crossed the porch and sat next to her on the swing. Gently placing his arm around her shoulder, he said, "Cora, are you okay?" A pause. "Well, I can tell you aren't okay. What is it?" His voice was deep and comforting.

After several more minutes of weeping and sniffling, Cora swiped her eyes with her fingers and looked up into Rex's dark eyes, soft for the first time. "I've just received some bad news from home."

"Florida?"

"No, South Carolina." The words choked her. "I found out my husband was shot and killed this morning."

"Husband?" Rex stiffened.

"Yes. I know...you didn't know I was married. Your parents didn't know either. We've been apart for over a year. He disappeared one night. He was a..." Cora began to cry again.

"Take your time." Rex moved closer to her and took her into his arms.

Cora relaxed against the strength of Rex's warm, muscular body. "We had been happily married, or so I thought for a while, when he was suddenly arrested for smuggling drugs into the country. I had no idea if it was true or not. He got out of jail on bond, and that night he disappeared. I've spent a whole year hoping and praying he'd return. I couldn't go on with my life until I heard from him. When I came to Lewistown, I was on my way to Florida to be with my parents. I still hoped Clark would come for me, but I'd nearly given up."

"He's been gone as long as my Patricia."

Cora turned toward him, gazing into his face so close to her own. She saw he was in anguish, too. "I'm so sorry. I shouldn't have dumped all of my problems on you." She wiped her nose on her hand.

"You're not dumping. I'm glad you did. It's nice to know someone else can relate to how I feel." He chuckled and gave her a wink.

"I've been expecting to hear this news for a long time. I thought I had prepared for it and accepted it even. Not until I actually heard he was dead, though, did I realize how much it still hurt."

"I can imagine."

"I think what hurts the most is he just up and left me. He didn't even say good-bye, or try to take me with him. He simply vanished. I thought our love was so strong. Finding out he'd kept things hidden from me was devastating."

"I'm sure he didn't want you to get dragged into his mess. He probably only wanted you to be safe."

"I guess so. He could've changed his ways, though."

"Probably easier said than done."

"Yeah, I suppose."

"I still grieve over Patricia, after all this time."

"But at least you found someone else." Cora weakly smiled.

"No, someone else found me." He slumped.

"What do you mean?" Cora cocked her head.

"I met Veronica at Wild Bill's, and she's wild all right. She drinks and smokes and uses foul language. She's quite different from my Patricia."

"How appealing. Why do you date her?" Cora shivered, remembering how Veronica's cold eyes cut right through her.

"She takes my mind off things. She's only out for a good time. I don't think I have to worry about her trying to lasso me, if ya know what I mean." Rex chuckled again, this time loudly, oblivious to Cora's condescension.

"I see." Cora moved away from him. "Well, thanks for hearing me out. You have a good shoulder for crying."

"Did I say something to offend you?"

"No, not at all. I'm a little frazzled right now. I think I'll go inside and tell your folks my news." Cora stood up from the swing.

The fact that Rex chose to be with this type of woman and that he was blind to Veronica's obvious plan to snare him weighed on her like a backpack full of rocks on a mountain hike.

"What will you do now?"

"I'll stay a little longer, if it's okay. I really love Susie. Spending time with her now will take my mind off things."

"I understand. I'm glad you're staying. I think it's better for Susie that you're here right now." Rex smiled.

Cora turned to leave. "Thanks." *I need to get past my obsession over Rex's lifestyle. I'm not his keeper.*

She returned to the family room and told R.L. and Pearl about Clark. They offered to fly her to Columbia for the funeral if she needed them to.

Soon after, she retired to her room and called her parents. "Hey, Mom."

"Cora." The ice in her mother's voice chilled her to the bone. "I wondered when you would call."

Cora wiped at a tear that began to fall from her eye. "I've been very busy at my new job." She didn't tell her about the kidnapping. "Did you hear the news about Clark?"

"Yes, I did. Are you planning to return home?"

"Not yet, Mom. I'm going to South Carolina for Clark's funeral. The Buchanans will need me to be there for them."

"I see."

Cora closed her eyes. "I'll be home soon."

"I understand. They are very important to you."

Cora sighed heavily. Here came the guilt. "I need to get this behind me. Tell Dad I said hello."

"Sure." Her mother hung up.

Cora cried herself to sleep, praying for God to bring her peace.

* * *

When Cora entered the terminal of the Columbus Metropolitan Airport after exiting the airplane, she looked for her driver. She'd flown to Columbia for Clark's funeral two days earlier and was ready to get back to the ranch. That morning Pearl had assured her someone from the ranch would pick her up. So Cora sat in a chair to wait as people rushed by on their way to undisclosed destinations.

As she flipped through a magazine, Cora reflected on the past two days. Her heart had soared when she saw Ben and Judy, although it had been under terrible circumstances. Much of their grieving had been done before Clark's death, though, so his funeral seemed nothing more than a formality. Seeing Clark's body had been one of the most difficult things Cora had ever done. How much he'd changed in only a year. Fifty pounds heavier, he wore his hair long to his shoulders and dyed black. He was hardly the same man.

Ben and Judy tried to convince her to return to Lake Murray, but she declined. She thought she'd possibly found a new life in Southern Hope.

Lord, is there a mission for me at the ranch? Or in the town somewhere? Is there a calling for me higher than working for the O'Reillys? Please reveal to me what it is you want me to do. If this is a time of rest and renewal for me, then please prepare the family for my departure when the time is right.

Cora glanced up from her magazine to watch a couple saying their good-byes as the gentleman prepared to board a plane. She smiled slightly at them. *Will they ever see each other again? There are no promises of such things.* Her heart ached over not seeing Clark one last time and over the realization that the last time she had seen him, she'd had no idea it would be the last. She didn't get to say good-bye. *It's probably for the best anyway.*

"Cora?" a deep voice called. Rex was standing in front of her.

"Rex? What are you doing here?" Cora inquired, standing. She straightened her shirt and fidgeted with her purse strap on her shoulder.

"I came to take you home." Rex shuffled his boots and straightened his Stetson.

Rex's smile warmed Cora's heart. *He said "home."* "You didn't have to do that. I know you were probably busy."

One of the airport personnel rode by on a motorized cart.

"I volunteered to come after you, Cora." Rex stared directly into her eyes.

He spoke my name. Her name rolled off his tongue like melted butter. Cora's heart pounded in her chest. The air left her lungs. "That's very kind of you." She tried to control her reaction. Rex was the most handsome man she'd seen in a long time, and her loneliness threatened to push her toward compromising her values.

"My pleasure. Let me have your bag." Rex took her bag from her. "Do you have any more luggage?"

"Yes, just one small suitcase."

"Okay, let's go get it. Then we can be on our way. Cook will be holding breakfast for us."

Cora smiled at Rex and followed him to the baggage claim, then out to the truck. His friendliness kept her eyes glued to him. It took almost an hour to get back to the ranch. Traffic was horrific. During the ride back, they talked about their tastes in music, movies, literature, and clothes. Rex told Cora about what had happened on the ranch while she was gone; she told him about South Carolina. They laughed and talked like old friends.

I'm glad I made the decision to come back to the ranch. Tomorrow holds promise.

When they arrived home, R.L., Pearl, and Susie greeted them on the porch. Cora sighed, glad to be back. In her peripheral, she saw the front door open and someone step out from the doorway. Cora saw her shoes first, then let her eyes move upward. Veronica stood in the doorway, hands on her hips, dressed as if she'd walked out of a fashion magazine.

"Hello, Cora. I see you've found your way back to the ranch." She sized Cora up, her translucent eyes reducing her to nothing more than a peasant.

"Hello, Veronica." Cora's elation changed to dejection, as if someone had punched her in the stomach. "Yes, I'm back." She smiled curtly.

Rex's neck stiffened, and he moved away from Cora, creating obvious space between them. He didn't even offer to help her with her bags. Like a direction shift of a spring wind, he went to Veronica and took her into the house.

Cora's mouth gaped as she stood beside Susie, her hand on top of the child's head, watching the two lovers. She could not understand why he changed so around Veronica. Maybe he was trying to have both of them. Maybe he only wanted Cora for conversation and companionship, and he wanted Veronica for the most obvious of reasons.

"Cora? How was your trip?" R.L. came down from the porch steps to help with her bags and frowned in Rex's direction.

Susie closely skipped behind her Grandpa's heels.

"Oh, it was as expected." She crossed her arms across her chest, giving herself a squeeze. "I'm glad it's over. Now, finally, I can start my life over." Bending down, Cora opened her arms to receive Susie and to give her a doll she'd purchased in South Carolina. She was thankful for this child who was going to be the lifesaver she needed. Susie hugged Cora's neck so tightly she could hardly breathe, but she loved it. A hot breeze blew across them. An airplane flew overhead, and Susie pointed at it, eyes widening in wonder.

"Come inside for breakfast. You must be hungry," Pearl said.

"Yes, I am, and tired." Then she turned to Susie, who was holding her hand as they walked into the house. "How about we take a nap after breakfast?"

"No way!" Susie shook her head dramatically, and everyone laughed.

"We'll see about that." Cora grinned at the child.

* * *

Two days later, on Sunday, Cora's rest reservoir still measured below empty. She'd been unable to pull herself away from Susie on Friday after her return, and Saturday had been almost as bad. She needed a bit of time to herself, so she decided to stay home from church. Pearl and R.L. took Susie into town for church and for lunch at Ms. Lottie's.

Cora stayed in bed and rested until her stomach wouldn't let her wait any longer. Then she put on her robe and went downstairs.

Jimmy was cleaning up the breakfast dishes when Cora entered the kitchen. "Good morning, Cora."

"Morning, Jimmy." Cora sat at the breakfast table, gazing out the bay window at the ranch. The early morning sun beamed onto the porch.

"How are you feeling?" Jimmy turned to study her.

"I think I'm getting back to normal. After the kidnapping and the loss of my husband, I'm definitely ready for life to be boring for a while." She laughed.

"I sure hope life calms down for you. Can I get something for you? I was about to head out for church, but I'd be glad to get you something," Jimmy offered.

"Oh, no. I wouldn't want you to be late for church. I'm staying in today. What did you serve for breakfast?"

"Bacon, eggs, toast, fruit, and coffee."

"What's left?" Cora's stomach growled.

"Some bacon. How would you like a BLT? I know it isn't quite lunch time yet, but sometimes a BLT is good this time of day."

"Jimmy, you're a genius. That sounds great. I'll get everything, though. You go on." Cora fluttered her hand at him and started for the refrigerator.

"Thanks. I hate to be late for church."

"See you at lunch."

Cora prepared the sandwich but couldn't eat much of it. Her nerves held her stomach hostage. She couldn't eat or sleep lately. Heading upstairs, she passed Matt's, Clarice's, and Rex's bedrooms. Their doors were shut, so she couldn't tell if they had gone to church or not.

Once in her room, Cora slipped her swimsuit on and headed back downstairs to take a swim before Susie returned. She hadn't been able to swim laps since she'd arrived at the ranch. Susie did not swim very well, and Cora felt she had to watch her constantly in the pool.

Outside, Cora put her thick towel down on the chair and smoothed sunscreen on her skin. She breathed in the aromas of coconut and lime. "Ahh..." When the sweat began to puddle in her navel and on her chest, Cora jumped into the pool to cool off. She swam about a half-hour, smiling up at the sun and lavishing the peace and quiet.

Then she heard Rex's truck pull into the driveway and wondered if he had been to church. Calculating what time it was, she knew he wouldn't have had time to return home from the city. *Why do I even care what he's doing, after the way he treats me? Best to avoid him all around.* As Cora splashed in the pool, Rex came around the house to enter through the back door. When he saw her in the pool, he stopped in his tracks and gave her a bright smile.

"Good morning."

It's not morning anymore. "Are you coming in from church?"

Judging by the way Rex looked, Cora knew the answer to her question before she even asked it.

"Morning. And no."

46

Cora said no more. His behavior after her return home from the airport had cut her deeply, and she didn't want to set herself up for more disappointment. She simply swam to the other side of the pool.

"What's up with you? Why'd you swim over there?" Rex squinted in the sun, his hair tousled and his shirt untucked.

"I just wanted to swim. Nothing's up," Cora dodged. In the water, she nervously kicked her foot. She knew what he'd been doing the night before. She was sure he'd been with Veronica, and that was why he hadn't returned home until now. She remained at the opposite end of the pool, playing with her hair.

"Are you mad at me?" Rex crossed his arms.

"Why should I be? You haven't done anything to me." She felt her eyes stinging.

"Right. You're absolutely right." Rex turned and walked into the house.

Cora slapped the water. "Ooh, that man!" *Why didn't I tell him what I think of him when I had the chance? Why did I clam up like that? Because...he is, after all, my boss. I knew it would be difficult to work for him. I never imagined the difficulty would stem from my lack of approval of his personal life, though.* She inhaled deeply. *But he likes the job I'm doing with Susie, and that's what matters. It's hard to work for a man who plays around. I don't know what to do.*

Cora climbed out of the pool, wringing her hair. Drying off with her towel, she reapplied sunscreen, and stretched out on the chaise. Closing her eyes, she let out a heavy sigh. *I have to learn to keep my big nose out of Rex's affairs. As long as I do a good job with Susie, that is all that matters.*

Cora was resting peacefully in her chair when suddenly fierce splashing in the pool startled her. She opened her eyes and jumped from her chair at the same time. Rex splashed in the pool, arms and legs flailing all over the place.

"Help! Help! I can't swim; I'm drowning!"

Instantly, Cora jumped into the pool to save him. There was no time to think. As she reached Rex, he almost drowned her, along with himself. She finally got him calmed down. Then Rex burst into laughter. Cora stared at him with her mouth open. She'd been conned. She shoved him powerfully and swam to the shallow end of the pool.

"Cora, come on, lighten up. I just wanted you to come in and swim with me."

"Well, that wasn't funny. I really thought you were drowning. What if that had been Susie? What if I'd thought she was joking? It isn't funny!" Cora's head spun from the adrenaline rushing through her veins.

Rex swam over to Cora. "Hey, I'm sorry. Are you okay? I didn't mean to frighten you like that. I was just playing." Rex's face was now inches away.

Cora stared into Rex's eyes—black as midnight, very intense, and spellbinding. "I'm fine, but I can't believe you did that. You know, I should drown you. Then you'd learn your lesson." Cora pushed Rex away playfully.

"Come here." Rex gently pulled Cora back.

For a moment, neither spoke. Cora couldn't help feeling tingly around him. He was so mesmeric and even more terrific-looking wet than dry. Even though she'd been mad at him a lot lately, her opinion had definitely changed since first seeing him at Ms. Lottie's. She now thought he looked great after working on the ranch, all dusty and smelling like the horses.

"What?" Cora felt herself slipping into Rex's arms.

"I said I'm sorry. I won't do it again." Rex pulled her closer.

"I hope not." Their eyes locked, and Rex's hold on her tightened. Her heart throbbed. She could feel it coming... "No." She pushed away from Rex.

"What is it?" Rex asked. "What's wrong?"

"Rex, you're my boss, and you have a girlfriend." *Whom you've been with in this very pool. What are you, some kind of gigolo?*

"Cora. You think too much. Veronica isn't my steady girlfriend. Besides, I'm not your boss." Rex tried to swim after Cora.

Cora reached the side of the pool and lifted herself out of it before Rex could catch her. "You are my boss." Cora turned around toward Rex and then pattered across the deck.

Climbing out of the pool after Cora, Rex replied, "I'm Susie's father. You're her nanny. But my father employs you. Not me."

Cora sat in her lounge chair, and Rex sat in the one beside her. Their knees touched.

"So I'm not your employee...but you do have a girlfriend. Anyway, I don't care if you think you're not steady. Veronica obviously thinks you are. She doesn't like me. I know she doesn't want me around." Cora towel-dried her hair.

"She doesn't matter right now. I want you around. You're great with Susie."

"Thanks." Cora gazed into Rex's chocolate eyes. *I love chocolate.* She looked away quickly. A hot breeze wafted across them.

"Why can't you look at me?" Rex questioned, pulling on the corner of her towel.

"It isn't you. I can't get close to anyone right now. It's too soon. I'm still sorting out Clark's death."

"He's been gone a year, Cora."

A bull snorted in the pasture.

"Yeah, well, he's been gone, but not dead. And I guess I don't get over things as quickly as you seem to. I can't just find someone, hop into bed with them, and forget all my troubles." Cora shot daggers at Rex with her eyes.

"Ooh, that hurt. Is that what you think I'm doing? Do you think you're my next conquest? You're wrong. I told you how I feel about Patricia. But you can't go to the grave with them. You have to move on."

"That's what I'm trying to do. But I can't do it the way you do! I couldn't leave my child for someone else to raise while I was out playing around with a wild woman. I mean..." She reached out to touch Rex in apology.

He jerked away. "So that's how you see it? Well, at least I know what you think of me. You don't like me!"

"Rex, let's drop it. I didn't mean it to sound the way it did."

"Tell me what you think!" Rex demanded. "Tell me!"

Cora sat in silence for a few moments, collecting her thoughts. "I think you're a charming guy. But I think you aren't living as you should. You never spend any time with Susie, and you're off at bars every chance you get. You don't even come home until morning. Staying out all night with a woman isn't exactly my idea of a good example." Cora crinkled her brow, waiting.

"You know very little about me." Getting up from the chair he sat in next to Cora, Rex stared down at her. The silence was deafening. "Raising Susie is now your responsibility. My parents knew I could not do it alone. That's why they hired you. You set the example for her and leave my life for me to worry about. Is that understood?" Rex glared at her, then walked away, not giving her a chance to respond.

"Rex!" Cora was open-mouthed. She couldn't believe what he had said. Did he really think she was now solely responsible for the raising of his daughter? Precious as Susie may be, Cora could not do what Rex demanded of her. The child needed her father. She had already lost her mother.

7

That night, after Cora bathed Susie and got her to bed, she went downstairs to the family room where R.L. and Pearl usually sat before bedtime. The lights were dim, and the television's glow flickered across the room. She smelled Pearl's popcorn and R.L.'s coffee. R.L. was flipping through a crossword puzzle book while Pearl cross-stitched.

Cora hesitantly interrupted. "Excuse me. Have you guys got a minute?"

"Sure. Come on in and have a seat. What is it?" Pearl said.

Studying their attentive faces, Cora fidgeted. "I don't know how to tell you this…."

"Oh, please don't tell us you're leaving," R.L. said.

"No. I don't want to, but…it's Rex. I don't think I can work for him. Earlier today, we had a confrontation. I may have overstepped my boundaries. I let him know how I feel about his personal life. I told him of my concerns about the type of father he is. He told me I shouldn't worry about how he lives his life, because I am now solely responsible for raising Susie. He said I should be the one to worry about being a good influence. I agree to a certain extent, but his influence matters most. It really bothers me that he stays out all night and never spends any time with Susie."

Pearl shook her head and R.L.'s neck stiffened. "We understand. Honey, we told you he would be difficult. The reason we asked you to come here was that we knew Rex was not doing his job as a parent. We knew we could not raise Susie properly because of our age."

"But I think this is doing both Rex and Susie an injustice. It's enabling him to stay uninvolved in her life. Susie already won't know her mother. Now she isn't getting to spend time with the only parent she has. Rex is being relieved of his fatherly duties. It isn't fair to Susie. One day she'll be grown, and she won't have any respect or feelings for her father." Tears puddled in Cora's eyes.

"You really care for her, don't you?" R.L. asked.

Cora walked to the mantel, taking in the family pictures. "Yes, I do. I care about Rex also. I want him to love his daughter. I want him to get over Patricia. I want him to find love for himself again one day."

"We wish he would find love. He has to find someone better than Veronica," Pearl said.

"And he hasn't been to church since Patricia died. It really pains us to see him living as he does. His life is so empty right now," R.L. added.

"He hasn't even been home in over ten months. Right after Patricia died, he moved himself and Susie back to the ranch," Pearl continued.

"Home? He has a house?" Cora remembered Veronica asking Rex to take her to his cabin.

"Yes, he built a house when he started dating Patricia. When they got married, he moved her in there. When she died, he came home. He's only been back to get things he needed. Most of the time, he sends one of us to get necessities," Pearl answered.

"I had no idea he had lived away. Where is his house?" Cora sat on the loveseat.

"You have to go behind the stables and over the hill. His cabin is on the other side of the hill. He put it back in the woods. He loved that place so much," R.L. said sadly.

"I'm so sorry. At least I had a year without Clark before finding out he was dead. I can't even begin to imagine the pain Rex has suffered." Cora buried her face in her hands. "I have wounded him so badly."

"Please, consider staying with us. I know it would do you some good to be with Susie. We love you so much already. We would hate it if you left," Pearl pleaded.

"I'll stay a little longer. I just don't know what to do about Rex, but I'll try to think of something. I'm going to go ahead and go to bed. Susie will be up before I know it." Cora walked out of the room, straightening her shoulders. Tomorrow would have to be a better day.

The foyer was dark, but she found her way to the stairs by the small lamp on the round table at the foot of the stairs. As she went up the steps, she heard Rex coming down the upstairs hall and prayed he would pass her by.

She ascended; Rex descended. They met in the middle. She looked at him and him at her.

"Hi." Rex stopped.

"Hi." Cora nervously halted in front of the O'Reilly family portrait.

"Cora, I wanted to say..."

"Please, don't." Cora held her hand up in protest.

Gently taking her hand in his, Rex continued, "Thanks for what you said today."

"Thanks?"

"Yes. Thanks."

"Don't thank me. I want to apologize to you."

"No. Don't. You struck a nerve. I didn't realize I'd been avoiding Susie."

"Oh," Cora meekly replied.

Then, shuffling his boots on the hardwood stair, he continued. "I've been thinking. How 'bout you and I take Susie to Calloway Gardens tomorrow? It's so nice this time of year." Rex still held her hand.

"Us? Just the three of us?" Cora looked at their hands.

"Sorry." Rex released her hand.

"No, it's okay." Feeling awkward about their contact, she leaned against the wall. "I think it would be fun. I've heard about it and passed the road signs before on the highway, but haven't ever been."

"Great, let's go after breakfast. I can get some men to cover for me tomorrow."

"Fine. We'll be ready after breakfast." Cora said as Rex began walking down the stairs. "Rex?"

He turned around. "Yeah?"

"Thanks." She smiled, then headed to her room.

* * *

"Susie, today we're going to Calloway Gardens." Cora buttered Susie's toast.

"Yay!" The girl threw her arms up in the air in a cheer, lost her balance, and almost slipped out of the kitchen chair.

"Be careful. So I take it you've gone there before?" Cora tucked a strand of her hair behind her ear.

"Yeah. There's lots of butterflies there." Susie took a big bite of her eggs.

"Butterflies, huh? Okay." Cora pulled the waist of her jeans up. Over the past year, with all of the stress over Clark, her clothes had started to get baggy.

Rex came into the house. "There's a butterfly house there. Butterflies hatch and fly all around freely."

"Wow! I can't wait to see them." Cora tried not to notice Rex's tanned skin.

"As soon as you ladies are finished with breakfast, we can go. I've loaded the truck." Rex shoved his hands into his front pockets.

Outside, Pearl and R.L. smiled at each other as Rex lifted Susie up into the big cab of his Ford pickup and buckled her in. He helped Cora in and shut her door. As he walked around to his side of the truck, he yelled, "See you this afternoon, Mom and Dad." His smile was a genuinely happy one…the first Cora had ever seen.

Just as they drove down the long drive, however, a sports car zoomed toward them. Cora looked at Rex, and his expression immediately changed. His neck stiffened, and he held his breath involuntarily. The car pulled up to the truck. Veronica sat behind the wheel. Cora let out a heavy sigh at the imminent change about to occur in Rex.

"What are you doing?" Veronica looked from Rex to Cora and back again with the eyes of a snake.

"We are going on an outing." Rex averted her stare.

"Excuse me?" Veronica blurted, slamming her hand on the steering wheel.

"Veronica! Relax, Susie is right here beside me. I thought it would be a good idea for Cora and me to spend some time with Susie." Rex winked at Cora.

Cora giggled, delighted that Rex had not altered his personality this time, and that Veronica was so steamed. Susie followed with a squeal.

"I just bet you did. Well, don't bother calling me tonight. I won't be home." Veronica sped away, scattering gravel and dust everywhere.

"Hmm, I guess she's mad." Rex put the truck in gear and continued down the drive.

* * *

As they drove through the admission gate of Calloway Gardens, Cora gasped at the flowering trees, plants, and green grass spread out as far as she could see. She couldn't take her eyes off the azaleas and other flowers.

"Rex, it's beautiful. I don't know why my family never came here."

"You probably didn't come here because you had the beach."

"You're right. Well, thank you for bringing us here."

"My pleasure." Rex found a parking spot near the Whippoorwill Lake. "Come on, Susie, let's go find a spot to have our picnic." Rex put the truck into park, grabbed the picnic blanket, and lifted Susie up and out of the truck.

"Let's go!" Susie shouted.

Cora laughed and stepped out of the truck. She grabbed the cooler and followed Rex and Susie to the lake.

"This looks like a good spot, "Rex said, setting Susie down and spreading the blanket out on the ground.

Cora helped him prepare the picnic site right at the edge of the lake. A gentle breeze blew, and it was cool enough not to worry about blistering in the sun. Susie began running with her arms held out to her sides imitating an airplane and chased butterflies. Her sundress sported butterflies of all types. Cora sat on the blanket and Rex began to chase after Susie. She watched them play together and smiled widely. Her speech seemed to have worked.

After Rex and Susie settled down on the blanket where Cora rested, she said, "Susie sure does love the butterflies."

"Yep, she sure does. Wait 'til you see her in the butterfly house. We'll stop by before we head home. It's really cool. There are examples of every life cycle and then, when they hatch, the butterflies fly all over the place." Rex opened the cooler, pulled out some soft drinks for them, and juice for Susie. He took out sandwiches, fruit, chips, and dip.

Rex and Cora talked while they ate. After Susie ate, she lay down on the blanket in the warm sunshine, flopping her legs back and forth. When Rex and Cora became aware that Susie had drifted into a nap, the two adults made themselves more comfortable. Rex lay on his left side and Cora on her right.

She picked a blade of grass. "Susie is so precious, Rex."

"Thanks. She really is a handful at times, though."

"I don't know of a small child who isn't a handful."

He groaned. "So, tell me about when you were kidnapped. What was it like?"

"It was pretty awful. I still can't believe it happened to me." Cora took a sip of her soda. "I had picked up my car from Bobby Millburn's shop and was heading home through some back roads he told me about. I started to get creeped out because the roads didn't seem like how he described them. So I turned around. But when I did, I blew a tire."

"I know you were scared. I wish Cook had followed you home."

"I know, but *Jimmy,*" she emphasized the name, "had errands and I had errands. Our schedules didn't mesh. Anyway, after my tire blew and that truck rammed into me, I got out to walk back to the main road and started to feel like I was being watched. Woods are so eerie when you're alone. That's the last thing I remember until I woke up in that disgusting cabin."

"What was that like?"

"You really do like the details, huh?"

"Yeah." He smiled.

Cora cleared her throat. "It was stinky and dark. I was tied to a cot and gagged. I don't even like to think about it."

"I'm sorry for bringing it up."

"No, that's okay. I wish the police knew who it was. It's driving me crazy." Then she stopped talking. "Listen, Rex, it's the meadowlark. Isn't it beautiful?"

"Of course. But not as beautiful as you are." He ran his finger down her cheek.

Cora felt herself blush. *Oh, I'm beginning to like this man. But he still has so far to go. I can't fall for him until he's more emotionally stable.* "Thank you."

54

The words tumbled out of her mouth.

"I mean it." Rex forced her to look at him by following her eyes with his own. He cleared his throat. "By the way, I really do appreciate you saying what you said to me yesterday. I know I was mad at the time, but after I thought about it, I knew you were right. It took me awhile to admit it, though."

"I wasn't trying to be right. I never should have pried into your personal life. I just thought Susie needed you."

"It's good feeling needed. I'm gonna try harder from now on to spend more time with her. I didn't realize I'd pulled away from her. Guess I didn't think it mattered at her age." Rex studied Cora's eyes.

"I'm glad to help." Cora dusted imaginary dirt off her jeans. That tingly feeling crawled up her back again. *What do I do? Should I get up off this blanket? Should I stay where I am?*

Rex leaned toward Cora cautiously. She stared into his eyes but did not move. Rex placed his fingers on her chin and moved toward her. "Your eyes are like a forest of evergreens. I want to stare into them nonstop."

"You do?" Cora drifted away, like a raft down a mountain stream toward a waterfall.

"Mmm-hmm." Rex closed his eyes and then kissed her cheek.

Cora's eyes involuntarily shut. She did not resist as Rex pressed his lips to her cheek. She hadn't felt a man's touch in a year. She groaned.

After only a few moments, Rex pulled away and regarded her with tenderness. She smiled weakly at him.

"Cora?"

"Yes?" She could hardly breathe. She felt herself slipping over the top of the waterfall.

Then Rex moved toward her again, a little less cautiously. He kissed her again, but this time on the lips. Cora responded, heat rising up to the back of her neck. She felt safe because Susie was close by but placed her hand on his chest just in case. Finally, he released her.

Cora collapsed back onto the blanket. She grasped her head with her hands. *Have I just crossed a line?* Looking over at this impressive man, she forgot all about her vow to stay away from him. She could think only of what a wonderful kisser he was, as she'd thought he would be. Gazing at his soft beard, she remembered the feel of it on her velvety skin. *I kind of wish he didn't have the beard so I could see his whole face.* She stared at his full lips, outlined by the beard, and then up to see his eyes pinned on hers. She sighed. Rex grinned. Her heart pounded. "You said that about my eyes to get me to kiss you, didn't you?" She laughed.

"No, never." Rex laughed in unison.

Cora nudged him. Rex lay on the blanket beside her, his arm lightly touching hers. They both looked up at the beautiful Georgia sky, brilliantly blue with columns of white, fluffy clouds.

"This is the most relaxed I've been in a long time."

"I'm glad you are. Have you had a lot of things on your mind?"

"Yes. Running the ranch has become so much like a business that it's not much fun anymore. Times are tough. It's getting harder and harder to survive as a cattle rancher."

Cora listened intently, not wanting to stop his flow of openness. "I've noticed more and more that farming and ranching is becoming…"

"A thing of the past? Exactly. I'm struggling with that. Dad and Matt run the office in Columbus. They deal with trade, contracts, and the whole business end of things. We sell meat, milk, purses, boots, and belts. About anything that can come from a cow, we sell. We also sell sperm from our prize bulls to breeders for bull riding. I just want to be a rancher. I don't want to deal with the business world. I like being on the ranch, not having to deal with too many folks."

"So, what's the problem?"

"Dad and Matt wanna open a dude ranch *and* a bed and breakfast. They say that's the only way we're gonna be able to stay alive. I wanna be a rancher. The dude ranch would seem to be a better fit for me than a sissy bed-and-breakfast inn, but I don't want a bunch of city folk comin' here playin' cowboy and cowgirl for a weekend, you know?"

"Oh, sure. That's got to be hard."

"It is. And I guess that's why I've been so grouchy lately. And why I haven't had time for Susie. I've been wracking my brain to find a solution."

"If there's anything I can do to help, I'd be glad to."

Susie tossed around on her blanket. Her nap was ending.

"Thanks. Hey, did I overstep my boundaries by kissing you?" Rex pulled a daffodil from the ground.

"I'm not sure what your boundaries are." Cora glanced in his direction.

Rex turned toward her and studied her face, then began to laugh. "What are you trying to say? It was okay with you, as long as it was okay with me?"

"I guess so." Cora sat up. "It was just a kiss after all, right? I'm only surprised that it…I didn't expect this to happen."

"I have enjoyed being with you here. I think you're a great person. I didn't know you were so pleasant. So, I wanted to kiss you."

"I see."

56

"Did I answer correctly? Do I get the prize?" Rex teasingly poked her waist.

"You idiot." She giggled. "I wasn't sure what you were trying to do or say or whatever." The meadowlarks sang in the distance.

"I wanted to kiss you. You're very lovely. I'm really growing to like you."

"Me, too." Cora accepted that Rex had only kissed her as a gesture of friendship. *Boy, he must want to be good friends.*

* * *

When they arrived home, Cora took Susie in the house as Rex unloaded the truck, whistling a tune. Susie told Pearl all about their trip to the park and offered her a handful of yellow and white daisies. Pearl glistened with pleasure as she heard her stories. Cora went to her room to freshen up while Pearl entertained Susie.

In the hallway outside her room, Cora ran into Clarice, sporting her designer blouse and new tight jeans. Her heels added six inches to her height and made her calves look like she worked out every day. "Hello."

"Hey, you're just the person I was looking for." Long earrings dangled from Clarice's ears. Her thin arched eyebrows looked freshly waxed.

"Me? Why me?" Cora rubbed the back of her neck with her hand.

"I wondered if you wanted to go with me tonight to Wild Bill's." Clarice tossed her hair, making pendulums out of her earrings.

"Thanks, but I'm really tired. We've been out all day with Susie." Cora shifted her weight to one foot.

"Yeah, Mom told me you and Rex were together. I couldn't believe it."

"We weren't exactly *together.* We thought it would do Susie some good to be with both of us at the same time."

"Rex's idea?" Clarice smacked her gum.

"Yes."

"I knew it. He's sly, isn't he?" Clarice said, popping her hip out.

"What do you mean?" Cora inquired, walking into her room.

Clarice followed her. "Rex likes you. I can tell."

"He dates Veronica. He obviously likes her more." Cora pulled off her sneakers, shuddering at the thought.

"No, he only *thinks* he does. You're more his type." Clarice put her manicured hand on her hip.

"Well, it doesn't matter. It won't go that far. I work for him, and that's all." Cora sighed.

"Okay, sure, whatever. Anyway, do you want to go with me?"

"I don't think so. I don't usually go to bars. But thanks for asking." Cora peered into the mirror on her dresser at Clarice behind her.

"Come on. I hate to go alone. It's a lot of fun. There's dancing and music. There's always a game of pool goin' on."

"Maybe another night. It is Monday, after all."

"Okay, then Friday night. We'll go to Wild Bill's then." Clarice turned to leave Cora's room like a tornado shifting direction.

"Clarice."

"I won't take no for an answer. Friday night after dinner." Clarice disappeared down the stairs and out the front door.

Cora frowned at her reflection. "Ugh, I don't want to go. I don't drink. I don't dance. I don't play pool. I'm not comfortable in places like that."

8

The third Friday in August marked Cora's sixth week at the ranch. The humidity was higher than in South Carolina and the mosquitoes pestered her ferociously, but not enough to make her want to leave. Georgia fit her the same way the bark fit the oak tree outside her bedroom window. The rolling hills covered with green grass and the flat land of crops restored peace to her soul. She loved breathing the fresh country air. Although quite different from the salty sea breezes of home, it was cleaner than the city air in South Carolina. She never wanted to leave this place.

After spending Monday with Rex, Cora's thoughts drifted continuously to her plans for her future. She looked at the clock on the wall more than ever before and flipped through the same magazines until she had the pages memorized. She took Susie to get a haircut and decided to get her hair trimmed, as well. The stylist introduced herself as Mindy, Clarice's best friend, and immediately filled Cora in on all the happenings of life in Southern Hope and Lewistown. The ladies Cora met buzzed about life around the area, making it easier for Cora to fall in love with her temporary hometown.

When Cora and Susie left the hair salon, they stopped by the library. Cora got a library card. *Why do I need a library card? I'm not staying.*

* * *

"Hey, Anne."

"Hey, girl. I didn't recognize your number."

"I got a new cell phone. Mine wouldn't work here."

"You got a new phone? Are you still coming home?"

Cora laughed. "Long story."

"What do you mean, Cora?"

"If I told you everything I've been through, you wouldn't believe it. I'll fill you in when I do come home." Cora grabbed her glass of lemonade off the kitchen counter and went out onto the back patio.

"You're planning to come, though, aren't you?"

"I am. I just don't know when yet. I love being here. It's renewing. Maybe you should come for a visit." Cora settled onto the lounge chair by the pool.

"Maybe I should. So what are you doing besides taking care of the granddaughter?"

"Taking care of Susie keeps me pretty busy. But I'm also taking time to find myself."

"I didn't know you were lost." Anne snickered. "I thought you got that worked out in church years ago."

"You're really funny. Seriously, though, I love this place and the family is so precious. I could stay forever. I love being on the ranch."

"But what's there for you? You'll never meet someone new if you stay there."

"Why? Are there no men here? You're silly. There are men everywhere."

"Yeah, cowboys! I can't see you with a sweaty, dirty farmer. You like businessmen in suits."

"First of all, the O'Reillys are ranchers, not farmers. Second, there are tons of businessmen in Columbus. But, if you recall, my luck with men in suits has not been too good. Besides, some of these men look pretty good in their cowboy boots and tight jeans." Cora's mind drifted to Rex. She cleared her throat.

"Anyone in particular?"

"No. No one I'm willing to mention yet anyway."

Will I ever go anywhere with my life if I stay here? I cannot remain Susie's nanny forever. What could I do if I stay, though? I don't want to leave, but there are too many people in PC, and Lake Murray holds too many memories.

* * *

"Clarice, is the invitation to go to Wild Bill's still open?" Cora met Clarice in the upstairs hallway before dinner.

"Why sure it is. Do you want to go?"

"I need something to get me recharged after the long week."

"Oh, goodie!" Clarice grabbed Cora in an embrace, engulfing her in her designer perfume.

Cora laughed. "Wild Bill's isn't exactly my type of place, but I think it would be fun."

"Okay. We're gonna have so much fun. We'll go after supper."

Later, Cora put on her blue jeans, a black silk blouse, and the Western vest with silver buttons she'd purchased earlier in the week. She squeezed on her black suede ankle boots, and hoped they were right for the outfit. Pulling her hair back into a smooth ponytail, she put on dangly silver earrings in the shape of cowboy boots—another find in town—and added a bangle on her right wrist. She rubbed the scar, remembering.

After darkening her makeup a bit, she gave herself an approving nod in the mirror. The dark circles had finally faded from underneath her eyes. Just as she placed her money and identification in her pocket, Susie came into her room, dressed in her plastic high heels with her feather boa wrapped around her neck.

"Cora, are you coming back home?" Susie held her teddy bear close to her chest.

"Of course I am, Sweetie. What would make you think I wouldn't be back?" Cora bent to Susie's level and looked her directly in the eye.

"My mommy didn't come back when she left." A frown settled across Susie's freckled face.

"Come here. I promise you I'll be back. You'll already be in bed when I get home, but I'll see you in the morning. In fact, if I'm not too tired, I'll even come in and kiss you good night when I get back." She brushed Susie's golden hair out of her face.

"You will?"

"I promise. Now, come on. Walk me out." Cora took Susie's hand in hers. She gazed intently at the little tot, wondering exactly what had happened on the day Patricia died. She was sure Susie had felt secure that her mother would return on that day. Whatever happened, it was obviously big enough to scar Susie.

When Cora and Susie got downstairs, Clarice stood in the foyer with Matt and another young man. Cora observed Matt in his jeans and dress shirt with a skinny tie and dress cowboy boots. Casual, yet still dressed to impress the ladies. His hair was perfect and his skin glowed like he'd gone for a facial. *Surely not.* She gave a quick glance in his friend's direction. Nothing much to look at.

"Oh, good, Cora, you're ready. Gosh, you look great. I mean it." Clarice came over to Cora, grabbing her right hand with both of hers.

"Thanks."

"This is Matt's friend, Justin." Clarice pointed with long fake nails the color of a red apple.

"Hey. Nice to meet you."

"You too."

"We're going to ride with them, if you don't mind. Mom feels better about us goin' if we have escorts." Clarice rolled her eyes, sweeping her lids with her long, fake lashes. "We can ditch them once we get there." Clarice flashed all of her teeth.

"That's fine with me if we ride with them," Cora said. "Or, we could follow them in my car. That way, if we want to leave early, we can."

"Leave early? Are you crazy? No one leaves early, Cora." Matt took her by the arm. "Let's go paint the town." He winked at her with his crystal blue eyes, shrugging his brows that she was sure he had waxed.

Cora smiled at Susie and kissed her good-bye, hiding her apprehension. She wished she hadn't decided to accompany them, but it was too late. Matt whisked her into his Jeep, and off they went.

All the way to Wild Bill's, Cora listened to Clarice flirt with Justin in the back seat. *I wonder if they're dating. If they are, why would Clarice want to separate from him at Wild Bill's? I have a lot to learn about Clarice.*

When they arrived at Wild Bill's, Cora waited a minute for her eyes to adjust to the darkness of the place. Laughter floated like sawdust in the air while people danced. The band played honky-tonk music, and she immediately wanted to tap her toes. Cora heard the bells and whistles of a pinball machine, and the clacking of pool balls hitting each other as someone played a game. Giant fans blew air all around and cigarette smoke filled the bar. Boiled peanut shells covered the floor. Cora liked the energy of the place but could have done without the smoke and the alcohol. The bartender stirred a mixed drink and offered it to a customer. Cora looked away, her stomach churning. They found a table and sat down.

"Well, what do you think?" Clarice put her mouth against Cora's ear.

Cora smelled Clarice's spearmint gum. "Wow, this place is huge. How big is it?"

"About 8,000 square feet, I think. It's made like a barn. The loft area up there is where you play pool and video games." Matt nodded toward the loft.

Cora continued to scan the place that reminded her of the pool hall she and Clark had frequented in their early days. A stabbing pain shot through her stomach. "I've never seen a place like this...not even near the beach in Panama City." Cora settled into her chair and watched people dance as the band played a two-steppin' song. She tapped her foot on the floor and slapped her hands on her knees involuntarily.

"Justin, dance with me." Clarice put her hand on her hip and popped her hip out of socket, her usual stance.

Cora watched as Clarice worked her charms on Justin. She quickly moved across the floor, pulling him by the hand. "Matt? Is Clarice dating your friend Justin?" Cora hollered over the loud music as she and Matt found a table.

"No, I think she'd like to date him. But, then again, Clarice would like to date every man in this place." Matt gave her a look Cora unmistakably understood.

One day she's going to find herself in a terrible situation, pick the wrong man to flirt with, and end up getting hurt or kidnapped like I was.

"Hey, Cora."

Cora glanced up to see who had called her name. "Oh, hey, Bobby. Matt, this is Bobby Millburn from town. Do you know him? He owns the car repair place near Ms. Lottie's."

"No, I don't know him." Matt looked Bobby up and down. He stood and puffed out his chest, shaking hands with him. The difference between Matt's soft, clean hands and Bobby's rough, grease-stained hands represented the gap between two classes of people.

"Nice to meet you." Bobby squeezed Matt's hand.

"Same here." Matt returned to his seat.

"So, Cora, how are ya doin'?"

"I'm doing fine. And you?" *Should I invite him to sit down?*

"Good. How's the car?" He stared at her through narrow slits, shadowed by thick, unkempt eyebrows.

"It's banged up a little bit from the accident, but it runs great. Thanks again for all you did." Cora smiled. *Why is he looking at me like that?*

"Sure. How are your wrists and feet doin'?" He stared at her hands.

"Healing up nicely. Thanks." Cora tapped her fingers on the table and quietly sighed.

"Okay. Well, I'll see ya later."

"Okay. Bye, Bobby." Cora waved at him.

"He's a strange character." Matt made a funny face at Bobby's back, curling up his lips.

"Oh, be nice. He's not so bad, Matt. He's probably better with cars than he is with people. He seems a bit introverted."

"Whatever." Matt shrugged. "Hey, you want to dance?"

"Oh, no, I'll just watch. You go ask someone else. I'm sure there are plenty of girls here you'd like to dance with. And any one of them would die for a dance with you probably." Uncomfortable, Cora peered under the table at the peanut shells. They felt strange underneath her boots.

"Well, probably." He stuck out his chest boastfully. "But the woman I want to dance with is sittin' right here with me." He winked at her.

"Please, Matt. You're just saying that."

"No, I'm not. If you don't want to dance, I'll stay here with you until you do."

"Really, you don't have to sit with me. Go, have fun." Cora shooed him with her hand, amazed at his vainglory.

"I want to dance with you." Matt got up from his seat and pulled Cora from her seat. Taking her by the hand, he led her to the dance floor. He took her other hand and began to lead her in the two-step.

The song they danced to ended about a minute later, and next a slow love song started. Cora laughed at the words, which said something about crying and leaving on a train. Matt released Cora's hands and placed his hands around her waist. *Oh, great!*

Cora cleared her throat and put her hands on Matt's upper arms. She moved in a little bit closer to him but kept a safe distance. "I really can't dance very well. I don't have much experience at it."

"I think you're doin' great. I've wanted to bring you here for a couple of weeks, just so I could hold you in my arms." Matt stared into Cora's eyes and suddenly pulled her up against him.

Cora put her arms around his neck and placed her head on his shoulder. That was the only way she could avoid looking him in the eye. He was wearing cologne that filled her nostrils pleasantly. He was a younger version of Rex as far as his looks went, except for his blue eyes and lack of facial hair. *How much more like Rex is he? What is Rex really like?*

Two women walked by and sang out their greetings to Matt, wiggling their fingers in a flirtatious wave. Cora felt his attentions turn to them. *The restless soul with wandering eyes.* She lifted her head from his shoulder and looked at him. She wasn't sure what to do next.

"You're kind of tense. I know what would relax you." Matt winked.

"Matt, cut it out!" *I can't believe this guy!*

"Can't blame a guy for tryin'."

"Whatever."

"Do you want to go sit down and get somethin' to drink?"

"Sure." Cora was relieved Matt had been the one to make the suggestion to stop dancing. "Thanks for encouraging me to come tonight. I really did need some time away from Susie. Taking care of a child all the time can be pretty tiring."

"I'm sure it is." He scanned the adjacent tables. At the table, he sat in the chair next to Cora, instead of across from her, as before. She scooted over a little to keep a comfortable distance.

"What do you want to drink?"

"I'll take a cola." Matt laughed in response to Cora's order. When he returned with two beers, she said, "No thanks."

"You weren't kiddin', were you?"

"No." She smiled weakly.

"I'll be right back." Matt went back to the bar and got Cora a soft drink. "I'm sorry, Cora. I thought you were only kiddin' me about the beer." Matt settled in the chair next to her, loosening his tie.

"No. I really don't drink. Most people can't believe it, but I don't."

"Why is that? Have you never tried it?" Matt pushed his beer mug over to her.

"No, honestly, I haven't tried it. I don't want to, either. I don't think I'm missing anything. I don't feel it's a good example for others. Since I've been taking care of Susie, I see things in a new way."

"I see. But Susie isn't here."

"Just the same, I'll pass."

"You don't mind if I have a beer, do you?" Matt took a big swig.

Cora could feel her upper lip turning up a bit in disgust. *How could he ask if I minded, and then drink it anyway before I could answer?*

Cora listened to song after country song until the once-entertaining sound of the steel guitar sounded much like an out-of-tune piano. Matt soon lost interest in her, as she'd guessed he would, and moved on to a woman at another table. Cora searched for Clarice in the dim light of the bar but never saw her. She gritted her teeth and tapped her fingers on the table, where she now sat alone. *I wish I'd brought my car so I could leave.*

After turning down several offers to dance, she surveyed the dancers through the cloud of smoke, noticing the obvious couples compared to the potential one-night-stands. Her heart ached for the ones seeking love in a bar.

Then she heard a familiar voice talking at the table beside her and turned toward the voice. *Rex!* He was dressed like a city cowboy. He greeted the people seated at the adjacent table, shaking their hands and patting their backs. Rex was very friendly...almost jolly.

Since the music was loud and she would risk him not hearing her, she didn't call out to him but merely waited to see if he noticed her sitting alone. She took a sip of her soda.

A few minutes later, Rex turned around. When he saw Cora, he instantly came over to her. "Cora? What are you doing here? Why are you alone?" Rex pulled out a chair and sat down across from her. "Do you mind?"

"Of course not. I came with Matt and Clarice and their friend Justin. But they've all left me, I hate to say." The music got louder, and Cora had to lean toward Rex and yell.

"Left you? They left here and didn't take you home?" Rex's jaw clamped shut.

Cora waved her hands in the air, protesting Rex's assumption. "No, no. I'm sorry. I didn't mean to imply that. They're dancing is what I was trying to say."

"And you?" He raised his right eyebrow.

"Nope. A few offers, though. I danced with Matt, but he soon tired of me and moved on." She played with the water droplets on the table.

"Why's that?" Rex leaned forward.

"A difference of opinion about beer."

"Did he try to put the moves on you?" Rex asked calmly.

"Yeah. No harm done, though. He didn't push the issue." Cora relaxed her shoulders for the first time that night. She looked into Rex's eyes, and he looked back. Their eyes locked.

"I'm glad. Matt's pretty slick with the ladies. He should stay away from you."

"Slick, huh? Must run in the family." Cora grinned, not asking why Rex wanted him to stay away from her. The question lingered on her tongue, however.

"Good one. Would you care to dance?" Rex invited.

"Of course, I would."

She got up from her chair and took Rex's offered hand, so warm and big with calluses, which proved he was a working man. His fresh scent filled her nostrils as they began the two-step, the same dance Cora had experienced with Matt. However, this dance was different. Her feet moved in unison with Rex's, shuffling across the sawdust floor, as Rex led Cora all around the room. When a slow song started, Rex pulled Cora in closer to him, and she did not resist.

Cora felt light-headed. If Rex felt what she was feeling, this could mean trouble. In the back of her mind, as they swayed to the music, was the fact that Rex was so different from her. It was obvious by his lifestyle. She wanted so much for him to change, but she knew she couldn't make it happen. She'd tried that with Clark, and it hadn't worked. *Lord, what's happening here?*

She closed her eyes and moved in closer to Rex, placing her head on his chest. His shirt was soft on her cheek. He was a head taller than her, and she could not reach his shoulder unless she stood on her tiptoes. His arms, strong around her waist, offered security from the world.

After the third song, Rex whispered in her ear, "Let's go sit down for a while."

"Okay."

Rex went to the bar, brought back cola for Cora, and water for himself. She smiled. Rex smiled back, but he said nothing. As they sat and talked, he played with the cuff on her shirtsleeve, and she occasionally rubbed her index finger across his hand.

They both jumped when Veronica threw her purse down on their table. Startled, they moved their hands away from each other. Cora looked wild-eyed back and forth from Rex to Veronica.

"How dare you bring her here! You knew I'd be here. What do you have to say for yourself?" Veronica hissed, eyes flashing lightning rods at Cora.

Standing, Rex walked around Cora and took Veronica by the arm. "Don't make a scene in here. Now sit down!" Rex shoved Veronica into a chair opposite Cora. Cora jumped. Then he reclaimed his seat next to her, throwing his leg over the back of the chair. "I did not bring her here. She came with Matt and Clarice. I just happened to run into her."

"Well, it sure looked like something else was happening here besides casual conversation. I've been watching you," Veronica sneered. Her painted eyelids and nails made her look like a saloon girl...a jealous saloon girl.

Rex said nothing. He only looked at Veronica.

Seconds went by like hours. Cora's heart pounded in her ears as she wondered what Veronica was capable of doing.

Matt came to their table. "What's going on, big brother?"

"None of your business, Matt." Veronica's words dripped with venom.

Matt held up his hands in mock surrender.

"Veronica," Rex said, as Cora heaved a sigh over the broken silence, "I told you the truth. It's obvious you don't trust me. Obviously you're not what I'm lookin' for in a woman," Rex said quietly, so as not to embarrass Veronica.

"What? And I suppose she is!" Veronica glared at Cora.

Cora shifted in her seat. Matt never took his widened eyes off Rex.

"I'm not gonna dignify that question with an answer." Rex turned to Cora and took her hand. "Come on, I'm takin' you back to the ranch."

Cora got up immediately and let out the breath she had held for over a minute. As the two left the bar, Veronica threw something at them, hitting them in the backs of their legs, but they didn't stop to see what it was.

When they got out to Rex's truck, they jumped in and he pulled away from the bar. Once they were down the road a bit, Rex spoke. "Cora, I'm so sorry."

"That's okay. It wasn't your fault. It just proves to me I don't belong in a place like that." She looked at Rex through the glow of car lights.

"You know somethin'? I don't, either." He chuckled.

Cora laughed along with Rex. In the dark cab of the truck, she could barely see his face as they passed a streetlight. She liked hearing him laugh, though. "I know it probably isn't any of my business, but is something going on between the two of you?"

"How did you guess? We haven't been getting along lately. She's turned into a possessive...well, you know what I mean? I don't like being around her."

"Why not?"

"I think it's you." Rex glanced over at Cora.

Cora swallowed hard, something she'd had to do a lot of lately. *I was afraid of this. Now what do I do? I finally find a man who's gorgeous and sweet most of the time, but his lifestyle is all wrong. But he did say he doesn't belong in the bars. Maybe he is changing.* She glanced over at him, shaking her foot nervously. "Me? What do you mean?"

"Two things really. First of all, you're a lovely lady. But, compared to Veronica, you're like Mother Teresa. And now I've gotten to know you and respect what you do for my daughter, I can't settle for someone like her."

"Thank you. That's a kind thing to say." Cora felt genuinely pleased to hear Rex's words. She traced her lips with her finger, remembering his lips on them. She stretched her legs out and crossed her feet.

"I'm also attracted to you. Not because of the type of person you are and how you are compared to Veronica, but for who you are, just for you. You have this glow about you. I can't be with her when I see there is someone like you."

"Rex, I thank you for what you're saying. But I told you before..."

"Cora, I'm not tryin' to make you go against your beliefs. I'm just sayin' I can't settle for Veronica when there might be a Cora out there somewhere for me. I know you'd never settle for me. I wouldn't want you to. You deserve someone much better than me."

As Cora looked at Rex, she saw sadness in his eyes, the laugh lines at the corners barely visible. "Rex, I think you're terrific. I never meant to imply you weren't good enough for me. We just have different values. And I'm still grieving too. We've talked about this before. I think we got off to a rough start. The more I know you, the more I like you. Especially when we were dancing tonight."

"Oh?" Rex smirked.

"Oh, yes." Cora boldly shrugged her eyebrows at him.

"Forbidden love, huh?" Rex pulled into the gates of the Southern Hope ranch.

"I guess so." They both laughed.

It was now midnight, and the O'Reillys were in bed. Once inside, they walked up the stairs together. "Good night, Cora." Rex stood at the entrance to Cora's bedroom.

As he turned to leave, Cora whispered to him, "Rex, thanks for bringing me home...and for the conversation." She leaned up and kissed him on the cheek. He leaned toward her to kiss her mouth, but she pulled away, uncertain where that might lead.

Once in her room, Cora dressed for bed and climbed between her sheets. But as soon as she relaxed underneath the covers, she remembered. She flung them back and slid from her four-poster bed. Pulling on her robe, she exited her room, walking quietly down the hall to Susie's room. She entered and closed the door behind her. *A promise is a promise.* When she turned around, she saw Rex. He was kissing his daughter and tucking her in. He was tenderhearted, more than she'd ever imagined.

Rex smiled at Cora as she walked over to the bed. The child lay so peacefully. Cora hated to disturb her even with a kiss. They made sure Susie was tucked in and then left her room. Once out in the hall again, they stood looking at each other. Cora noticed Rex studying her robe. Loneliness threatened to overtake her. The past year without Clark had left not only an emotional void in Cora's life, but a physical void, as well. She feared their kiss had stirred a forbidden fire. She said good night again and scurried down the hall to the safety of her room.

When she climbed back in the bed, her tiredness from before was something of the past. She turned on her television and flipped through the channels. She settled on the late-night news in time to see a report about another missing woman, this time from Lewistown, where Ms. Lottie's place was.

Oh Lord, God, please! Let them catch this guy! Please don't let anyone die because of this psychopath.

9

The following morning, Cora awoke with a smile, remembering her ride home with Rex the night before. She stretched and her spine tingled from her encounter. The August sun blazed in through her curtains, dancing across her bed. She stretched again, yawned, and protested having to get up.

Cora rolled over in her bed. Snuggled up next to her and sleeping soundly was little Susie. She gently brushed the child's hair out of her face. Suddenly she remembered the news story about the missing woman. *Lord, please protect this precious child from this kind of tragedy. She has already been through so much.*

Slowly, Susie's eyes opened.

"Good morning, little one. Did you sleep well last night?"

"Yes, ma'am." Susie wrapped her arms around Cora's neck. Her Snow White nightgown felt so soft on Cora's skin. Her hair smelled like lavender.

"Well, good. How did you end up in my room?"

"I missed you. I had to see if you came home."

"Oh, Susie, I told you I'd return. I came in last night and kissed you good night." Cora tapped Susie's nose. "I guess we better get up. Breakfast will be ready soon. You stay here in my bed while I go shower. Okay?" Cora climbed out of bed reluctantly.

"Can I go to my room and play?"

"Of course you can, Sweetie. I'll be in to dress you when I get myself ready." Cora went into the bathroom and shut the door.

"Can I come in with you?" Susie asked from outside the door.

"No, darling, you run along and play. I'll be in soon."

Susie left Cora's room, and Cora proceeded to get ready for breakfast. She lavished her shower, washing away the smell of cigarettes from the night before at Wild Bill's. She dried her hair, put on a little foundation and mascara, and then dressed in her jeans and black T-shirt. She slipped her sandals on and went down the hall to Susie's room.

Half an hour later, Cora and Susie entered the dining room where R.L., Pearl, and Matt waited for breakfast.

"Good morning, girls," R.L. greeted.

"Morning." Cora sat in her usual seat, Susie by her side. Cora looked for Rex, but he was nowhere in sight.

"Good morning, Cora." Matt winked at her.

Blushing, Cora greeted him. *Why is he acting like that? Is he flirting with me? Could he be laughing because I left Wild Bill's with Rex last night? Surely, he doesn't think something happened between us.*

Soon after, Rex entered the room. Instead of taking his seat across the table from Cora, as he usually did, he sat next to her. Matt cleared his throat and chuckled, making it clear to everyone what he thought. Rex shot Matt a disapproving glare through narrow slits, and then turned to Cora and gave her a huge grin. Cora noticed R.L. and Pearl eyeing each other and smiling. Something was definitely going on.

"So, Rex, have you decided which direction you'd like us to take with the ranch?"

"No, Matt. And I hardly think this is the time to talk about it." Rex grimaced.

"Well, you and I haven't exactly been on the same side of the planet lately. When do you think we're gonna talk about it?" Matt took a loud sip from his coffee.

Cora's gaze flitted back and forth between brothers. The tension between the two was undeniable. How could Matt switch from playful flirt to hard-headed businessman so easily?

"We can talk privately in Dad's office later or I can come into town and we can meet. Breakfast after a late night out is not the time."

"Matt, Rex is right," R.L. cautioned.

"As always." Matt looked away.

"Excuse me, ma'am." Jimmy entered the dining room from the kitchen. "Miss Clarice hasn't come down yet. Should I serve breakfast, or do we wait for her?"

"It's 8:20 a.m. already. She knows breakfast is at 8:00 a.m. We'll go ahead and eat," Pearl answered.

"I wonder why she hasn't come down yet. You think she's feeling okay?"

"Oh, R.L., you pamper that girl too much. Rex, didn't y'all go out last night together?" Pearl asked.

"Yes, ma'am. Well, I joined up with them later." Rex drank a sip of his coffee and added sugar and cream, then buttered his toast, cut it in half, and gave Susie one piece.

"Maybe she's tired. She may have had too much to drink, although I hope that isn't the case. What time did you get in?" R.L. questioned Rex.

"I brought Cora home early. I didn't go with them; I went there later, by myself. I don't know what time Matt and Clarice got in last night. Matt?" Rex turned to his brother.

"Uh, I got in at 2:00 a.m." Matt's face turned red. He picked at his eggs with his fork.

"What do you mean *you* got in? Where was your sister? You went there together." R.L. glared at Matt.

"I took someone home, and Clarice said she'd be fine." He shifted nervously in his chair.

"Son, I can't believe you left her there. Why didn't you go back and check on her?" Pearl slammed her hand down on the table and Cora jumped.

"Mom, she can take care of herself."

"I'm going up to check on her. I can't believe you were so irresponsible!" Pearl got up from the table. "Excuse me, Cora." She stormed out of the room.

The rest of the family began eating breakfast in silence. Cora could hardly eat, sick that something might have happened to Clarice. She turned to Rex, giving him a worried look. He touched her arm gently. Cora thought about the missing girl report but said nothing for fear of spreading panic to the family.

Within a few minutes, Pearl came bounding down the stairs and into the dining room frantically. "R.L.! Clarice isn't in her room. It looks as if she didn't come home last night. Where could she be? I shouldn't have gone to bed last night without checking on her."

"Now, honey, I'm sure she's fine. She probably stayed in town with a friend." R.L. turned toward Rex. "Rex, can you go look for Clarice?"

"Yes, sir, I'm on my way. Cora, go with me." Rex looked in Matt's direction and groaned.

Cora looked at Pearl. "What about Susie?"

"Go."

Rex and Cora were heading out the front door when Clarice stepped onto the front porch. Her untucked blouse was unbuttoned past her cleavage. She carried her boots in her hand. Her makeup was almost entirely gone except for her smeared mascara. A blue pickup disappeared down the driveway.

"Where have you been?" Rex demanded of his sister, who was giggling.

"None of your business," Clarice stammered, trying to push past her brother.

Grabbing her arm, Rex turned Clarice toward him. Cora noted bruises on the girl's face. "It most certainly is my business. Mom and Dad are worried sick about you. For all they know, you're dead. Look at your face. What happened to you? Now tell me where you've been!" Rex kept his eyes on hers.

"I met somebody! Okay? I went home with him." Clarice looked at her brother, tightening her jaw.

"Clarice! How could you?" Cora gasped. "Did you know someone else was kidnapped last night? It could have been you." Rex and Clarice both turned toward her, surprised by her outburst. "I'm sorry, but I can't believe it." An earthquake rumbled through Cora because of her disappointment in Clarice.

"Oh, please, Cora, get a life. Like you've never done anything like this before. What do you think I went to Wild Bill's for, anyway? This isn't the first time I've done this. It's just the first time I've gotten caught." Clarice crossed her arms across her chest, causing her top button to unbutton, revealing more cleavage.

"What? Young lady, do you realize if Mom and Dad knew you'd stayed out like this before they would lock you in your room? Not to mention what else could have happened to you." Rex pointed his finger in her face.

"So what? I'd find a way to get out if they locked me up. I'm an adult, anyway. And nothing would happen to me." Clarice tapped her boot defiantly on the porch.

Cora went over to the porch swing and sat down. She stared in disbelief at what she was hearing. She never imagined Clarice would be promiscuous. She had hoped she was only a flirt.

"Clarice, you're not an adult if you can't support yourself. You can't pay your way. You live off Daddy."

"I hate you, Rex!" She stomped her foot.

"Go inside! I'm not helping you out of this mess."

"Rex! Come on. I didn't mean it. That's not fair." Clarice grabbed his arm.

"Fair? How fair is it that Mom and Dad are in there, frantic? This is the fairest thing I could do for you. Maybe this will straighten you out. Now get in there!" Rex pointed toward the door.

When Clarice reluctantly opened the door and walked in, the sound of R.L.'s voice yelling at Matt filtered out.

Hearing Susie crying, Cora ran past Rex and Clarice to get to the child. When Susie saw Cora, she ran from her gramma's arms and into Cora's. Cora whisked the tot outside on the porch to swing. She didn't want Susie to hear the explosion that was soon to occur.

It was half an hour before Rex came out onto the porch. He wiped the sweat from the back of his neck. He walked over to the swing and sat next to Cora, taking Susie into his arms. "Hi."

"Hi." Cora looked straight ahead. A hot morning breeze blew across her face.

"Thanks for bringin' Susie out here. I don't like her to be around when there's fightin' goin' on."

A cow mooed in a far-off pasture.

"You're welcome. I didn't think I really belonged in there, nor did I care to be." Cora rubbed her hands back and forth on her legs. She surveyed the cracked paint on the porch flooring.

Grabbing one of her hands in his, Rex gazed straight into her eyes. "Don't be nervous. Everything will be okay."

"I'm not so sure, Rex. Did Clarice go home with a friend? A boyfriend, I mean?" Cora asked.

"Not exactly." Rex looked down at the ground.

"Good." She blew out a puff of breath.

"No, not really." He raised his eyes to hers.

"What do you mean?" Cora watched Susie as she jumped down from her father's lap.

"She went home with a stranger."

"A stranger? No! How could she? I can't believe she'd do that, knowing there's a kidnapper on the loose. Did she—"

"Yes, and evidently she's done this before."

"Oh. What did your parents say?" Cora stared into Rex's dark eyes, genuinely concerned for his sister.

He exhaled. "Well, at first they were thrilled to see her alive. But when they saw she was unharmed, except for those bruises, they demanded some answers. They were very disappointed in her for not callin', for goin' home with someone she didn't know, and for doin' what she did while she was with him. They were also furious with Matt for leavin' her there. Turns out he met a woman and took her home. He stayed at her house for quite a while, if you know what I mean."

"So, both of them...?"

"Yes, evidently so."

Cora buried her head in her hands. "I feel awful for leaving her there last night."

"No, no, you're not to blame. Clarice is a big girl, and she knew what she was doing. One night wouldn't have made a difference. Besides, Matt was responsible for both of you last night. When I brought you home, he was no longer responsible for you. But he was still to look after Clarice."

"I still feel bad. Maybe if I'd stayed, Clarice wouldn't have left with that guy. And maybe Matt wouldn't have gone home with someone he didn't know."

74

"Don't bet on it. They both think of themselves first. You heard Clarice. She said she went there looking for a man. She would have left with him no matter what. And, if you'd stayed with Matt, you might have ended up like the woman he spent the night with—used and discarded."

"Nothing would have happened between me and Matt, I assure you. I think he knew that too, because he quickly grew tired of sitting with me at the table. I wish I'd never gone with them. I wanted to drive my own car, but they insisted I ride with them. Truthfully, I wish I'd never gone at all. I'm not used to things like this." Cora's stomach flip-flopped.

"I know what you mean. I never went to Wild Bill's until after Patricia was gone. It was all new to me, too. You'll get used to it."

"Oh, no, I won't." She held up her hands in protest. "I'm not going back there again. I told you last night I wasn't cut out for places like that." Cora got up from the swing to check on Susie, who had run to play on the walkway.

"Cora? Wasn't there anything good about last night?" Rex came after her.

Cora turned. "Oh, yes. I was able to get to know you a little better. But, you're still a mystery to me."

"Me? You're the mysterious one."

"I don't think so." Cora giggled.

The front door opened, and out came Matt with Clarice right on his heels, yelling at each other, saying things Susie should not hear.

"I'll talk to you later, Rex." Cora rushed down the steps and took Susie's hand. She led her up the steps and into the house. Susie began to cry.

Once upstairs and in Susie's room, the two played until lunchtime. They talked, and Cora tried to answer Susie's questions about her family's arguments as best she could. She and Susie had their lunch served out by the pool. After they ate, Susie went down for her nap.

Cora went into the kitchen and used Jimmy's computer to email Anne and tell her about Clarice. She had to get the events of the past twenty-four hours off her chest.

10

"Mrs. O'Reilly?"

"Pearl."

"Pearl." Cora smiled. "Would you mind if I take a few hours away to ride one of the horses around the ranch?" Cora, wound tighter than a ball of yarn, needed a break from the Clarice episode.

"Of course not. Susie will be fine here. You go ahead."

Cora changed into her old jeans and a worn T-shirt and walked toward the stables. On Saturdays, most of the ranch hands headed into town for the day, so Cora didn't worry about going to the stables by herself. Only Rusty, one of her favorite hands and one she trusted, would be there. Cora stopped to watch the baby chickens at the chicken coup. She reached down and patted a kitten on the head.

Rusty gave Cora a gray horse with black spots. "Her name's Millie, and she is the gentlest one we have on the ranch."

"Thank you." With Rusty's assistance, Cora mounted Millie and was on her way. Her body melded into the saddle, which freed her mind from worries of falling off Millie in her gallop, so she could enjoy the cloud-sprinkled sky and scrubby pines. The ranch seemed to go on forever, the rolling hills various shades of green. Wild flowers bloomed in every field Cora rode through. Cows dotted the landscape at every turn. Gravel paths popped up sporadically, edged by barns, bales of hay, and ponds.

By the time Cora looked at her watch, over an hour had passed. *I really should head back.* She was a little afraid to be so far away from the ranch by herself. The wildlife...the kidnapper...creepy ranch hands who might be watching her. Sighing, she reluctantly turned Millie around and retraced her path. She was about halfway to the stables when, all of a sudden, Millie began to kick and twist like a bronco.

"Steady, Millie. Calm down!" But Millie did not heed Cora's call. Unexpectedly the horse bolted like lightning over the hill behind the stables.

"Slow down, girl! Please! Millie, Millie!" Cora pleaded. She tried to remain calm so as not to excite Millie any more than she already was, but it was no use. Now she could only hold on as tightly as she could.

Millie ran and ran until she topped the huge hill, then headed straight down it, ignoring the path already cut out. Cora closed her eyes and ducked down as far as she could against Millie's mane. *Lord, please let Millie stop running long enough for me to jump off.*

Then, without warning, Millie raised up on her back legs and Cora fell off. As she hit the ground, landing painfully on her side, she looked up to watch as Millie ran over another peak. Cora winced with pain. Her brain felt as though it was rattling in her head. She lay on the ground and began to cry. She'd never felt pain like this before in her life. Fire shot through her body. She wasn't sure where her injuries were, but she knew she couldn't move. She only hoped someone would come for her soon.

* * *

"Cora, Cora? Wake up. Are you okay?"

Cora heard someone calling her from a distance. She opened her eyes and tried to move. "Ouch! I can't move." Suddenly she was aware of Rex gently touching her face.

"What happened?" Rex checked to see if Cora was bleeding anywhere.

"Millie threw me." Cora tried to move again.

"Millie? How?"

"I don't know. Something scared her, I think. She just bolted. I held on as long as I could."

"Where do you hurt?"

"I think it's my side. I landed on my ribs." Cora coughed.

Immediately, Rex scooped Cora up off the ground and walked away from the direction of the ranch.

"Where are you taking me?" Cora breathlessly held her side.

"To my cabin."

"But where...?" Cora began and then turned her head toward the direction Rex was walking. She saw a beautiful log cabin tucked away amongst a cluster of oak trees towering above. "Oh, Rex! It's beautiful."

Clearly pleased, Rex carried Cora into the cabin and laid her down on the couch in the living room, in the back of the cabin, which boasted wall-to-wall windows from the floor to ceiling, both made of pine. Outside, through the windows, Cora saw a bubbling creek about five feet wide, and Millie munching on grass. She let out a low grumble.

Rex headed toward the kitchen. "I'll be right back. Don't try to move."

Cora obeyed. She looked around with wide eyes despite her pain. Inside, a cobblestone fireplace graced the back wall, and the furnishings of pine and rattan added to the rustic feel. The chairs were sea green and white striped, and the couch printed with pastel roses. The overstuffed recliner in the corner, Cora assumed, was Rex's chair. Although the cabin was quite masculine in design, an air of femininity floated about the place. Silk flower arrangements and custom frames with family pictures adorned the end tables. Bowls of potpourri, which still held a faint scent, fragranced the cabin, reminding Cora of the mountains in the Carolinas.

Rex came from the kitchen carrying a glass of water and some tablets. "Here take these. I've called the doctor, but he won't be here for another forty-five minutes. Looks like you may have bruised your ribs. He said it didn't sound as though you'd broken any, so that is good."

"Thanks." Cora took the medicine from Rex. "What am I taking?"

"Just some aspirin. It's all I have here. Sorry I couldn't offer you something other than water, but I don't have anything in the fridge." Rex's eyes clouded.

"That's okay. I'm so glad you found me. How did you know where I was?" Cora tried to shift into a more comfortable position.

Sitting on the end of the sofa, Rex put Cora's feet in his lap. "I didn't know where you were. I happened to be out this way, and something told me to come toward home. I'm not usually here. It's a miracle I found you. Luckily I got to ya before you dehydrated or a snake got ya." Smirking, he brushed dust from her boots.

"Please, don't get your hands dirty." Cora ignored his comment about the snake, although it did send a shiver up her spine.

Rex removed her boots. "There, that's better."

"Rex, you're impossible. Now tell me…why didn't the doctor want me to come to his office?"

"I told him I didn't want you to be moved. I felt like you need to rest."

"Thanks. Again." Cora drank her glass of water and reached to set it down on the coffee table. She winced.

"Here, give it to me. So, we have some time to talk. Whatcha wanna talk about?"

"How did things turn out with Matt and Clarice?"

"Be glad you left when you did. Matt was furious with Clarice for not coming home. Clarice was angry because neither of us took up for her. I don't know what to do with either of them." Rex ran his finger along the top of Cora's socked foot.

She shivered again. "What do you mean? Why, in your opinion, is what they're doing so wrong?" She asked because she wanted to test Rex.

"Because they shouldn't go home with strangers. Or with anyone, for that matter." Rex blushed.

Cora noticed his embarrassment. "Oh?"

"What do you mean?"

"No offense. I just thought..." She looked away.

"What? Veronica and me? No way!"

"Really?" Cora's eyes sparkled.

"No, never! What gave you that idea?" Rex shifted to face her.

"You did stay out all night with her that one night, so I assumed.... And you didn't exactly deny it that morning at the pool."

"You got me on that one. I guess I was too prideful to admit what I'd really been doing. Let me set the record straight." The sun popped out from behind a cloud and beamed in through the windows, casting directly on Rex's tanned face. His dark eyes were like deep pools.

"Wait! You don't have to explain anything to me. Really," Cora interrupted.

"Yes, I do. I like you. And I want you to know the truth about me. I know I came across cocky in the beginning, and I meant to. You see, when I first met you at Ms. Lottie's, I thought you were the prettiest thing I'd ever seen. Not just because of your looks, but your personality as well. I came home and told Mom about you. I don't know why, but I did." Rex paused.

"I'm shocked. I didn't think you even noticed me."

"Oh, yes, I noticed you. Anyway, when Mom and Dad brought you home, I knew they were trying to match-make. It made me mad that they were interfering in my life, so I rejected the very thought of you. I could tell right away the type of woman you were, respectable and all. So I pretended to be a stud so you wouldn't like me."

"And that was all an act?" Cora mused.

"No, not all of it. I *am* a stud." Rex smirked.

"Go on with your story, before I kick you." Cora snickered.

"What else do you want to know?" Rex glanced around the cabin at the display of memories.

"The rest. The part about you and Veronica. I thought you were serious with one another."

"No way. That's what she wanted you to think. She was jealous of you from the start."

"I knew that much. She was too insecure acting for me not to figure that out. So, you didn't bring her here?" Cora pushed.

"No, why do you ask?"

"I wasn't going to say anything to you, because I didn't want you to think I was eavesdropping. One night, right after I came here, I went out on the back porch—hoping to find you, actually—and I heard voices in the pool. It was you and Veronica." Cora looked away from Rex.

"And? What's the question?"

"I heard her asking you to bring her here, and when you said 'no,' she..."

"...tried to get me to be with her in the pool?" Rex completed her thought. He closed his eyes and shook his head from side to side.

"Yes." Cora continued to look away, knowing she'd caught him in a lie.

"You obviously didn't stick around to hear what happened after that."

"No." Cora peeked back at Rex.

"I told her I wasn't ready to be with her. I said I hadn't completely gotten over Patricia, and I felt marriage should come before sex." Rex stared directly into Cora's eyes with such intensity it made his eyes water.

"Really? You're not just saying that?"

"Believe me, if it wasn't true, I wouldn't say it. This is too embarrassin' for me to talk about."

"Why embarrassing?" Cora inquired.

"Because I'm a man. Real men are supposed to get right back in the saddle, if you know what I mean."

"I'm a fool. I thought the worst of you. I'm sorry." Cora reached for Rex's hand.

Taking her hand in his, Rex accepted her apology. "That explains why you pulled away from me in the pool last Sunday. You thought...oh, I'm so sorry."

"I thought you were a gigolo." Cora chortled.

"Well, I'm not. I even have a confession to make. When you saw me that mornin' at the pool, I was returnin' from Ms. Lottie's. I wasn't out all night with Veronica. I stayed with Ms. Lottie." Rex colored. "I go there a lot to get away from the ranch."

"You're her boy."

The two laughed and talked until the doctor came to check on Cora.

As the doctor suspected, Cora had only bruised her ribs. He wrapped her tightly and told her she should rest for a week. When she asked about her duties with Susie, he told her someone else would have to tend to the child. Rex reassured Cora he'd watch after Susie. Cora knew then she had made an impact on Rex's life. He was finally becoming a better father.

A couple hours later, when she was alone, back in her room, Cora blew out a frustrated grunt for thinking romantic thoughts of Rex. Only two weeks had passed since Clark's funeral, and she seemed to have forgotten, practically overnight, about him. *You should be ashamed of yourself. When I'm better, and I have enough money, I had better hightail it out of here and head home to Florida. Starting a relationship with Rex, as nice as he may be, would not be a good idea at this time.* She knew what she had to do.

* * *

Per the doctor's orders, Cora stayed in bed to rest the next day. She hated to miss church since she'd done so the week before. A heaviness fell on her heart. *I wonder if I made the right decision in coming to the ranch. I made it out of defiance to Mom and Dad, after all. If I had stayed with Ms. Lottie, I wouldn't be developing a potentially destructive relationship with Rex, and I'd at least be closer to church. Well, what's done is done.*

As Cora lay in her bed, reading a book, someone knocked on her door. "Come in." She straightened her covers, pulling them up over her chest.

"Good mornin'. Here's your breakfast." Rex carried a tray of food.

"Rex? What are you doing? You don't have to pamper me like this." Cora's breath caught in her throat. She stared at his dark eyes, tanned skin, tight jeans, and boots. She swallowed hard.

"It's my pleasure. Someone has to take care of you. Mom and Dad are gettin' ready to leave for church, and so is Jimmy. So that leaves me." Rex grinned and set the tray over her lap.

"But you need to go to church with Susie. What about Clarice or Matt? Or...or...Juanita?"

"Cora? What's wrong? You don't want me here?" The sparkle left his eyes.

"No, it's not that." She shook her head.

"It must be somethin', if you'd rather have Clarice or Matt take care of you. And Juanita has the day off anyway." Rex waited for her excuse.

"I feel funny being alone in the house with you. What will people think? What will your family say?"

"I don't think anyone will think a thing since you're in the condition you're in. Nobody's around for miles. Now, eat!" He nudged the tray closer.

Cora surveyed the silver tray Rex had brought to her. "Mmm, the food does smell good." She noted the bud vase with a pink rose in it. "Thank you, Rex. The rose is lovely, too." Cora looked at him and melted.

"I thought it would be a nice touch. Is something else botherin' you?"

"No. I guess not. Maybe it's just the pain medicine."

"I'm goin' to go downstairs. I'll be in my office for a while. I'm workin' on a few plans for the ranch. Dad and Matt want me to come up with a design for the workin' ranch." He groaned.

"Oh, that sounds so cool."

"I'm not thrilled about it, but they're forcin' my hand."

"I hope you get some work done."

"Me, too. I'll be back in about thirty minutes to get your tray, okay?"

"Thanks." Cora smiled as Rex left her room.

After enjoying her breakfast, she stretched out in the bed with her cell phone between her ear and shoulder and called Anne.

"Hey, Cora. What are you doing?"

"I'm in bed." She ran her fingers through her messy hair, combing out the tangles.

"In bed? What for?"

"I got thrown from a horse on the ranch yesterday and practically killed myself."

"Are you okay?"

"Yeah, just sore and bored." She yawned.

"Have you got anyone there to take care of you?" Anne teased.

"You're so funny. Yes, Rex is here. In fact, he's home playing nurse today." She sniggered.

"Very cool. Life gets better and better for you, huh?"

"Yeah, having an injury after being thrown from a horse...that's a real treat." The two laughed until Cora's sides ached.

"Are you going to be okay, though?"

"Oh, yeah. The doctor said my ribs were bruised, and I need to chill out for a few days."

"Did you call your mom?"

"No way. I don't need her rushing up here taking over. I'll call them soon. I can't go there right now. Hey, listen, I hear Rex coming up the steps. I'm going to let you go and call you later, okay?"

"Sure thing."

"Bye." Cora closed her cell phone and quickly pulled herself to a sitting position in the bed.

When Rex returned for her tray, Susie trailed right behind him. "I want to stay home from church so me and Cora can play."

"No, not today, girl." Rex patted her on the top of the head.

"Please, Daddy?" Susie begged.

Cora interjected, "Susie, I can't take care of you until my ribs are better. You'll have to go to church with your gramma."

"Yes, ma'am." Susie leaned up and kissed Cora on the cheek before leaving her room.

"I'll see you later, honey." Cora stuck her bottom lip out at Rex and then grinned.

"Okay, dear." He hooted and winked at her.

"I meant Susie!" Embarrassed, she slapped the air.

"Do you need anything else?"

"No, I'm fine. Thanks."

"Get some rest. I'll be back in a while."

Cora's mind swirled with thoughts about the decision she must make. She fluffed her covers, fidgeted, flipped through her Bible, and thought of ways she could help out if she stayed at the ranch. She turned on the television only to see a report of another missing woman—this one from Lewistown. The woman's description was similar to hers: dark hair and green eyes. *Hold on. Is there a pattern here?*

Cora began to put the pieces of the puzzle together.

11

Cora carefully moved herself out of her bed, unable to stay there any longer, and ambled to the terrace outside her bedroom. She chose a wicker chair as far against the wall as she could, so she could hide from anyone returning home from church. She listened for Rex coming up the stairs, too, so she could sneak back into her bed quickly. She knew Rex would scold her if he caught her out of bed.

Suddenly, the loud noise of a car racing down the driveway, spinning its tires as the gears changed, alerted Cora. She started to jump up from her seat but winced. At second glance, Cora saw that the car was Veronica's. Before she had a chance to try to move again, Rex flew out the side door of the house and onto the driveway to meet Veronica. Cora pushed herself as far back into her chair as she could, trying to remain quiet.

As Veronica squealed her car to a halt, missing Rex by only a foot or two, he called to her, "What are you doin' here?" Cora could tell by the stiffness in his neck he didn't want to see her.

Getting out of the car, one long leg at a time, and removing her dark sunglasses, Veronica spoke. "Boy, what a way to greet your girlfriend. I'm here because I have tried to call you, but you never return my calls. I assumed you weren't getting my messages. I knew everybody would be at church. I knew we could be alone."

Cora closed her eyes. She didn't want to see or hear them talking. *I wish I could be invisible.*

"You're not welcome here."

"What?" Veronica stomped over to Rex.

"I mean it, Roni, go home!"

"Why? It's that...that...woman, isn't it? She's turned you against me."

"Look, leave Cora out of this. She did not turn me against you. She's an innocent party in all of this. After the way you acted Friday night...well, put it this way: you turned me against you with no help from her."

Cora opened her eyes and peeked through the rails. Rex turned to enter the house, but Veronica grabbed his arm. When they disappeared under the terrace, Cora could no longer see them. She ducked quickly into her room but allowed the French doors to remain open. She still wanted to hear if she could.

"What do you mean by that?"

"Veronica, *you* chased me away," Rex insisted. "You held on to me so tight I couldn't breathe. You were too pushy when it came to certain things. You refused to give me time to get over Patricia."

"Oh, Patricia, Patricia! I'm so sick of that woman's name. What was so great about her anyway? You act like she was a saint, when we both know she was a tramp."

"You shut your mouth." Rex's voice was coldly angry. "You don't talk about Patty like that. She was the mother of my child. She was not a tramp."

"How do you really know you're Susie's father? I suppose you've forgotten about her little affairs with the men at Wild Bill's. And that she drank so much because of her guilt that she ran off Connors Peak and killed herself? Forget about her. You're wasting your life worshipping her memory. And, might I add, a memory that's seen through rose-colored glasses," Veronica hissed.

Cora couldn't believe what she heard. *Is this true about Patricia? How can it be? Rex acts as if she could walk on water.*

Rex spoke with tears dripping off his voice. "Roni, you've hurt me for the last time. If you loved me, you wouldn't talk about my wife like that. You'd forgive her as I've done. I want you to leave, and don't ever come back."

"What do you know about love? You worked day and night on this stupid ranch until Patty was bored out of her mind. That's why she'd go to Wild Bill's. That's why she looked for someone to love her. You didn't meet her needs."

"You're such a liar! Get off my property! Get out of my life!" Rex yelled.

Cora heard the door to the house slam shut. Veronica got in her car and zoomed down the drive. Her heart ached for Rex. She wanted nothing more than to go to him and comfort him, but she could not. She couldn't let him know she had overheard his fight with Veronica.

Then Rex knocked on Cora's door. She was still standing by the terrace door when he entered. "Can I come in?" he asked and then burst into the room.

"Yes." Cora sat on the chaise at the foot of her bed. Rex sat beside her. He buried his head in his hands and began to weep like a lost child. Cora said nothing. She only stroked his hair and waited patiently for him to speak.

"Cora, my life is such a mess. I've made a disaster out of everything. I can't please Dad or Matt. I'm a bad father. And now…Veronica was just here."

"I know."

He looked up at her. "You know?"

"I couldn't help but hear the two of you. I'm sorry."

Gazing deeply into Cora's eyes, Rex collapsed in her arms. She groaned under his weight against her sore ribs, but she reached out to him anyway.

"Did you hear everything?"

"Yes."

"Then I don't have to explain."

"No, you don't. You don't have to talk at all."

Cora looked at the clock. Ten minutes passed. Rex rested in her arms. He shook with emotion, and Cora's heart opened to him. She could not go if Rex needed her.

"It's all true, what Veronica said." Rex sat up straight and wiped his eyes. "I wasn't home enough for Patty. She did start goin' to Wild Bill's. She became a drunk and didn't come home every night. She usually came back the next morning. It was no secret. One night, after we'd had an argument about her lack of work around the house and caring for Susie, she left. That night she didn't return. The next morning I got a visit from the sheriff, sayin' she died at Connors Peak. She was drunk, and her car went over the cliff. We don't know whether she planned it, or if it was an accident. People at Wild Bill's said she was pretty rowdy that night, complainin' about marriage and motherhood." Rex rubbed his face vigorously and then looked up at Cora.

"I'm sorry. I don't know what to say." Cora placed her hand on his shoulder.

Rex stood and walked over to the terrace. "You're sayin' everything I need to hear." He turned around to face her. "What I mean is you're just bein' here for me. You aren't passin' judgment."

"Who am I to pass judgment? My husband was a drug dealer. A bounty hunter shot and killed him. Who am I to judge someone else's spouse?"

Then Rex laughed. He came back inside to where she stood.

"I didn't mean to spoil the mood," she apologized. "I wasn't trying to be funny."

"You're amazing. Did you know that?"

"No."

"I'm glad you said what you said. You made me forget about her."

"Patricia?" Cora looked at Rex's face.

"Veronica....and...Patty, too. I feel much better."

"I'll tell you what I think."

"What?"

"They ought to close Wild Bill's."

Rex chuckled. "Do you feel like joinin' the family for lunch? They'll be home soon."

"I'd like that. It will take me awhile to get dressed, though, so you'd better find something to do with yourself until I come down."

"You yell at me when you're ready to come down, and I'll help you down the stairs. I'll be workin' in my office. Okay?" Rex insisted.

"You got a deal. I'll be ready in a few." Cora pushed Rex out the door and shut it behind him. *You've definitely got to leave,* she told herself. *This man is not over his wife yet, and if you stay, you'll only get hurt. And so will Susie.*

Cora proceeded to get dressed for lunch, wincing several times along the way. When she finished dressing, she called to Rex and he came to help her down the stairs.

The family arrived home from church.

"Where are Clarice and Matt?" she asked.

"They didn't go to church today. They're both out somewhere with friends." Rex narrowed his dark eyes.

Cora cooed at Susie's stories from church, her interpretation of the Bible story, and was thrilled the child had opened up to her so easily. She really hated to leave this place, but maybe her mission was complete. She had successfully brought a father and his child closer together.

* * *

"Cora, I'm glad you feel like playing again."

"Me too, Susie."

"I missed you while you were sick."

"I missed you, too."

"Cora? How long have you been here?"

"Let's see, it's August 24th. I think that would be seven weeks now."

"Seven weeks?"

"Yes, almost two whole months now."

Cora had secretly planned her trip home to Florida and hoped to leave in another week or two. She almost had enough money saved to fly home. She was excited to see her parents. After the events of the last week at the ranch, Cora appreciated them more than ever before and knew she needed to attempt to restore her relationship with them.

While the family ate breakfast, and discussed the events of the past week, the doorbell rang. Juanita, the housekeeper, answered the door, and then called to Cora. A courier waited on the porch for Cora to sign for a registered letter.

Cora puckered her mouth, wondering who would send her a letter of this type. She excused herself and went into the study. The sender was the law firm she'd worked for outside of Columbia. When she opened the envelope, a letter from an attorney in the firm slipped out.

When Cora came to, everyone was crowded around her, calling her name. She saw Rex first. "What happened?"

"You passed out."

"I did?" She rubbed her head.

"What is it? Bad news from home?" Rex came to her side.

Still clasping the letter in her hand, she sat up with Rex's help. He moved her to the wingback chair near the window and made sure she was comfortable. "No, it isn't bad news." She looked at the letter again. "Oh, boy." She grasped her forehead with the palm of her hand. "It's shocking news, I guess. I don't know what to think."

"Tell us, if you don't mind," R.L. said.

"This is a letter from Clark's attorney in Columbia. He had a will I didn't know about. He left everything he owned to me and to his parents and had a life insurance policy for $500,000.00. It's kind of bittersweet, but I'm rich!" The pain from the past, the struggles to makes ends meet, suddenly disappeared.

"Oh, my, you're rich!" Pearl exclaimed.

"What are you gonna do with all of the money?" Clarice spoke to Cora for the first time since the fiasco after Wild Bill's. Laughter filled the room at this expected question from Clarice.

"First of all, I guess I'll make that trip back home to Florida. I need to spend some time with my parents." Cora looked from one face to another, trying to read their expressions.

Suddenly the sun coming in through the windows hid behind the clouds floating by outside. The room darkened, as did the mood.

Immediately Susie burst into tears. She ran to Cora and threw herself into Cora's lap. "No. Don't go. I love you."

Cora hugged Susie and began to cry, too. "I have to go, Susie. Only for a short time, though. I need to be with my friends in South Carolina and then my mommy and daddy for a bit. I'll be back, because I'll have to get my car."

Cora glanced at Rex for help. He avoided making eye contact and shuffled his boots on the floor. He appeared more devastated than Susie. The bridge they'd begun to build that crossed the chasm crumbled before Cora's eyes.

"No. I need my mommy, too. You're my mommy." The child clung to Cora.

Cora looked at Rex once more, surprised by his child's statement, but he turned and stalked from the room. The front door slammed; then Rex's truck cranked up and left. She glanced at Pearl and R.L. for understanding, and they smiled sympathetically.

Cora's head throbbed the entire day. She tried to read her Bible and pray, but she couldn't concentrate. She sent Anne an email before taking a hot shower to relieve the tension in her neck.

Hey, Anne. You'll never believe what happened today. I got news that Clark left me half a million dollars. Yep, I'm rich. For some reason, I'm not super happy, though, and I'm more confused than ever. Now what I've been planning for weeks can happen, but I'm not sure I'm doing the right thing. I know in my heart if I leave, I probably won't return. I should be fine with that. I was only passing through anyway. But now I'm attached to Susie. She's so precious. And, yes, I also know that all little girls are precious. I should cut my ties now and go home for good. But I want to stay. Yet if I stay, I'll fall for Rex completely. I know I will. Since I'm so unsure about his beliefs, and know he's not completely over his wife, staying has to be out of the question. I can't stay just because Susie needs me. Please pray for me. I don't know what to do. Cora

Cora called Ms. Lottie to tell her how much she appreciated all she'd done for her and that she would miss her. She prodded Ms. Lottie for a hint about Rex's feelings, but the older woman never betrayed his confidence, if he had confided in her at all.

Cora stepped out onto the back porch for a cup of coffee. She hoped to find Rex there. She sipped from her cup and waited for him. As she relaxed, she heard the familiar sound of the meadowlark, and her heart sank. She would really miss the tranquility of this place, and the soothing song of the bird. She knew that anytime she heard a bird sing, she would think of Rex...and how they had surprisingly grown close to one another.

Although she sat for a long while that evening, Rex never came.

* * *

The next day, the last Friday in August, Cora packed her jeans and shirts into her bag, getting ready to fly to Columbia again, this time for the reading of the will and to receive her insurance check. From there, she would go straight to Florida. As she put her shoes in her suitcase and stuffed her socks in the pocket on the top flap, she sighed, thinking about Susie and how she had continued to ask why Cora had to leave. Cora repeatedly explained to her the reasons. She told her she would try as hard as she could to come back and reminded Susie of how important it was to take care of her daddy. She wanted Susie to feel responsible for him, so she'd draw closer to him and not concentrate as much on Cora's departure.

"Is everything coming together for the trip?" Pearl stood in her bedroom doorway. Her perfume floated in and warmed Cora's soul.

"I guess I'm almost packed. If it's okay with you, I'm going to leave my car here." She met Pearl's eyes. "I'll probably come back before heading to Florida. I'll drive home, I guess."

"That's fine. Do whatever you need to do. If you decide to fly straight to Florida and stay, just call. We'll get Rex to drive the car back." She winked.

"Oh, okay. But I don't think that will be necessary, and I don't think he'll want to do it anyway." Cora searched the dresser drawers for the last time. "How is Rex, by the way?"

"Oh, he's just being Rex."

"Since the day I heard the news, he's stayed away from me. I know he's avoiding me because he even eats his meals at the cabin." Her mind flashed back to the days, one after another, that she'd seen Rex in the pasture working. If she waved, he turned his head. If she came down the stairs, he went out the front door. If she waited outside his office, he never came out. Cora shook her head, and her thoughts came back to the present.

"I wish I knew what to say, Cora. I don't know what's going on with Rex."

"I know he's mad at me because I'm doing exactly what he asked me not to do on the first day I was here. And the thing is: I never said I wouldn't come back. But he shut me out, and now I feel like I can't come back." A tear slid down her cheek.

Pearl entered her room and embraced her. "It will be all right, Cora."

With mixed feelings, Cora now finished packing her suitcases, set them by her bedroom door, and descended the stairs for breakfast. Susie had spent the morning with Pearl, so Cora could finish getting ready. When she was halfway down the curving staircase, she caught a glimpse of Rex heading out the front door, his Levis and Stetson hat burned into her memory. She called to him, but the door shut anyway. She had to talk to him. They hadn't spoken in a week.

Rushing down the stairs, she headed out the front door, passing the aromas of bacon and pastries and the family in the dining room without saying a word. "Rex!"

He did not acknowledge her. The summer sun hit Cora square in the face. She held her hand up to shade her eyes. "Rex O'Reilly, you stop right where you are!"

He turned to look at her. "What?"

"What? Is that all you can say? I'm leaving in an hour, and that is all you can say?"

"What do you want me to say, Cora?" Rex's eyes blazed.

"What's wrong? Why are you shunning me like this? I had hoped we were closer." Cora tried to make eye contact.

"You don't get it, do you? You're leavin', goin' home, never returnin'. You're no longer a part of our lives." Rex glared at her.

"So, it's over and done with, huh? As if I never existed?" She put her right hand on her hip.

"Why should I try to make you stay? You're gonna go anyway. Nothin' I could do would make you stay." Rex turned and walked away.

"Really? I guess you don't know me like I thought you did." She followed him down the steps.

Rex stopped and turned toward her. "I don't know you at all. In the grand scheme of things, this was just—it—you're—" He grunted. "Look, we both helped each other out when we needed someone. We're friends, that's all. Nothing ever happened between us. You made sure of that." Rex turned to head for his truck.

"Wait! Rex! Why are you mad at me? If you say we're just friends, then you should be happy for me that I got the money so I could move on with my life. I'm closing one chapter and starting another. Like you said, you can't go to the grave with them. Besides, I never said I wouldn't be back. You didn't even give me the chance to tell you my plans and help me decide if I had a reason to return."

Rex fell silent and stared at the ground. Then he stiffened his neck. "I'm mad because you're hurtin' Susie. I told you two months ago I did not want you here if you were only gonna turn around and leave. You stayed anyway, and now you're leavin'. It doesn't matter if it's only for a little while. You're doin' exactly what I didn't want you to. You hurt Susie, you hurt my family, and..."

"And what, Rex? Say it."

"There's nothin' more to say—except have a nice life." Rex walked to his truck and jumped in.

"Have a nice life? What? I thought you'd take me to the airport. I thought we could spend a little time together before I had to leave."

"Why? I don't want to be around you anymore. Go find someone else to chauffeur you around." Rex slammed the door to his truck and cranked the engine. He sped off so fast that Cora fell backwards in the drive trying to avoid his truck and the flying gravel.

Cora sat on the drive for a few minutes, the sting in her heart worse than the sting in her hands. *Why is Rex so angry? It has to be more than Susie. He has to be bluffing, like he did when I first came. Why can't he show his true emotions?* She held her head high and refused to let the tears flow, blinking them away. She got up off the ground, dusted her clothes and her hands off, and walked back into the house.

During breakfast, Cora tried to hide the hurt she felt from her argument with Rex by talking with everyone and sharing how she would miss them all. Susie would be the hardest to leave.

Cora thought about driving her car to the airport since Rex had left, but she called a cab to come pick her up. She did not want anyone else to take her. She wanted to say her good-byes at the ranch.

12

As the plane touched down on the runway, Cora wrung her hands, thinking about seeing her parents for the first time in three years. She tried to forget about the last few conversations with them, since they had been such a slap in the face. She wasn't sure what to expect, but she wanted to forgive them for their attitudes toward her.

In Columbia, South Carolina, she settled her business. She had intended to stay only one night with Clark's parents, but they insisted she visit with them longer. It had been the right thing to do. Now she felt rested and prepared for what might lie ahead. She looked out the window at the planes passing on the runway. *Has it really been eight days since I left the Southern Hope?*

Cora slipped off her right shoe and inspected the blister forming on her heel. *Why did I wear these red flats?* She thought about how Ben and Judy wanted to know everything about her stay in Georgia. It had taken her two days, but she eventually told them about the man who had made such an impact on her life.

"I'm really confused about Rex. Do you think I'm looking for love too soon after Clark's death?"

"Clark has been gone in your mind long before you actually heard the news of his death, Cora," Ben answered. "In ours, too," he added sadly.

"You have to follow your heart. No one can tell you what is right for you," Judy affirmed.

When the flight attendant announced over the intercom that the passengers could exit the plane, people stood to retrieve their bags from the overhead storage. A child walked past Cora and sneezed right in her face. Cora held her breath. The person next to her in the aisle reached up to get her bag, hit Cora in the head, and walked down the aisle without apologizing.

Now, as the plane emptied of passengers, Cora marveled at how different Clark's parents were from her own. *I dread my parents telling me what to do with my money and my life. I know when I see them the criticism will begin. I wish they were more like Ben and Judy.* She closed her eyes and said a silent prayer that all would go well.

As Cora exited the corridor, she adjusted the strap on her bag to keep it from cutting into her shoulder. She walked past families waiting for their loved ones and limo drivers holding signs, and fumbled in her purse for her baggage claim ticket. When she looked up, there, standing in front of her, were her parents—Brenda in her black Jones New York suit with Vera Wang pumps and Walt in his Armani, cell phone in hand. Cora jumped. *How did they know when my flight was coming in? I didn't even tell them what flight I was coming in on. I wanted a little extra time to get prepared for our reunion.*

"Mom! Dad! What are you doing here?" she managed. "How did you know when I was arriving?" Cora forced herself to smile and hug her parents.

"Well, dear, are you not happy to see us?" Brenda questioned, her elegant hands dripping in diamonds and tipped with manicured nails.

"Oh, don't be silly." She dismissed the thought with a wave of her hand. "Of course, I'm glad to see you. I'm just shocked you two drove out here to meet me. You didn't have to."

"We knew you didn't have your car. It made sense for your dad and me to pick you up."

"Oh, of course. Thanks. How long have you been waiting?" Cora averted her eyes from her mom since that nerve in the back of her neck was already twitching.

At that instant a man walked between Cora and her parents, oblivious to their conversation, and knocked Brenda's purse off her shoulder. She narrowed her eyes at him.

"About thirty minutes. These cheaper airlines are always late. You have money now. Why didn't you fly First Class with a more respectable airline? Better yet, why didn't you let me arrange your trip for you?" Walt, ever the businessman, inquired, his salt-and-pepper hair styled to perfection. He looked at the clock on his cell phone and sighed.

"Delta flight 732 boarding now for Mexico."

Cora looked up at the ceiling. *Mexico sounds nice about now.* Not even one minute had passed, and they had both succeeded in getting on her nerves. "Dad, why don't we go and get my bags? We can talk about my choice in airlines later. At least I'm home, right?" Cora tried to be pleasant but squinted her eyes at her dad at the same time. She walked a pace ahead of them, feeling like a gazelle running from a cheetah.

On the way home, Cora watched the mile markers slowly click by, sealing her doom. She sat in the back seat of Brenda's Lexus, taking in the familiar scenery. Leaning her head back on the headrest, she closed her eyes.

At first the classical music on the radio soothed her nerves, but Walt's erratic driving and fussing about the traffic retied them in knots. Brenda fussed at him for fussing at drivers who could not hear him. Their voices blurred in her ears. She dreamed of eating dinner and going to bed. It was only 7:00 p.m., but Cora's body ached, and her mind could think no more.

"We're stopping at Franklin's on the way home to eat dinner. What do you think about a nice, expensive meal for a change?" Brenda turned her head toward the back seat.

"I was hoping to go straight home. I'm so tired I could just eat a pizza in front of the TV." *Why do they assume I haven't had a nice meal while I've been gone?*

"Pizza? Television? Honey, that's no kind of meal. You need some lobster or crab to welcome you home." Walt slammed the brakes on to avoid hitting the truck in front of them. "Okay, we'll stop somewhere else, where we can get in quickly."

"Mom, Dad, I appreciate you wanting to take me out, but how about tomorrow night? I'm wiped out from the flight and dealing with the airport. Really, I'd love a slice or two of pizza and my bed."

Brenda finally made eye contact with Cora and held her eyes prisoner for over a minute. Cora's gaze didn't waver.

Brenda looked away first. "Okay. We'll call from the car and order it now. It should be there shortly after we get home." Brenda turned back around.

Thank you, Lord. Thank you. As they neared home, Cora inhaled the salty sea air. "Are we going to the beach house tonight or staying in town?"

"We'll go home tonight. We can go to the beach house tomorrow."

"Okay." Cora rested her head against the seat again and closed her eyes.

* * *

After filling her stomach and talking with her parents for a while, Cora excused herself to her room. She called Anne to tell her she was home and phoned Pearl, as well. It had been years since she'd slept in her old bed, and she couldn't wait to fall asleep. Although her mother had changed the decorations in her room to an Asian theme, the bed was still the same.

Thank you, Lord, for getting me home safely. Please be with me as I attempt to heal the broken relationship I have with my parents. And help me know if I'm supposed to stay here or go back to the ranch and, if so, in what capacity that would be. Before her eyes shut for a final time that day, Cora read Psalm 71:20. "Though you have made me see troubles, many and bitter, you will restore my life again; from the depths of the earth you will again bring me up."

* * *

The next morning, Cora awoke to the smell of breakfast cooking on the stove and coffee perking in the gurgling pot. She rolled over and sat up in the bed, remembering the feeling of having Susie curled up next to her. Dragging herself out of bed, she threw on her robe. In the bathroom down the hall she brushed her dark hair and washed her face. She touched the delicate skin beneath her eyes. The dark circles looked like they were returning. Cora went back to her room and slid on her house shoes, then headed for the dining room.

"Morning." Cora yawned.

"Morning. Did you sleep well?" Brenda asked.

"That bed is as wonderful now as it always was." Cora sank into a chair at the dining table, a different table than had been there before.

"Well, if you hadn't run off with Clark Buchanan, you'd have no reason to have missed that bed," Walt commented from behind his morning paper.

Cora's mouth dropped open. *If this is supposed to make me want to stay, they're crazy.* She knew nothing to say in defense, so she shut her mouth. She tried to eat her breakfast without choking, even when the bacon threatened to wrap around her vocal cords. She was so angry she could barely swallow her food. *Why won't they forgive me for marrying Clark?* At that moment, she wanted nothing more than to get away from her family and be by herself.

"Cora, I thought we could go shopping today while Dad is at work. I'm sure you could use some better clothes. There's a new boutique at the mall, and the clothes there would help you dress more your age." Brenda took her seat at the dining room table.

"Oh, Mom, we don't have to do that today. My clothes are fine. Really." Her insides bubbled like a volcano. "Besides, I thought I'd try to call some of my old girlfriends and arrange a get-together. Anne has been waiting to see me."

"Well, so have I. For years! But if that's what you want to do with your time, go ahead." Brenda took a sip of her hot tea and gazed out the window, blinking tears away.

"I do. Thanks for understanding. We'll go shopping another day. I'll be here for a few weeks." Cora excused herself from the table. Wanting to scream, and feeling pulled between her mother's wishes and her own, she went to her bathroom to take a shower. She slammed the door behind her. *Surely, I can do that right.*

While Cora showered, guilt crept up from her toes and threatened to overtake her. *I know I should want to be with Mom, but I want to see my friends, too. Why should I have to choose? There are plenty of hours in the day.*

A short while later, after brushing her damp hair, she dug her address book out of her purse and thumbed through it, deciding which friends to call. She called Anne first to see when she could meet, then began calling her other friends. Before long she'd rounded up nine girlfriends for dinner that evening, including Anne.

Cora next found Brenda, pruning the roses in the back yard, wearing her designer hat and garden gloves. She went outside to help and tried to make casual conversation, but her mother's near silence was an old attempt to spread the plague of guilt. Cora needed a big vaccine against it. Her parents were not currently attending church anywhere, so she did not go to church either that day. Instead, she watched her mother meticulously care for her roses.

I wonder if their lack of fellowship with other Christians is why they're so sour all of the time. I will pray for them more often.

* * *

Cora's insides jumped like popcorn in a pan of oil by the time she got to Antonio's that evening. The ocean view and brisk sea breezes electrified her senses. She waited in the lobby for the hostess, then followed her to a table on the patio by the beach. She sipped her water as she waited for the others to arrive. The ocean waves soothed her nerves, reminding her that her troubles were small in the grand scheme of life.

When Anne arrived, the two best friends squeezed each other's necks until they nearly broke. Cora's other friends arrived soon after Anne did, and the hugs and hellos flew like balloons on the breeze. Everyone applauded when Cora said dinner was her treat.

"You should have seen my parents when I told them I was going out with all of you tonight." Cora pushed her hair behind her ears, and the wind whipped it across her back.

"What do you mean? Like how Pete acted when I asked him to put the kids to bed tonight without me?" Alicia burbled, slinging her blonde locks over her shoulder.

"They wanted to take me out to eat. Actually, they wanted to go last night on the way back from the airport, but I was too exhausted. I was in no mood to be with them tonight, either." Cora and Anne exchanged a knowing look.

"That's how my mom is when she finds out I'm going out with friends." Jo's amber eyes stared directly into Cora's.

"Mine always want to know when I'm getting married. I mean, you have to have a guy first!" Denise chimed in.

"What's the problem? Why are they driving you crazy?" Karen asked.

Cora reached for a garlic roll. "First, they arrived at the airport, when I never even told them when I was coming in. My father, the big travel agency detective, found out my flight information. Then, not one minute after I saw them, they were already jumping on me about my choice in airlines. It's been nonstop since then." Cora sipped her cola; water droplets formed on the glass.

"They're probably just concerned about you," Janet said.

"But they sure have an irritating way of showing it." Cora straightened her silverware.

"When you're a parent, you'll understand." Janet caught her napkin from flying off the table.

"Maybe. I'd thought about staying at the beach house a night or two before coming home, but they surprised me." She tapped her foot to the Caribbean music in the background.

"They would have caught you. The neighbors would have called them." Anne broke her long silence, her blue eyes like the sky over the gulf on a summer day.

"I know."

"Enough about your parents. I want to hear about Clark. We haven't seen you since you left with him." Denise grabbed a roll from the basket.

"Nothing much to say, really."

Denise focused her eyes on Cora. "Oh, come on. He does business with the law firm you work at, comes in all suave and debonair, whisks you away from us, and you say there's nothing to talk about?"

"Yeah, a drug dealer posing as an export businessman coming in to take advantage of the young and trusting legal secretary. Real suave. Export business, my foot!"

Anne giggled. "Bitter, are we?"

"Oh, shut up!" Cora stuck her tongue out at Anne. "You guys know the story. Clark entered my life like a tornado, uprooting every bit of common sense I'd ever had. His stupid blond hair and gorgeous blue eyes suckered me in, and his charm won my heart. I was too trusting for my own good."

"Go on," Karen said.

"When we moved to South Carolina after we got married, Clark's parents lived only a few miles away. Having them around made me feel at home, and when Clark traveled on business, I stayed with them. I grew really close to them because they accepted me unconditionally. I used to style Mrs. Buchanan's hair and do puzzles with his dad. We were happily married, and then one day they arrested him for drug dealing."

Cora exhaled. "Looking back at the picture from my twenty-fourth birthday, I see in Clark's eyes something not quite right—something unsettled. Less than a month after that, the police arrested him on drug charges. Supposedly, according to reporters, Clark's export business fronted for a drug operation. His dad put up bail and Clark came home, while waiting for his trial. The next night, he slipped out of the bed and disappeared. I haven't seen him since. His dad almost lost everything because of him. In fact, I paid them back with some of the life insurance money. He was gone a year when I decided I had to leave and start over. I had hopes he might return, but I knew if he did, he'd go straight to jail. I was headed home in my car when I broke down in Georgia."

"What happened then? This is more excitement than I've had in a long time." Jane played with the strap on her sundress.

"I stayed at a bed-and-breakfast for a bit and met a real nice family there that offered me a job. So I stayed. That's where I've been for the last couple of months." Cora took a big breath.

"What kind of work did you do for them?" Mary prodded.

"She flirts with their grown sons." Anne sniggered, making full eye contact with Cora.

"Anne! I do not." Cora smacked her hand playfully.

"Well, from the description of them, I'd flirt with them if I was there."

"Maybe."

"Maybe, huh? Anyway, tell us what you do. Why did you leave?" Karen asked.

Cora shrugged her eyebrows. "You don't really want to know all the boring details, do you?"

"You bet we do." Alicia nudged her gently.

Cora crossed her eyes and stuck her tongue out playfully. Just as she began, the waitress came to take their orders. When she walked away, Cora continued, "Here's the story. When my car broke down, it was going to take a few days to repair it. So I found a room at a bed-and-breakfast inn. When I found out the estimate on the repairs and that it would take a week to get the car, I knew I wouldn't have enough money to pay for it and my expenses, too. So I started working for the lady who ran the inn. I almost had enough money to come home, but I called Mom and Dad and asked them to send me a little more. We got into a huge fight, and they refused to send me any money. I planned to stay with Ms. Lottie and work for a while until I could come home." Cora took a bite of her roll.

"Maybe you need to go to a counselor."

"Are you kidding, Peggy? My counselor would need a counselor. Do you want to hear the rest?"

"Yes," they all chimed in.

Denise followed a tanned, shirtless man in shorts and flip-flops with her eyes. The others laughed at her. She blushed.

"Okay. A man named Rex came into the inn one day to eat. Although I didn't know it until later, he was interested in me. He went home and told his parents about me, and they came into the inn to meet me. A few days later, when they heard I needed money and couldn't afford to stay at the inn any longer, they offered me the position of nanny for their grandchild, Rex's daughter. His wife died a year ago."

"Ooh, so does he have the hots for you?" Anne's blue eyes sparkled like crystals.

"I don't know. Not really. He had a girlfriend, who I will not waste my breath or your time telling you about. Anyway, I told them I'd try it for a while and see how I liked it. I ended up falling in love with the little girl. Her name is Susie, and she's three, almost four." Cora's throat choked up, and tears welled in her eyes. "Then, one day, when my car was ready, I drove to town with Jimmy, the cook, to get it. On the way home, I got lost on these back roads and blew my tires on something. Then someone crashed into my car. When I got out to walk, someone came up behind me and hit me over the head..." Cora paused, a tear sliding down her cheek.

Peggy urged her on. Everyone wanted to know about Cora's time at the ranch and her kidnapping. After she finished telling them about her near-death experience and the other missing girls, Anne begged her to tell them more about Rex. Cora could not fool her lifelong friends. They all knew she had feelings for this man. She finally shared with them everything that had happened with Rex. They threatened to hang her if she didn't go back to Georgia to be with him.

* * *

Cora punched the code into the keypad by the gate and waited for the gate to open. She pulled through in her mom's Lexus with her friends following in their cars behind her. She looked up at the three-story beach house, the pink stucco, and red tiled roof, and shook her head at the extravagance. She pulled the car into the garage, careful not to bump the door on the support pole.

"Oh, my gosh! I forgot how great this place is," Peggy reminisced.

"Yeah, great. It's a bit too rich for my taste." Cora shrugged.

"What do you mean?" Alicia asked.

"I mean, they've got this house and our home five miles away. Do you know how many starving children they could feed for what they paid for this house?"

"Oh, Cora, get over it. Just enjoy the opulence. It's not going to go away," Anne blurted honestly.

"I guess." She stuck her tongue out at her.

They climbed the stairs to the front porch, which was on the back of the house and faced the beach. Cora stopped and leaned against the rail, looking out at the sunset. The sea breeze blew through their hair and kissed their skin.

"It's so great that your parents are letting us stay here tonight," Karen said. "I'm glad my parents didn't mind watching the kids."

"Yeah. I wish Jane had been able to stay," Cora said.

"Well, her husband wouldn't let her stay the night out." Janet groaned.

"Wouldn't *let* her?"

"Yeah. A big story going on there." Jo shifted her overnight bag to her right shoulder.

"You'll have to get her to fill you in," Mary added.

Cora opened the door and led the way into the beach house. Soon high-heeled shoes and wooden sandals clicked on the Italian marble floor. "Why don't we put our things in the master bedroom? We'll probably crash in the living room, don't you think?" Cora tossed her purse on the sofa.

"Probably," Anne agreed, kicking off her shoes by the door.

"I'm tempted to sleep out here." Denise lingered outside on the porch.

"Me, too," Peggy chimed in.

"It's probably too muggy out there." Alicia rejected the idea for herself.

"And we'd get bitten by mosquitoes," Mary offered.

"You guys are such moms." Jo giggled. "Let's go for a swim."

"Okay." Cora picked up her duffle bag.

"Wait, let's see what kind of food your mom has first…in case we need to run back out," Janet said.

"I'll look in the pantry." Cora walked into the kitchen and flipped on the light. She walked over to the pantry and opened the door, noticing the new stainless steel appliances. She shook her head. "Here's a box of brownie mix, some marshmallows, popcorn, tortilla chips, and a jar of cheese sauce." She opened the refrigerator door. "There's soft drinks and water."

"Any beer or wine?" Karen asked.

"No, I don't think so. Why? You'd drink it?" Cora crinkled her eyebrows at her friend's suggestion.

"Sure." Karen turned to face her with hands on hips. "When I can get a night away from the kids, I want to enjoy myself. With an ex-husband, I need a drink every now and then. Wouldn't you drink?"

"No way! We could make some coffee, though."

"Okay. Whatever." Karen sighed.

"Let's bake the brownies and then go for a swim." Mary walked toward the kitchen.

"Let's go for a walk on the beach first before it gets too late, and then bake the brownies and swim." Denise kicked her shoes off.

"Sounds good to me." Anne stood and grabbed her duffle bag off the floor.

* * *

After their walk on the beach, they came back into the house to bake the brownies. "What time is it, Cora?"

"Denise, how many times have you asked me that? It's 9:30 p.m."

"Sorry. How long will the brownies take to bake?"

"The box says twenty minutes, and if you don't distract me, I can get these whipped up and in the oven in just a couple minutes."

"I'm going to put on my bathing suit." Denise headed for the bathroom.

"Me, too." Karen picked up her overnight bag.

"Is that my cell phone ringing?"

"Yep," someone called out from the bedroom down the hall.

Cora ran to her purse, grabbed her cell phone, and checked the caller ID. "It's Mom," she announced to her friends first, then hit *redial*. "Hello? Yep, we're here. Okay, well, y'all have a good night. Yeah, I'll be home midmorning." Cora hung up the phone and stared at Anne. "Wow! For the first time in forever she treated me like an adult."

"It's about time." Anne laughed.

"I'm starting to smell those brownies." Alicia headed toward the kitchen.

"Me, too. Let me go check them. I think they still have about ten minutes." Cora followed.

"Are we going to go swimming now?"

"Denise, you're driving me crazy," Mary said.

Cora pulled the brownies out of the oven and then put her suit on. "Let's go. The beach towels are in the closet downstairs by the back door."

Once they were all downstairs, Cora flipped on the floodlights outside and the entire pool area lit up.

"Wow! That pool is gorgeous." Peggy stepped out onto the patio first.

"Is it heated? I can't remember." Janet followed.

"Yep. I think they keep it heated all the time."

"Yay!" Anne blew her a kiss.

One after the other, they all jumped into the pool—cannonballs, belly flops, dives. The laughter and splashing felt as good to Cora as the water and ocean air did. "So, tell me what's going on with Jane and her husband."

"I told you, you would have to ask her," Mary said.

"I'm not going to do that. Tell me."

"He's gotten real possessive these days." Peggy dove in the deep end.

"And you really think it's all of a sudden? That's rarely the case." Cora dogpaddled to the shallow end of the pool.

"What do you mean?" Jo asked.

"I mean, he's probably always been possessive of her, but she loved feeling important to him. Now they have the kids, and she's busy running them all over the place. He's probably checking in on her and where she is at different points in the day, and it's getting on her nerves."

"How did you guess?" Janet sat on the steps in the shallow end inspecting her body in her bathing suit.

"Oh, I've seen it before. I had a friend in South Carolina who experienced the same thing. She was basically doing everything for the kids with no help from her husband. She never heard from him during the day because he was at work. But at night, while she was at the ball field or the basketball games and he was home getting drunk, he called her constantly and made her feel like he didn't trust her."

"What happened with them?" Alicia swam to the ladder.

"He left her for a younger woman with a mousy personality—someone he could control."

"So he was controlling the whole time?" Denise asked.

"Yep, she thought he liked checking in on her because he cared."

"My husband checks in on me, but he's not suspicious of me or controlling." Alicia climbed out of the pool.

"That's because you're married to the best husband there is," Karen said.

"Yeah, well, my ex never checked in on me. He never called when he traveled out of town on business. Turns out, he had another family in Oregon," Janet said.

"What?" Cora exclaimed.

"Yep. He never checked on me because he didn't want me to check on him," Janet replied.

"I never knew what Clark was doing. I never would have guessed it."

"What's the secret then?" Peggy asked.

Cora thought about it for a minute. "God has got to be first in your life before you can even have a relationship with anyone else. And he's got to be first in his life, too. Your faith can't carry him or a relationship. And you've got to have your security and your identity in God, not a man. When you find a man who is chasing after God the same as you are, go for it. When God is at the center, then the relationship can survive anything." Cora sighed, thinking of Rex for the first time in a while.

"And know what you're getting into, too. Make sure there's nothing weird in his past that you can't deal with." Anne added.

That night Cora could barely sleep. She savored everything she had heard over dinner and scrutinized every word that rolled off her tongue. Her mind turned somersaults—her parents, Clark, her second chance at life, Susie, and most of all, Rex. It seemed that even in Florida this man held her thoughts captive. *If he is so wrong for me, why does he continuously pop into my head?*

Cora's weary eyes burned from the chlorine. She tried to sleep, but all she could see was Rex's face every time she closed them. Her right hip hurt from lying on the thin mattress of the sleeper sofa, and she felt like Jacob in the Bible who wrestled with the angel. After hours of tossing and turning, fighting with her satin sheets, she finally fell into a sound sleep....

* * *

The next morning Cora put her key in the lock and turned it, opening the front door. She looked down at the doormat that said *Welcome. Am I really welcome here?* Entering the house, she shut the door behind her. The heavy cloak of dread covered her. She sighed. Her parents were out on the patio, so she crept quietly into her room, hoping to catch her breath before any confrontation.

Cora tossed her things down on her bed and reached for the telephone. Clearing her throat from the phlegm in it—her sinuses definitely still needed to adjust to the sea oats—she dialed the number. As the telephone rang, Cora nervously rapped her fingers on the nightstand by her bed and frowned at her reflection in the mirror on her dresser. The chlorine from the pool made her hair feel like straw.

Finally, a voice answered. "Hello."

"Hi! It's Cora. Who's this?" She smiled, although no one could see her face.

"Rex." His voice was flat, lifeless.

"Hi. How are you?" Electricity shot through her body, followed by melancholy longing to be back there.

"Fine. And you?"

"Oh, getting acclimated." Cora shifted in her bed, peering out the window at the bright morning clouds.

"Acclimated? Don't you mean settled?" The ice in Rex's voice chilled Cora.

"No. I told you I wasn't staying here permanently, Rex. I'll be back in a few weeks." She rubbed the scar on her forehead with her hand.

"Why? You've got all the money you'll ever need. You don't need the job."

"Money isn't everything, Rex. Besides, I didn't say I'd be back at the ranch, I said I'd be back in Southern Hope or maybe Lewistown. I need to get my car. If you don't want me back at the ranch, I might stay with Ms. Lottie again. Would you prefer I stay here?"

"I want what's best for Susie."

"And I thought I was great for her."

"I said what's best. I want someone who will stay."

"I think you're looking for a mother for Susie...or at least someone who can fulfill your role so you don't have to think about being a parent to her. I didn't think that was my job." Her blood boiled.

There was a pause, then Rex asked, "How do I know you won't pack up and leave again if you come back?"

"I guess you don't. If you could allow yourself to trust me long enough, you'd know I love your family and I want to be there. I feel so at home there. More at home than I've felt anywhere in years." She swiped away the tears.

"Then why did you leave?"

"I told you. I had to settle Clark's will, and I thought I should see my parents! And seeing my parents is something I will need to do for the rest of my life, no matter where I live. Imagine if you lived away. You'd have to check on them every once in a while, too. It's selfish to expect me not to do the same." Cora ran her fingers through her hair, pulling at the ends of it. She looked again in the mirror and frowned.

"It seemed quite final to me."

She rubbed her fingers on the base of the lamp on the nightstand. No dust. Not a speck. *Of course.* "That's the impression you gave me, all right. It was like you wrote me off before I was even gone. I thought you'd take me to the airport so we could talk and spend some time together. We had gotten so close...or so I thought. But when I got this money, you shut me out. It really confused me and it hurt."

Silence rang on the line for a minute, then finally Rex said, "You were so happy when you found out about the money. You said you needed to go home. I thought you wouldn't be back."

"Well…"

"So…I cut my ties."

"You sure did. You never gave me the chance to explain my plans and to ask where I fit into your plans, if at all. You hurt me terribly."

"Sorry." The silence filled the space between them like the sand in the sidewalk cracks in town.

"Well, I'm here now. I'm trying to mend my broken relationship with my parents. It seems I leave a trail of broken ties everywhere I go. You know, I can only handle one troubled relationship at a time."

Rex remained quiet on the other end of the line, so Cora rattled on. "I'll be back in Georgia, and I'll be back at the ranch to get my car but not to stay unless you want me to." Hot tears stung her eyes, and a tremble distorted her voice. She leaned back onto the headboard and crossed her legs at the ankles.

"Why would you want to come back? Is Susie the only reason?" Rex's voice was soft, hesitant.

"Should there be another reason, Rex?" Cora was tired of the games. She buried her head in her hands—something she seemed to do a lot of these days.

"I guess not. We both know you think I'm a bad person."

"I never said that, Rex."

"It came across that way. And I thought I'd explained my behavior when we first met, but you still pulled away from me." He groaned.

"You didn't exactly make an attempt to have a relationship with me either. I thought we were moving in that direction. I'd forgotten all about how things were when we first met. I was ready to start over." *Should I jump on the next plane, or hang up on him and never speak to him again?* "When I found out about Clark, it gave me the closure I needed. It let me know it was okay to move on. But when I found out about the money, you shut the door. It's almost like you wouldn't want me unless I was dependent on you."

After another silence, Rex spoke again. "Cora, that's not how I feel. But I don't know what you want from me. I don't know if I could even give you what you want. I don't even know what I want. I've made such a mess of everyone's lives."

"First of all, here's what I need. I need a little bit of space. I needed to come home and now I'm here. That was in my original plan before I ever met you. I need to enjoy the beach and my friends and try to reconnect with my parents. Secondly, I need you to be completely honest about your feelings. Be honest with me and with yourself. I'm tired of games. Do you want me to come back, Rex? Do you want to see if there's something between us?" She sat up on the edge of the bed and switched the phone to the other ear.

"Do you want to?"

"Rex! Please." She slammed her fist on the nightstand. She heard her mother walk past her bedroom door outside in the hall. The loose floorboard betrayed her position. "Rex?"

"I don't know, Cora. I need to talk to Mom and see what she thinks about you comin' back to care for Susie."

"Oh, so, you would only want me to come back if I'm needed for Susie? You don't want to see if there's anything between us? Well, let me know." Cora's heart constricted. Like the storm clouds that rolled in on a late summer day, she knew a storm of another kind brewed ahead.

"Yeah, I will. Bye." Rex ended the call.

"Bye," Cora said to the buzzing line. The click sounded so permanent. *What did I expect him to say? Even if he'd said he wanted me back to be with him, that wouldn't be enough. I have to know he believes in the same things I do. I don't want to tell him that's what I want, because he might pretend to have my same beliefs just to get me. What am I supposed to do?*

"Cora? Are you all right?" Brenda tapped on her bedroom door.

"Yeah. I'm fine." Cora sat on her bed hugging her pillow.

"May I come in?"

"Sure." Cora swiped away the remnants of tears. This scene seemed like a rerun of her teen years.

"Are you really okay?"

"Yeah. No. I don't know." She shrugged and threw the pillow to the end of the bed.

"Do you want to talk about it?"

"No, not really."

Brenda sat next to Cora. "I know I'm not your choice in person to talk to, but I'm here."

"I know, Mom. I really can't explain what I'm feeling right now. I need to process my thoughts before I can talk about them."

"Oh, I see. I understand. How about we go shopping today? That will make you feel better."

Cora jerked upright and slapped her legs with her hands. "No, Mom, shopping will not make me feel better. Buying things and spending money doesn't make things go away."

Brenda's mouth gaped. "I'm trying to help in the only way I can."

"Well, don't. Please!" Cora buried her head in her hands, and Brenda left her room, quietly shutting the door behind her.

She knew it wouldn't take long for her father to step in.

She was right.

"Cora?"

"Hey, Dad." Cora looked up at the man who was virtually a stranger. The years of trying to please him had carved a path of resentment between them.

"How's it going?"

"Okay, I suppose." She didn't want to disappoint him.

"Your mom said you were having a bit of a rough time this morning." He winked.

Oh, she did, did she? "Yeah, I guess so." Cora felt like a mouse caught in a cookie jar.

"Did it have to do with your night out with your friends last night? I worried about you getting with them."

She shook her head. "Actually, no. We had a great time last night, Dad. We went swimming in the pool, took a stroll on the beach. It was great."

"Did you lock everything up?"

"Yes." She bowed her head, and her insides threatened to explode.

"So, are you having money problems? Have you spent everything you got from Clark?"

"No, Dad. I'm not having money problems and I haven't spent everything. I'd have to be very frivolous to have spent everything."

"So I suppose you simply don't want to talk to us, huh?"

"Not right now, Dad. I just got home and I need to decompress a little. The last few months have been a whirlwind, you know?"

* * *

Cora braced herself for more continued grilling over their belated lunch.

"Cora, I've invited the ladies from the Country Club over tonight. They're so anxious to see you and to maybe find an eligible bachelor suitable for you." Brenda chopped vegetables and put them into the sizzling oil in the sauté pan.

"Mom! What are you talking about?" Cora put down her coffee cup and stared at Brenda in disbelief.

"Cora, you are not getting any younger. Clark's gone, and it's now time to redeem yourself." She smiled at Cora.

"Redeem myself? What do you mean?"

"I mean, it's time to move on, and there are some good gentlemen still left here in the city who are back from college and ready to settle down."

"Mom, I don't need anyone to find me a boyfriend—or a future husband, for that matter. Seriously! You're unbelievable."

Brenda laid down the knife and swiveled to face Cora head-on. "Well, what do you want me to do?"

"Give me a little space, Mom. I just got home, and you're trying to plan every minute of my life out for me. I never said I was back here to stay. I'm not saying that I'm not, but it's my decision. Maybe I want to travel for a while. I don't know. But it's my decision to make. I have to do what's right for me. I have to do what God wants me to do. I'm not going to make another mistake."

"Okay. Okay. I'll leave you alone." Her mother threw her hands up in surrender.

Cora leaned on the bar overlooking the kitchen. "Mom, you and Dad have been great. I appreciate everything you've done for me. But I need a bit of breathing room. I need to acclimate myself. I haven't been under your roof for years. I've been married and then single and independent. I need some time."

Her mother stiffened. "I don't know why you even came home if you weren't ready to be with us."

"Truthfully, I wanted to stay at the beach house for a few nights before coming home and had planned to do so, but you guys surprised me and picked me up at the airport." She apologized for her truthfulness with her eyes.

"Then why don't you go there? We certainly don't want you here if you don't want to be here."

Cora turned to see Walt standing by the kitchen door. "Dad!"

* * *

At the beach house, Cora flipped through the channels on the television, stopping on each one no more than a few seconds. "Five hundred channels and there's still nothing to watch." She clicked the power button, turning off the big-screen television and tossed the remote onto the sofa. Closing her eyes, she rested her head back on the arm of the sofa. Her foot mimicked an earthquake that never stopped. She rolled her head around, hearing the popping and crackling in her neck.

Sitting up suddenly, she spotted her Bible on the coffee table and picked it up. Walking to the patio door, she pulled it open and stepped into the healing, ocean air. She drew a deep breath. "Now, that's more like it."

Cora sat in the chaise and opened her Bible. She pulled her new sunglasses off the top of her head and put them on. The glare of the pages made her eyes burn. "That will make reading out here easier." She smiled and began to read Proverbs.

"Mom? Dad? I'm back," Cora announced two days later as she opened the front door of her parents' home and closed it behind her.

No one responded. She followed the smell of freshly brewed coffee to the kitchen. "Mmm." She picked up a mug and poured herself a cup.

Peering out the back window, she saw her mother pruning her roses again. She opened the sliding door and stepped out. "Hey, Mom."

"Hello." Ice formed on her lips as the words slid from them, despite the warm temperature.

"I'm back."

"I see that you are."

"I really enjoyed my couple of days at the beach." She tried to catch her mother's eye.

"Good." Brenda never looked up from her roses.

13

During the next week, with October on the wind, Cora took long walks on the virtually tourist-free beach and visited St. Andrews State Park and the county pier with Anne. At the jetty, huge ships dredged up sand and pumped it onto the beach to rebuild the beach after the spring storms. Cora's heart felt like that sand…being dug up from the depths, certain feelings having been undisturbed for years.

She read her Bible and prayed more than ever, but she remained restless. Although Panama City was beautiful this time of year with the cool breezes and mild days, she continued to think of Georgia and the fresh start there for her.

Who am I kidding? I can't live in Georgia without being with the O'Reillys. And I guess I won't be going back to be with them since Rex never called me back nor has anyone else. Rex probably didn't even tell them I called.

Cora could rest no more in her room on this rainy late September day. As she headed down the hall to talk to her parents, she studied the pictures on the wall. Only a few of her were framed and hanging there—nothing like the ones of Rex, Matt, and Clarice at the ranch. The only ones of her were those from beauty pageants and piano recitals. There were no markings on any of the door facings of her height changes throughout the years. The O'Reillys had marked Rex, Matt, Clarice, and now Susie.

"Hey." Cora entered the sitting room. Outside the window the fall tropical storms brewed, much like her troubles brewed inside her.

"Hello." Brenda glanced her way.

"I need to talk to you." Cora sat in the blue wing-backed chair.

"What is it?" Walt puffed his pipe.

"I'm not sure why, but I'm not happy here." Cora's voice shook.

"It's about time you admit it. Your mother and I have known it ever since you've been home."

"Are we bothering you? Do you need to get your own place?"

"Do you need to stay at the beach house permanently?"

Cora formed her words slowly and carefully. "No, Dad. At first, I thought that was it. But it's not living here at home that's the problem. It's living in Florida. It doesn't feel the same. I truly want to be in Georgia." She sat up straight and stretched her back. The tension never seemed to go away.

"What? Living on a ranch with who knows what kinds of people? Cowboys and ranch hands? Cow manure and tractors?" Brenda let out a disgusted sigh. "I thought we raised you better than that."

"We thought you were home to stay."

Cora eyed Brenda in disbelief at her shallowness, and then Walt. "I never said that."

"I was going to talk to you about investing your money and taking over the travel agency. That way, you'd be settled." Cora opened her mouth to interrupt, but Walt continued, "I've been planning to retire for a long time so your mother and I could travel. How could you deny us that?"

Cora was quiet as the options, or the lack of them, ran through her head. The unwanted responsibility weighed heavily. Finally, she spoke. "I told you in the beginning I was just home for a visit. I think it's time we get honest with each other. Me being here is not what you expected, and it isn't what I thought it would be either. I never intended on moving back home. I wanted to come for a while to clear my head and to be with you both. Originally, I thought I'd go back to South Carolina."

"Anywhere but here, huh?" her mom threw in snidely.

"Mom, I'm trying to open up here and share what's going on in my head. Something is missing. I don't know if the problem is between us, or if it's just me. But I'm not happy here." Cora waited to see if they would say anything.

They merely looked at her in confusion.

She rubbed her forehead, feeling the tender scar from the accident. "I don't know if I belong permanently in Georgia or not, but I do know I want to be there now. Caring for Susie was remarkable for me when I was dealing with my feelings about Clark. The love of a little child is so special." Cora shifted in her chair. "There's a problem, though—Susie's father. I care for him a great deal. I think he cares for me, too. But he's bitter toward God. He's a widower, and he's having a hard time opening up to me. But I'm drawn to him anyway."

"Like a moth to a flame," her mother said. "Why are you always mixed up with worthless men?"

"Why do you always have to have a man in your life? Can you not just be Cora for a while?" Walt got up from his chair and stalked from the room.

"Dad! I've been alone for over a year now. Besides, Mom's been trying to match me with someone at the Country Club. Wait! Stay and talk to me."

"Cora, let him go. He can't talk to you. He wants you to stay. He wants you to be his little girl...the little girl he never really had." She looked away.

Cora stared. Her mother was crying. "Mother, what is it?"

"There is so much you don't know." Thunder clapped, and Brenda jumped.

"What do you mean, Dad wants the little girl he never had? I am his little girl. I always was. Why is he so hard on me? He's always been that way." Cora knelt in front of her mother.

"He wanted you to be like him. But you grew up so fast and were gone from us so quickly. We haven't been a part of your life for so long. You've shut us out. Your father and I wanted a chance to have what we never had."

"But Mother, the reason I left when I did is because you two drove me away. I didn't want to leave. You could not accept my love for Clark. You never let me make my own decisions. I always felt I was doing everything wrong. I know you guys were right about him, but still..." She sighed. "I never measured up to what you expected of me. Why is that?"

Brenda let out a sigh that matched Cora's sigh. Silence hung heavily in the room like a storm system while Brenda rubbed her hands together repeatedly. "For a long time now I have felt you needed to know something about your childhood, but your father insisted I not tell you. I feel the time has come. In fact, it is past time to tell you. What I am going to say will hurt you deeply, but it will also explain to you a lot about your past. So please be patient with me."

"What is it, Mom? Tell me." Cora scooted her chair closer.

"Please, sit beside me on the couch."

Cora moved beside her, never taking her eyes off her mother's face. "Please tell me. I have to know why I've felt so unworthy all of my life."

"I don't know where to begin, except the beginning."

"Okay."

"Years ago, when your father was first starting his business, he worked very long hours. After we were married for a few years, we started trying to have a baby. But he was always tired and didn't feel like—"

"I get what you mean, Mom." Cora blushed.

"We had not been successful after trying for quite some time, and I was so frustrated. I think maybe I was even a little crazy. You see, I had always wanted babies. You never think you'll be unable to have them."

"What happened?" Cora gazed deeply into her mother's blue eyes.

"Your father got tired of my constant crying and moping around the house so he started spending even more time away. I hardly noticed. As long as he was there when it was time to go to bed and to try to make a baby, I was happy."

"Okay. But you had me eventually, right? You and Dad survived the tough times. Everybody goes through times like that."

"Yes, we did survive those times, but not unscathed."

"What do you mean? And how does this apply to me?"

"Your father found another woman. A woman who didn't cry all the time.

A woman who would make him laugh. A woman who could make him happy. A woman who could make him a father."

"What!" Cora jumped up from the couch. "What are you saying? Dad got this woman pregnant? I have a brother or sister somewhere out there?"

Brenda sat in silence, focused on the floor.

"Wait, I still don't see how this would change the way he feels about me. Does he love that child more than me?"

Brenda's eyes stayed pinned to the floor. "You do not have a brother or a sister." Lightning flashed.

"I don't understand. Did the woman lose the baby? Or did she abort?"

"No." Brenda got up and walked toward Cora. She placed her hands on Cora's forearms. "You are that baby. You are your father's child by this other woman." Brenda burst into tears.

Cora pulled away from her mother. Tears streamed down her own face. *I am a result of an affair?* She faced Brenda again. "No! This cannot be true. How can this be? You're not my mother?" She shook her head violently.

"I am. I raised you."

"What about my birth mother? Where is she?" Cora sobbed.

"She died giving birth to you. They were only able to save you." Brenda closed the space between herself and Cora and reached her arms around her.

"Don't." Cora yanked away from her. "Why didn't you ever tell me this? All my life I've known you didn't love me like you should. I've always felt there was something holding us apart. I tricked myself into thinking it was Dad. But it was you. Why didn't you just tell me so I would have understood why you despised me?"

"I couldn't. I don't. I wanted to. I-I knew it would devastate you. As it has. Your father didn't want you to know. Not ever. He'd always been extra hard on you because he wanted me to love you. He thought if you were the best at everything, I'd forget about his immorality." Brenda collapsed on the couch.

Memories of piano and dance recitals, modeling shoots, and pageants flooded Cora's mind. "I have to get out of here. I need some air." Cora stormed from the room.

"It's raining outside. You don't need to be out in this weather."

Cora ran to her room and grabbed her purse. When she sprinted back through the living room, Walt was standing by the window. He turned to look at her. She paused only a moment, staring at the man who had betrayed her all of her life. Then she hurried from the house, slamming the door.

"Cora!" Walt yelled.

* * *

Three hours later, Cora pulled her father's spare car into the driveway. His new car was not there, but an unfamiliar truck was parked behind her mother's Lexus. As her headlights shined in the dark through the fog, they revealed the tag on the back of the truck. It was a rented vehicle. *I'm in no mood to even greet someone, much less entertain.* Cora flipped the visor down and opened the mirror to check her face. She frowned at her reflection. The dark circles were back.

Cora sat in the car for a minute, holding the keys in her hand, trying to think of something to say when she entered the house. So many emotions raged through her mind. *I can no longer stay here in this house. But where will I go?*

Cora climbed from the car and ran to the front door through the stinging rain. The cold and foggy dampness chilled her to the very core. She longed for a cup of hot cocoa. She put the key in the lock and turned the doorknob, unlocking the uncertainty of her future. When she entered the foyer, she took off her raincoat and hung it on the hall-tree. No one greeted her at the door. She looked back out at the truck in the drive and called, "Where is everyone?"

Cora shut the door and was proceeding down the hall and toward her room, when out of the corner of her eye, she saw someone standing in the living room. The hair on her arm bristled.

When she turned, she saw a man—a tall, dark man. The lights were off in the room, the only light coming from the hall. She couldn't quite make out the identity of this person, but something about him was familiar. *Rex?*

She paused, squinting, thinking this must be a guest of her father's. "Hello?"

14

"Hello, Cora."

Cora's breath caught at the medicinal sound of the voice. "Rex? What are you doing here?" She stepped into the living room, moving closer.

"I came to see you. I wanted to say I'm sorry." He cleared his throat.

"Oh." Her knees weakened.

"I'm sorry, Cora, for being so rude. For hurtin' you."

"That's okay. I'm sorry for the things I said too." Her emotions were reeling. "How did you get here?"

"I flew and rented a truck."

"That explains the truck outside." She motioned outside. "How did you get in? How long have you been here? Have you been waiting for me?"

"Your parents let me in. And, according to them, I arrived about fifteen minutes after you left."

"Rex, I've been gone for hours. You waited?" Her mind spun like a merry-go-round.

"Yeah."

"Where are they?" She stepped closer, tilting her head to the side.

"They went out to dinner. They said you might not want to see them when you returned—that you might want to be alone with me." Rex held his Stetson in one hand and rubbed the rim of it with the fingers of his other hand.

Cora walked over to turn on the lamp on the table next to where Rex stood. When she turned around, his appearance caught off her guard. Her throat went dry as if she'd eaten a bag of pretzels with nothing to drink. Rex stood there in black jeans, a button-down shirt, with a big belt buckle shining in the dim light and his dress cowboy boots. It was not what he wore, however, that thunderstruck Cora the most. When she looked up at his face, she didn't recognize him at first. His beard had been shaved, leaving only his thick mustache to line his upper lip. His fresh haircut kept his unruly curls and waves neatly in place. Cora felt herself melting at the very sight of him. She never knew he was so handsome. He had a strong square jaw and chiseled cheekbones. Did the personality fit the looks, or was it the other way around?

Cora's eyes finally shifted to Rex's own dark eyes...eyes as dark as they had always been, but soft and caring at this moment. She gazed into them, mesmerized by his tenderness. She never wanted to look away.

Rex returned her stare gently. In the dimly lit room, he moved toward her. "Are you okay?" He delicately stroked her shoulder.

Goosebumps ran down her spine. "I suppose. I'm in shock over you being here and over the way you look. I can't believe you shaved."

"I wanted to look nice for you." He smiled, revealing a dimple on his left cheek.

"Well, you do." Cora felt her face redden at her boldness.

Smirking a bit, Rex said quickly, "Thank you." Then somberly he said, "Let's sit down." He led Cora to the camelback sofa. "They told me what happened. I'm sorry."

Cora looked up at Rex. She saw in his eyes the same compassion of the night she'd found out about Clark's death. Suddenly she burst into tears. Rex wrapped his arms around her and held her tightly. Cora allowed him to hold her and cried without reservation. This man was so big and strong, yet soft and gentle at the same time. He smelled of musk, which put Cora's senses into a frenzy of frustration. *Lord, please let this man be the one for me. He makes me feel so safe.*

Rex slowly released Cora but did not let her move too far away. "Do you want to talk?"

"I don't know if I can. But I'll try. I want to." She sighed. "I'm so hurt, so betrayed. How can a woman raise another woman's child and not tell her? I would have been better off if I'd been given away at birth. I never felt like my mother loved me fully. I always knew there was something keeping us from having a close relationship. I finally grew to believe the type of relationship we had was normal for a mother and daughter. My father always seemed unhappy with me. Supposedly, he wanted me to be perfect so his wife would love me more. The years of dance and beauty pageants and ice-skating...all to please her for him. I finally learned through caring for Susie that there was much more to being a mom than mine had been."

Rex was listening intently to her without looking away. At last he spoke. "I'm so sorry I hurt you, Cora. You've been through so much. What can I do for you? How can I help?"

Cora looked into Rex's deep dark pools. "You've helped more than you know already."

"Good." He smiled, the dimple popping out again.

"But you can do one thing for me."

"What's that?"

"Never let Susie feel like she doesn't measure up."

"I will do all I can." He nodded in agreement.

"Thank you. And thanks for being here."

"I'm glad I came."

"That reminds me, why are you here, really? I mean, I wouldn't think you'd come all this way just to say you're sorry. Is everything okay at the ranch?" Cora shifted sideways to face Rex. She brushed her hair out of her eyes and self-consciously patted her nose and wiped her eyes.

"Yes, everything's okay at home. Except for the fact you're not there. The place hasn't been the same since you left. I came because I want you to come back with me."

"You do?" Cora's heart beat so fast and loudly, she could barely hear herself think.

"Yep. I had a talk with Mom, thinkin' she would help me forget about you. Instead, she helped me see how blind I was being." He chuckled. "Actually, she told me I was a fool."

"What do you mean, Rex?" Cora nervously squirmed.

"I'm very full of pride...and stubborn."

"No! I'd never have known if you hadn't told me." Cora slapped Rex on the arm jokingly.

"Come on, now. Be nice to me. It's hard for me to open up." He gave her a sad puppy dog look. "Anyway, it took me so long to warm up to you because of Patty. I knew instantly there was something different about you. And when you came to the ranch, I really liked the way you and Susie were together. But I wasn't lookin' for a replacement for Patty as my wife or as Susie's mother. I started havin' feelings for you, and I didn't want to. I didn't know how to act. You were such a good person, and I had changed so much. Her death made me bitter. I knew you would never accept me because I had become so...I don't know." He grunted and rubbed his hands together.

Cora smiled at Rex because his words were right but said nothing.

He continued, "Then we did get closer, and I liked that. But when you found out about the money and said you needed to go home for a while, I couldn't handle it. I felt rejected. I knew if I let myself care for you, I'd get hurt again. Then I realized I already did care for you. It would hurt worse to lose you than it did to lose Patty, because you'd still be alive somewhere out there away from me. I knew I could never adapt knowin' you were here in Florida goin' on with your life or even somewhere in Georgia or South Carolina, when we could have a life together...I mean, *try* to have a life together." Rex gazed at Cora.

Cora still said nothing. It wasn't often Rex spoke his true feelings, and she did not want him to stop.

"What I mean is, I want you to come back with me. I want you to help care for Susie. I'd love to have your input with the ranch. Or you could do your own thing. I don't care. I want the chance to get to know you better. If you decide you're not happy at the ranch, I want you to find a place and be happy. If you're still not happy, then…well, I'll have to let you go. But I can't stand the thought of never findin' out if we could make it together. I need you."

Cora's mouth hung open. Her eyes focused on his as tears poured from them. *Of course, I want to be with him. But there is so much still to find out about him. Can I move back to the ranch and be with him without losing control? Can he accept the fact I won't be with him in a physical way? What should I do?*

"Rex, I really want to be at the ranch. I told my parents this afternoon I wanted to return because I wasn't happy here. I told them I needed Susie and your family. I tried to explain to them about you, but they wouldn't listen. I tried to put my feelings for you into words, but there are no words. It's kind of crazy, you know? I, too, want to see if something's truly happening between us or if this is nothing more than attraction or maybe just desperation because we're both lonely."

Rex nodded in agreement.

"I hurt them when I told them I didn't want to stay here. They can't understand why you all feel more like family to me than they do. That's when my mother, if I can still call her that, told me about my father's affair. Now I don't know if I should leave. If I leave them now, it will probably sever our ties forever. I'm not sure, but that might be what I want anyway. I know deep down inside, though, I can't leave on bad terms with them. It has killed me to be away from you like this. I know it would do the same to me to leave them." Lightning flickered gently outside, followed by a distant rumble of thunder.

"I understand. And I agree. You have to mend the broken relationship. It's like back on the ranch when there's a hole in one of the fences. You can't leave it because it gets bigger."

"Yeah, I know. I can't leave the way things are now."

"Remember, while holes in the fences are bad, fences themselves are good things. They set those boundaries. They keep in what needs to be in and they keep out what needs to be kept out. I think maybe you need to mend the fences and then you all can move on with the next phase of life. I've had to do that with my parents and me livin' back at home. They don't own me just because I live there. I'm still an adult man who's a father."

"True."

"Of course, lately I haven't been actin' too much like a man. But I'm changin' things. So, do ya think you would want to come back after things are better with your folks?"

"I want to be there, Rex. With you." Cora gazed into his dark eyes of coal, the magnets pulling her toward him.

"You do?" A laugh escaped his lips. "I can't believe it. I totally don't deserve you." He took her hands in his.

"Don't say that. You are a good person. You're so considerate and caring. You have helped me so much. Really. It seems like, ever since you've known me, you've seen me do nothing but cry and get hurt."

"That isn't true. I've seen you smile a lot, especially when you're with Susie. I know you love her. It makes me feel—I don't know—loved."

"That isn't the only reason you want me to be there, though, is it? For Susie?" She let go of his hands.

"I want you to be there because I want you." He grabbed her hands. "I want to spend time with you gettin' to know you." Rex looked into Cora's eyes until his own misted.

"Rex, I don't know if I can be what you need. I'm scared I might not be able to keep you happy."

"What do you mean? You're more than I could ever need."

"I mean, I can't *be* with you." Cora searched his eyes for mutual understanding.

At first, Rex appeared confused. Then his face turned red. Cora giggled to see him blush. His eyes widened, and he shook his head back and forth. "Cora, I never meant to imply I expected a physical relationship. You must think I'm awful. You should know by now, after everything that happened with Veronica, I would never ask that of you until you were ready."

"But I wouldn't ever be ready." She looked away.

"What?" He raised his right eyebrow.

"Not unless our relationship turned into something more...more permanent." She glanced up at him and their eyes locked.

"Do you mean marriage?"

If she could have crawled under the couch, she would have. She did not want to presume Rex would ever want to marry her. She felt like a fool, but she nodded.

"Cora, that's what I meant to say. I just didn't want you to think I was bein' too pushy. I wouldn't want to be with you unless we were married. And hopefully, that will happen." Rex looked down at his folded hands.

"What are you saying?" Cora placed her hand on his.

"I hope we become close enough to want to get married."

"Really? You feel that way about me?"

"Yeah."

"Boy, this is deep, isn't it?" She wiped the remaining tears away.

"Yeah, it is. But we needed to talk about it. I want you to know my intentions. I want to make you feel the same way the song of the meadowlark makes you feel."

"How did you know I love that bird?"

"I noticed how it affected you when you heard it sing."

"I miss hearing that bird." She slumped.

"I miss you bein' there to hear it. Please come back with me? I would love to have your input. We're gonna open a bed-and-breakfast, even though I don't want to, and it looks like Ms. Lottie's gonna come stay with us and help run it."

"When are you leaving?" The rain no longer came down. Only the sound of the gutters dripping the remnants could be heard outside.

"Not for a few days. I planned on stayin' until I could talk you into goin' with me." A deep laugh escaped his mouth.

"Oh, you're good." She crossed her legs, finally relaxing. "Where are you staying?"

"I got a room. Don't worry about me. Please come back with me. I already bought your ticket." He placed his hand gently on her shoulder.

"You did? Well, aren't we presumptuous?" she taunted.

"No, just hopeful." He winked at her.

"There is one other thing I have to know before I can make my decision."

"What?"

"How do you feel about God? Please be honest with me. You haven't been to church with your family since Patricia passed away. You haven't gone at all since I've been there. Not that church attendance is everything, but it's a good indicator. I need to know." Cora knew this could be the end of what was about to begin between the two of them. However, she also knew if she did not get this out in the open before leaving with him, she might make the same mistake as she did with Clark. She held her breath.

Standing up from where he sat next to Cora, Rex walked across the room and faced the window, staring out into the night. After a minute, he turned to face her. "Cora, I am a believer, like you. But I have found it very difficult to believe in anything since Patty died. I felt like God let me down. Instead of turnin' toward him, I turned away. I've known for a while now I needed to turn back, before it was too late. I just didn't know how to do it. Since I've known you, though, I've known a peace I never knew before. You've taught me a great deal about faith."

"Having faith is what gets me through this crazy life."

"I feel like I've been given a second chance."

"Tonight, when I was out driving around wondering what to do with my life, I knew something would work out. I knew God was weaving things together, even though I couldn't see them. I had faith things would fall into place. Then I came home, and here you were. I needed you. I just didn't know how to make that happen."

"I needed you, too, Cora. Will you let me into your life?"

"I would like to try it."

"I don't know if I can ever be as good as you, though."

"Rex, we're all striving for the same thing. The point is, we keep at it. You have to promise me you won't try to hide your feelings from me anymore. Please tell me what you're thinking or feeling, so we can deal with it together. We've wasted so much time already. Okay?" Cora got up off the couch and walked over to Rex.

"Okay. It's a deal." Rex winked at her. "Not to change the subject, but are you hungry?"

"A little, I guess. Would you like me to cook something for you?"

"Absolutely not. I'm takin' you out to eat." Rex grabbed Cora in a bear hug.

"I look terrible, though." Cora wrapped her arms around the man of her dreams, her heart warming.

"You're the most beautiful woman in the world. You could never look terrible."

"Let me at least go patch up my makeup and change clothes. I'll be right out." Cora tried to pull herself out of Rex's grip.

"Not until I do this." Rex bent his head to kiss her.

Cora melted into his arms. She had almost forgotten how wonderful it was to feel the kiss of this man. The softness of his face without the beard warmed her heart even more. His scent filled her nostrils, tranquilizing her. Then, gently, Rex released her.

"Now, you can go." He smiled; the dimple even more prevalent now.

She ran her fingers through his curls. "Now I don't want to go," Cora enticed, but she turned and headed toward her room.

Once in her room, she touched up her face and then looked for something that complemented the way Rex was dressed. She picked her new jeans and sweater her mother had brought home for her from the mall. She smiled the entire time she dressed. *Rex came for me. He opened up to me, too.*

Cora joined Rex in the living room after only a few minutes. "Wow! I thought you couldn't get any prettier."

"Why thank you, sir." Rex opened the front door for Cora, and she stepped outside. "Nice rental by the way."

They left the house after Cora wrote a note for her parents telling them where she was going. In the truck, on the way to the restaurant, she sat in the middle next to Rex. He tried to keep his arm around her, but she had to lean too far up uncomfortably. So instead, she pulled his arm from behind her and wrapped her hand inside his arm. "The only thing that would make this ride more perfect would be some good country music." Rex winked at Cora, and she rolled her eyes.

At dinner, they talked more at length about their immediate future, the ranch, the bed-and-breakfast, Susie. They also laughed about childhood memories and the difference between their growing up—Cora at the beach and Rex in South Georgia on a ranch; Rex with hard-earned old money and Cora with white-collar new money. Rex filled her in on the latest happenings of Clarice and Matt. Their dinner included sampling each other's seafood and sharing a veritable chocolate explosion for dessert. Cora could not take her eyes off Rex's smooth face, nor could she stop staring into his fiery eyes. Rex kissed a drop of chocolate off Cora's mouth.

Cora asked Rex to come back inside with her when they returned to the house. She wanted her parents to get to know Rex better. She also needed him with her. He agreed to stay with her for as long as she needed him.

* * *

"Well, Rex, here goes," Cora said as they pulled into her parents' driveway.

"What are you gonna say to them? Are you still mad? Or are you okay with what you learned today?"

"I don't know what I'll say. I guess that will depend on how they are when we get inside. I don't think I'm fuming anymore, though. I'm so much happier now that you and I have worked out our differences, so I think I can be more understanding with them." Cora smiled at Rex.

"Let's go, then." Rex opened the truck door and slid out. He held out his hand to Cora, and she climbed out on his side of the truck.

They walked slowly up to the front door. Little beads of sweat formed on Cora's upper lip. She was still apprehensive about going inside. She quickly said a silent prayer as she and Rex entered the foyer. While they were hanging up their jackets on the hall-tree, Walt and Brenda came into the foyer from the sitting room at the back of the house. For a moment all four stood, not saying a word.

Then, finally, Walt removed his pipe from his mouth. "Cora, I am truly sorry for not telling you. I wouldn't blame you if you hated me forever. I should never have let this lie go on for so long. Your poor mother's been heartbroken since you left. I should have never put her in the position of having to tell you."

The weight of a thousand freight trains lifted off Cora's chest as Walt shouldered the blame for his family's disharmony.

"Why don't we all go in the sitting room to talk?" Brenda held out her manicured hand, pointing the way.

"I'll stay in here." Rex gestured toward the living room.

Cora looked at him and was about to speak, when Walt spoke instead. "No, son, we'd like you to join us. You are obviously a part of Cora's life, so you need to hear all that is going to be said."

Rex nodded. They all walked into the sitting room. Brenda disappeared into the kitchen and swiftly returned with a pot of coffee and cups.

Cora reached to pour a cup of coffee. "I've had a lot of time to think about everything you told me today. I've been very bewildered. I drove around for hours, crying and yelling. I felt so betrayed. I wasn't sure what would happen after today."

"We want things to change between us. We want things to be better. We've both been too hard on you all of your life. We've made you pay for my sin. That was wrong. It was not your fault. I wanted so much for your mother to love you that I tried to make you perfect. I know I was too rough on you. I want you to forgive me." Tears flooded Walt's eyes, and he reached out for her hand.

She accepted his hand, feeling the softness of hands that had never seen a hard day's work. "I've known all of my life that something wasn't right. I've even noticed many times how I look nothing like Mother. I always thought that the Sinclair genes were just extra strong. I wondered why I had no siblings. I knew I had to work too hard for your love. Most of the time, no matter what I did, it wasn't enough. I grew to accept this and assumed it was normal." Cora sipped her coffee.

Rex sat silently beside her, hat in hand. His eyes never left her face.

"Can we start over?" Brenda looked into the depths of Cora's eyes. "I know you may not want to call me your mother anymore, and I will understand if you don't, but please don't shut out your father. He feels terrible about this, and we want you in our lives."

"We can get past all of this, Dad, Mom." Cora looked at Brenda. "You are my mom. You may not have given birth to me, but you did raise me. Maybe you weren't the best of parents. Who is, though? We all make mistakes in our lives. We shouldn't be penalized for them." She gazed at Rex. "We all need to learn to forgive and forget."

"Cora, I know what you are saying. I never let you forget about your mistake in marrying Clark. I'm sorry. I know you truly loved him. It wasn't your fault he turned out the way he did. I'm sorry he died. I deeply regret we did not offer you our support when you found out about his death. I know you must have been hurting." Walt puffed his pipe.

Rex sat on the couch beside Cora, holding her hand but not saying a word. She relaxed because of his presence. "I know you two want to have a fresh start with me, and I want that, too. But I do want to return to Georgia." She cringed at the potential response. "I hope you agree with me that we can have a fresh start with me in Georgia. It's not an either/or situation."

"Of course, we understand you want to be with Rex, and with his little girl. We want you to be happy. Go, and enjoy yourself. But you better call and write us often." Brenda offered a genuine smile.

"And we have email now too so you can send us photos of what you are doing."

"Do you really mean it?" Cora perked up. "Dad? Is this okay with you, too? I thought you wanted me to stay here and run the company."

"Your mother and I made some decisions this evening. We don't want to transfer our business dealings to you. That's not fair. We both want to travel," Walt said. Then, turning toward Rex, he continued, "You'd think that, since I own a travel agency, we'd travel all the time. In reality, though, I work all the time, and we never go anywhere. We've decided to sell the business and to travel in a motor home until we are too old and have to do something else. When we decide to settle down, we'll probably choose a location near you, Cora. I think we'll keep the beach house as a vacation home, though."

"That sounds great, Dad. How do you like the idea, Mom?"

"I love it. As long as you won't miss your childhood home."

"No." Cora breathed in relief. Not much of this home held fond memories.

"This will give you the space you need away from us, and it will give us some growing time. We've neglected our relationship for far too many years." Brenda sipped her coffee and smiled at Walt.

"Well, Rex, what do you think of this crazy family?"

"I think it's no crazier than mine, Mr. Sinclair. I have yet to figure out why Cora wants to be with us. Our house is always in a crisis."

"It is not, Rex O'Reilly. You're such a liar." Cora jokingly smacked him on the arm.

"At any rate, I'd like to extend an invitation to the ranch to you both.

You're welcome anytime. Wherever your daughter is, you are welcome."

"We thank you, and we may possibly take you up on your invitation," Walt said.

Placing her cup on the table, Cora slapped her legs and stood. "I don't mean to be rude, but I'm exhausted. I think I will walk my dear Rex out and head to bed." Cora yawned.

"Why don't you stay the night here, Rex?" Brenda offered.

"Oh, thank you ma'am, but all of my things are back at the hotel. I'll be fine." Rex put his Stetson on his head, adding almost a foot to his height.

Cora and Rex walked to the front door. They talked only for a few minutes before Rex leaned down and kissed her good night. "I'll call you in the morning. We still have a lot to talk about. Maybe we can go for breakfast?"

"Yes, sir, that would be great." Cora gave this tall gentleman a salute. "Good night. Sleep tight. Don't let the bed bugs bite."

"Oh, thanks. There probably are bed bugs at my hotel. But seriously, I will sleep quite well now I know we're good." Rex tipped his hat.

"Yep, we're good." Cora shut the door and walked into the house to go to bed.

* * *

The following morning, Cora awoke smiling in the warmth of her bed. Her Bible readings from the night before remained in her thoughts. She shivered in anticipation of spending her day with Rex and with her parents.

Soon after Cora had showered and dressed, the telephone rang.

"Good mornin'," called the deep, raspy voice on the end of the line.

"Good morning, Rex. Did you sleep well?" Cora flirted.

"I missed you, but I did sleep quite well."

"No bed bugs?"

"No, thankfully, no bed bugs."

"Good." She giggled.

"I'm happy to know we are gonna be together."

"I am, too. Are you coming here to the house?" Cora brushed her dark, shiny hair. The new shampoo her mother gave her had transformed her hair after the chlorine had burned it.

"Yes, if you'd like me to. We can get breakfast like I said last night."

"That sounds good to me." Cora heard a knock at her bedroom door. "Hang on. Come in."

"Oh, I'm sorry, I wasn't aware you were on the phone. I'll come back."

Brenda backed out of Cora's room.

"Mom, what do you need? I'm on the phone with Rex." She waved her mother into her room.

"I was checking to see if you were having breakfast here or not."

"Rex and I were going to go out."

"Why don't you invite him here, if you'd like?"

"Do you want to eat here? Then we could go out afterwards," Cora inquired.

"Sure. Sounds great. I'm on my way."

The line went dead, and Cora hung up the telephone. "He said he'd like to eat here. He's on his way. Are you sure you want to feed him? He eats a lot of food," Cora ribbed.

"I'd love to feed him. Come on and help me in the kitchen."

Cora followed Brenda down the hall and into the kitchen. She smiled because Brenda was in such a happy mood. The patio doors were swung open, and the breeze blew inside.

"Where's Dad?" Cora scanned the kitchen and dining room.

"He went out for a while this morning. He said he had to get something. He wanted to get it before you left."

"I'm not leavin' today. At least I don't think I am. Rex bought me a ticket to return with him, but he said there were a few days before the flight."

"You might want to leave sooner. You probably are anxious about getting a start on things and seeing where your life will lead."

"I guess. I want to be with you two also, though. Besides, Rex and I aren't exactly getting married. We're just going to see if things work out."

"Oh, I see." Brenda regarded her with a furrowed brow.

"It isn't what you think, Mom. We aren't sleeping together. And...there are no plans to do so. Rex knows I will not do that unless I'm married. And he feels the same way. We've only known each other a few months, and it's been pretty rocky. We're just now admitting there's something here. I must say, though, that if we feel we are right for each other, marriage will come quickly, no doubt." Cora smiled.

"I understand exactly what you are saying. A grown man will have a difficult time waiting."

"And a grown woman, too." Cora elbowed Brenda, and the two giggled. *I can't believe I'm having this conversation with Mom and that we are laughing together.* Cora set the dishes and silverware out on the table.

"I'm back," rang a voice from the foyer.

"Dad? Is that you?" Cora sprinted through the kitchen to the entrance hall.

"Yes. Good morning. Did you have a good night's sleep?" Walt kissed her on the cheek with more warmth than she'd ever felt from him.

"Yes, I sure did. What have you been out doing so early this morning?"

"I had to pick up a few things. You'll find out later." Walt hid the packages he held behind his back.

"Dad!"

"Go help your mother with breakfast." He smiled and waved her away. "Is Rex coming to eat with us?"

"Yes." She pouted.

"Good. I got something for him, too." Walt headed to his study.

Going back into the kitchen, Cora chewed her bottom lip as she tried to solve the mystery. "Mom, what do you think he bought for us?"

"Now, now, patience." She shook her finger at her. "He'll show you when he's ready."

"I can't stand the suspense." Cora blew her bangs out of her eyes.

"Get busy scrambling those eggs, and you'll forget about it soon enough." Brenda handed Cora a plastic spatula. "Then you can move the dishes out to the patio. It's a great morning to eat outside."

* * *

When Rex arrived, the family sat down to breakfast on the patio. The conversation matched the cheery calls of the sea birds. Cora continued to smile at everyone because things were going so well. *Did I step into someone else's happy home life? It's as though the past twenty-five years of my life never existed.*

After finishing his breakfast, Walt sat back in his chair and lit his pipe. "Well, you two, we've told you our plans about selling the business and then traveling. What are your plans?"

Cora looked at Rex to see if he'd answer, unsure of what plans he'd made.

"We can do whatever Cora would like. I've already purchased her a ticket for the trip home. I know that sounds a bit conceited, but I did it hopin' it would sway her to return with me. The flight's scheduled for tomorrow at eleven in the morning. If she wants to stay here a bit longer, that's fine, but I've got to return to the ranch." Rex turned toward Cora. "So, it's up to you."

"What would you two like me to do? Do you want me to stay a few more days?" Cora looked at her parents. *Maybe they won't mind if I fly back with Rex. I really want to go home with him.*

Pouring a second cup of coffee for herself, Brenda responded. "I'm glad

128

you came home. I'm just sorry that most of the time you were here we wasted on foolishness. But as much as we would love you to stay, I think you should fly back to Georgia with Rex. Now that we've gotten to know him and we've dismissed our initial reaction to the thought of you being with someone you met recently, I know you should go. The two of you would be miserable without each other."

"You're right." Rex took Cora's hand in his. "I've known Cora all summer long, and I have been interested in her. But I was too stubborn to let her know it when the time was right." He smiled at Cora. "If I hadn't let my pride get in the way, Cora probably wouldn't have left the ranch so upset like she did."

"Rex, we've discussed this. I didn't exactly make it easy for you. I was running as fast as you were."

Walt grinned and held up a hand. "Now that you have both stopped running, and you've caught each other, what do you expect will happen?"

"Sir, I'd like to have your daughter stay with my family at the ranch as long as she wishes to stay. I hope we become very close, now that I've dealt with my pride. My daughter loves Cora very much, and Cora cares for her also. I feel we have something here, if Cora wants to be with an old cowboy like me."

Cora smiled at Rex and then at each of her parents, pleased with their acceptance of Rex and with his kindness and gentleness.

"I hope you stay together. I know you lost your spouse, just as Cora did, and starting over has to be difficult. I'm sure your daughter plays a big role in your decisions also."

"Oh, yes, ma'am. I've gone out with a few women since my wife's death, and Susie has liked none of them. Of course, now I see why. They were all terrible for me. Susie instantly took a likin' to Cora, I think, especially because she was her nanny before she was a friend to me. Susie had her all to herself. I think it will be easy for her to accept Cora as more."

"You two keep us informed. We want to know what's going on with you." Walt stood from his seat at the table. "I've got to head to the office and get some work done. I should be back for lunch."

"Wait a minute, Daddy. You haven't heard what my decision is."

"Okay, go ahead." Walt smirked at her.

"I think I will return to Georgia with Rex tomorrow."

"Surprise, surprise," Walt mocked.

"I plan to help out with some changes to the ranch and still work with Susie. I'm not going to be just Rex's girlfriend. I'm anxious to get started with my new life."

"Sounds like a great plan." Walt started to leave the dining room.

"Aren't you forgetting something, Dad?"

"No, not that I know of."

"I believe you have something for us both."

"Oh, I suppose you are right. I did go shopping, didn't I?" he teased. "I'll be right back." He stepped up into the house, heading for his study.

When he returned carrying boxes, Cora's face lit up. "What's in them?"

"Open them and see."

"Both of you open them at the same time." Brenda leaned forward.

When Cora and Rex opened the boxes, they each found matching snakeskin boots. They gasped when they saw the expensive gifts.

"Sir, I can't take these. It's too much. You hardly know me," Rex protested.

"Yeah, Dad, these are too much," Cora agreed.

"I thought long and hard about a gift for you both. This was the best I could do on such short notice. You will both accept them as our token of love and apology for everything," Walt insisted. "I hope they fit."

"Okay, thank you. But are you sure?" Cora laughed inside because her father must have already assumed she would return with Rex, or he wouldn't have bought them.

"*We* are sure." Brenda regarded Walt with the adoring eyes of a schoolgirl.

Noting that exchange of affection, Cora smiled.

"Of course, we're sure. Now I have to go to work. I'll see you two later." Walt shook Rex's hand and then left the patio.

"Well, what are you two going to do today?" Brenda got up from her seat and collected the breakfast dishes.

Still in shock over the gifts her father had given them, Cora answered, "First of all, I'm going to help you with the dishes. Rex, why don't you go watch television in the den? I won't be but a few minutes."

"No, you don't," her mother insisted. "You two go on and get started with your day. I'm sure you had already made plans."

"I had thought about riding around and showing Rex the sights. I'd like him to see where I grew up. I wanted to take him down to St. Andrews, too. And to the beach house maybe."

"That would be lots of fun, Cora. Let's go."

"Mom, are you sure you don't want me to help you?"

"Go on. Have fun. But plan to have dinner with us tonight. We've made reservations at Franklin's. I won't take no for an answer."

Cora eyed Rex, who gave his nod of approval. "Okay. Sounds like fun."

"Thanks for taking me sightseeing." Cora sat next to Rex in the rental truck, basking in the warmth of the sun coming through the windows, and tapped her toe to the steel guitar playing on the radio.

"Sure thing. It's my pleasure. I love seein' where you used to hang out. It gives me a glimpse of the stuff that made you who you are, Cora." He winked at her, the laugh lines around his eyes more noticeable in the daylight.

"If you'll go left on Thomas Drive here, we can go to St. Andrews and walk out on the pier. We used to do this all the time when we were in high school."

"I bet you caught lots of fellas here, huh?" Rex cut his eyes toward her while he turned onto Thomas Drive, passing the T-shirt shops and shell shops. Rex looked twice at the seafood restaurant straight ahead.

"No, not really. Well, maybe," Cora provoked.

They drove through the gate at the entrance to the park and pulled around to the pier parking lot. They walked out onto the pier, the autumn wind gusting, and seagulls diving at the prospects of acquiring bait from the local fishermen. Cora pulled her jacket closed and sucked in a deep breath, filling her lungs with the salty air.

"Wow! This is so beautiful. You know, I've never been to the beach before."

"Why? It's only four hours away." Cora let the wind blow its salty healing across her face.

"We always had the ranch to work. When you have all the animals and ranch hands we've had, you can't take time away. It's too hard to find people who can run things. And every summer my cousins would come for their vacations."

"Did you not ever go away with your friends on school trips or anything?"

"Nope." He took in a deep breath; the wind blowing through his curls.

"Well, what do you think? Isn't it amazing?"

"I think it's the greatest thing I've even seen, and I'm glad to be sharing it with you."

"Me, too. I think this is the best place to see and feel God's presence." Cora grinned at Rex like a child. "I should've brought the bread to feed the gulls. I left it in the truck." She snapped her fingers in regret.

"Do you want me to go get it?"

"No, that's okay."

"Maybe next time." Rex put his arm across Cora's shoulders, and she leaned into him as they walked on the weathered wood of the pier.

Funny, isn't it? she couldn't help but think. *Rex and I are kind of like this beaten pier, with years of pain and turmoil carving a place in our lives. But, like the pier, we're still here, and we're solid.*

"Next time?" She looked up at him.

"Yeah, when we come back to visit your parents." He looked out at the sea, shoving his left hand into his front pocket, his brown eyes soaking in the beauty.

"That sounds like a good idea." She smiled. *Next time? So he's thinking about the future, huh?* "I still can't get over my parents and how they're taking all this change. I thought they'd resist letting me go, especially after all the revelation of the past two days. But they seem somehow at peace now. Almost like they were only being that difficult and clingy because of their secrets."

"Oh, I'm sure their own guilt about things made them act the way they did toward you. That's human nature. We always want to blame others for the things we've done wrong. And if we can't put the blame on them, then we want to make them as miserable as we are for no reason."

"Wow, you're like a genius or a philosopher or something," Cora joked.

"Ha! Actually, I'm an expert." Rex leaned over to kiss Cora's forehead.

After enjoying the view from the pier for a while, they turned and walked back to the end. Cora pulled off her shoes and rolled up her pants legs. "Let's go look for some shells for Susie."

"Okay." Rex pulled off his boots and rolled up the bottom of his jeans. He carried his boots with him and followed Cora.

"Watch out for the jellyfish. They're washed up all over the place. You don't want to get stung by one." Cora stepped around a clear and purple jellyfish approximately two feet in diameter. "Look! Out there, just ahead. Dolphins!" She pointed to her right.

"Where?" Rex shielded his eyes from the glare of the sun.

"Wait, they'll come up again. They're feeding. They love this area of the bay. There they are!" She pointed again.

"I see them. That's wild!" Rex snickered like a little boy.

They stood side by side, watching the dolphins surface for several minutes.

"My ears are hurting a little from the wind," Cora said finally. "You ready to go?"

"Sure, if you are. Where do you want to go next?"

Cora showed Rex where she'd played as a small girl in the park. They parked the truck and walked for a while, stopping to swing in the swings like children. As they sat on a bench feeding pigeons, Cora stared into Rex's eyes, watching for any flecks of regret or hesitance. "I have a question to ask you."

"Okay, go ahead." Rex threw breadcrumbs to the birds.

"When I return home with you, should I still be Susie's official nanny? Should I stay at the ranch or with Ms. Lottie?"

"I don't want you to be Susie's nanny officially. You're my girlfriend—I hope. Between my parents and me, Susie should not need a nanny any longer. If I had been the type of father I should have been, she'd never have needed one in the first place." Rex scratched his bristly chin.

"That's not entirely true, Rex. You did have to work for a living. She would have needed someone to care for her while you were working. Besides, you would never have met me."

"That's true." He nudged her with his shoulder.

"Now, back to my question. Since I won't be caring for her any longer as an employee, what will I do?"

"Well…"

"I'll need to earn money…wait, I really don't need it right now, do I?"

"No, ma'am, you sure don't." There was that dimple again.

"Hmm, I can't just return as your girlfriend. I can't stay at the ranch in that capacity. People will assume we are…"

"I know. We don't want anyone to get the wrong idea," Rex agreed, pausing to think. He held his chin between his thumb and forefinger.

"How about I stay with Ms. Lottie in town? Then we could still see each other, but no one would get the wrong idea," Cora proposed.

"I'd go crazy with you bein' that far away. You have to stay at the ranch."

"Rex, I can't go back and stay at the ranch just so I'll be there when you need to see me. If things don't work out between us, I'll be stuck. It would make the whole situation so awkward." She looked at him for an answer.

"I'll move back home."

"But, Rex, that's too much for you right now. Are you ready to go back?"

"I am now. Knowing you feel the same about me as I do about you clears up a lot of things in my head. And it will give me some quiet time to figure out a plan for the ranch. I also have to think toward preschool for Susie. So the time back at home will do me good."

Throwing bread out to the pigeons, Cora turned to Rex. "What do you mean? How has this changed your feelings about moving back home?"

"I've been afraid to go back because of the memories of Patty. I thought I couldn't deal with it. But these past few weeks of bein' without you were just as bad. I realized before I came after you I had never dealt with my grief. I closed myself off from everyone, and I was angry with God. When you came to the ranch, and Susie loved you so, I thought I'd finally gotten rid of my last tie to

Patty. I was glad I didn't have to take care of Susie. It didn't take me long to realize you were very special, but I refused to care for you. So I chose to stay with Veronica because she was the complete opposite of you. I thought I wanted a relationship with someone who would expect nothing from me emotionally." Rex took a sip of his cola.

"You don't have to run from your pain." Cora rubbed the scars on her wrists.

Rex ran his fingers through his hair. "I guess that's what I'm tryin' to say. I know now that when you run and hide, the problem only gets worse. I need to move back home so I can deal with the pain of losin' her, if there's any left inside me."

"I agree. I think I've finally come to terms with Clark's death. Some questions will never be answered, so I have to let them rest. I guess I could stay at the ranch. But if I stay there, Susie won't understand why I'm not her caregiver any longer. I don't mind at all spending time with her. I love going to the library and teaching her to read. Are you sure you wouldn't want me to continue to be her nanny?"

"Absolutely not. I want you to go home with me and be free to do whatever it is you'd like to do. If you're carin' for Susie all of the time, you'll not have the chance to...I want you to enjoy yourself."

"Okay. I think I'd like to have some time just to be me. I'd love to read a book or two, learn some more about the ranch, and maybe even find a new hobby." Chills rushed up Cora's spine at the thought.

After their talk in the park, Cora showed Rex her old schools and her favorite hangouts from high school. She wanted Anne and her other friends to meet him, but there wasn't enough time. They ate lunch in the mall and shopped for a while but stayed away from the tourist shops, though Rex did buy a hermit crab for Susie. They held hands as they walked and laughed freely.

After shopping for a while, Cora suggested, "Let's head home. But let's drive by your hotel first, though, and check out. There's no reason for you to stay at the hotel when you'll have to come pick me up in the morning."

15

That evening the conversation between the two generations never stopped. Cora grinned the entire time. Rex's eyes sparkled when he snorted at Walt's jokes. Cora marveled at the light-hearted nature of her father—something new for him. Brenda stared at Rex throughout the meal and listened to his every word. He answered questions in a polite Southern drawl.

As Cora watched the ease with which her parents interacted with Rex, her mind drifted. *I still wish Mom was my birth mother, and they had not kept the secret from me. I wish I could know more about my real mother. But I'll have to be content with the way things are. I know someday they'll tell me more.*

At eleven o'clock, everyone retired for the night. Rex stayed in the guestroom down the hall from Cora's room. Once Cora got dressed for bed, washed her face, and brushed her teeth, she called Anne to say her good-byes. She tossed and turned all night—staring at the clock every fifteen minutes or so, fighting with her pajamas and sheets, knowing Rex was so close....

* * *

The next morning, Cora and Rex got ready to head to the airport. Cora fidgeted all throughout breakfast over leaving. The last time she'd departed from her parents was when she had left with Clark. This time she knew she was doing the right thing, but she still felt butterflies in her stomach.

"Bye, Mom. Bye, Dad. I'll miss you." Cora hugged each of her parents tightly as they stood by the front door.

"We'll miss you, too, Cora." Walt shook Rex's hand as he smiled at Cora. "Rex, it was great meeting you. You are a good man."

"Thank you, sir. It was a pleasure meetin' you both." He tipped his hat to Brenda.

"I'm so glad you came home, and we had this time together." Brenda wiped tears from her eyes. She leaned up and gave Rex a peck on the cheek.

"Me, too," Cora said. "I love you both."

"I love you, Cora." Brenda squeezed her again. "And Rex, you take care of my girl, okay?"

"Yes, ma'am. I sure will."

"I love you, too." Walt sniffled, then grabbed her for one last hug.

As Rex pulled out of the Sinclairs' driveway in the rental truck, Cora waved good-bye. She smiled bravely, but a tear still slid down her cheek.

"Are you okay?" Rex asked gently.

"Yes." She wiped the tears away from her eyes. "I guess I'm realizing how much I'll miss them. I never thought I'd hear myself say that, but it's true now. This is so different from the last time I left."

"I'm real proud of you. You've grown up since you've been home."

Cora frowned. "What do you mean? Should I take that to mean I was childish before?"

"Not at all. I mean you've been through a lot of junk in a very short time. Then, on top of everything, to go home to your parents, seeking comfort and support, only to find out all that you did. That only added to your pain. You've been through a growin'-up time without realizing it. You came out on top. You should be very pleased with yourself." Rex grinned.

Her brows relaxed. "I see what you mean now. Thanks for that. I give God all of the credit, though. He's been doing a lot of work on me. I guess I *have* grown. I learned to accept my parents as they are, and to love them no matter what. I would have done that a long time ago, had I been able to see the future."

"Sometimes it takes a major blow to make us realize what we have. At least you didn't lose one of your parents to death. You still have a chance to start over with them."

"I know. I'm very thankful for second chances. Really thankful." Cora giggled at Rex and placed her arm around his neck.

"What do ya think about skippin' the whole airport scene?" He glanced over at her.

"What do you mean?"

"We could drive home in less time just about than it would take us to get on the plane, wait, land, and drive to the ranch."

"If you're up for driving, it sounds great to me."

"Okay. Let's gas up then."

"What about the truck?"

"We can return it when we get home."

To start their road trip, Cora and Rex got a large fry and two chocolate shakes. Rex turned up the country music on the radio and sang like a lonesome cowboy, emphasizing the howling and yodeling at the end of each line.

Cora giggled until her side ached, seeing yet another facet of Rex's personality. "I think I've got a slow-talking cowboy on my hands, just like that Loretta Lynn song we heard the other day."

"If you're goin' to say it, say it right…slow-talkin' cowboy."

"So, I have to leave the g off the end of the word?"

"Yep."

Cora clapped her hands like a child. "I am so excited about getting back to Georgia and spending more time with you."

"I'm glad you're comin' back with me. I'm not lookin' forward to goin' back to work, though. It's gonna be hard to concentrate with you there."

"I'm sorry." Cora teased. "I can stay away from you, if you want me to."

"No way! We'll have the time change soon and it will be dark earlier so our days will be shorter on the ranch. That gives me more time to spend with you in the evenins'."

"Yay!"

"One problem is that it rains so much this time of year. We have to really watch the horses so they don't colic." Rex put on the blinker and changed lanes to get out from behind an eighteen-wheeler.

"Is that dangerous?"

"It can be. A horse can die quicker than you'd think. Especially when we have freezin' temperatures. The hay will mold and rot so quick. It can be a mess."

"Maybe we won't have a bad winter this year. We'll have so much on our minds with getting the B&B going, we don't need to have to worry about the ranch and the horses on top of that."

"I love how you say *we*. You're already a part of the place."

"Thanks." Cora adjusted the air vent in front of her.

"We do need *some* freezin' temperatures, though. If we don't have a real good hard freeze, the mosquitoes and bugs will be a nightmare to deal with come spring and summer."

"It's always something, isn't it?"

"Oh, yeah. It sure is."

* * *

After they stopped for a bathroom break, Cora sat next to Rex in the middle of the truck with her head on his shoulder. She loved the clean smell of him and the strength of his size. He could pick her up and rescue her from trouble or toss her to the ground and tickle her with ease if he wanted to. She held his hands in hers, noticing the scars and calluses on them. He was a hard-working man. Cora still could not believe he had shaved his beard. Words could not describe how he looked to her.

Just as Cora began to doze on Rex's shoulder, he tapped the brakes hard to avoid running up on the back of an eighteen-wheeler. Cora jumped.

"Sorry. I didn't mean to throw you through the windshield."

"That's okay. I was going to end up with a crick in my neck anyway." She scooted over to her side of the truck. "Do you mind if I read for a little bit?"

"No. Go ahead. Whatcha readin' lately?"

"Oh, a lot of Proverbs and Psalms in the Bible. I also love Acts and Romans."

"I love Romans. Why don't you read it out loud?"

"Okay." Cora turned to Romans and began to read. As they sat apart in the truck, they held hands.

By the time they drove across the Florida-Georgia line, torrents of rain began to come down. Cora put her Bible in her bag on the floorboard and squeezed the armrest tightly.

"Are you okay?" Rex glanced over at her and then back to the road.

"Yeah, I just hate traveling on the highway in a rainstorm. It makes me so nervous."

"There's nothin' to fear. Rex is at the wheel." He winked at her.

"Okay." The swishing of the wipers back and forth across the windshield calmed Cora's nerves. She silently prayed for safety. Eighteen-wheelers zoomed by, knocking the truck about in the wind.

"How about we get off the highway for a bit and let this storm pass? Want some coffee?"

"That sounds great." She sighed and relaxed her shoulders.

By the time they finished their coffee and shared a donut, a double rainbow reached across the sky in the distance.

* * *

Less than two hours later, Rex turned off the main road onto the dirt road leading to the Southern Hope.

"I can't believe we're really here!" Cora gushed. "That I'm back! When I left here, I knew I wanted to come back, but I didn't think I would, except to get my car. I knew you didn't want me here." Cora unbuckled her seat belt and slid over next to Rex.

"Well, I'm glad I came after you. If I hadn't, there would have been a lot of misunderstanding goin' on between here and Florida. I did want you. I just didn't want to want you. I wanted you to reject me so I'd have an excuse for not fightin' for you."

138

"This is crazy!"

"It sure is." Rex winked at her.

"I can't wait to see your parents and Susie. Do they know I'm coming?"

"No, I didn't tell them. They'll be so excited," Rex answered, smiling. "I know I am."

"Me, too. How do you think Susie will react to me not being her nanny?"

"I gave it a lot of thought last night, while I was tryin' to sleep in the room next to you." He stabbed himself in the heart with his fist. "I think it would be best if we didn't actually tell her you aren't her nanny anymore. You spend as much time with her as you want, of course, and then between Mom and me, she'll never be without someone."

"That's a good idea. I was afraid if we sat down and told her, making a big production out of it, it would only hurt her feelings. I'd never want her to feel rejected by me."

"That's exactly what I was thinkin'. You don't mind still spendin' some time with her?" Rex squeezed Cora's hand.

"Goodness, no. Besides, it's almost wintertime now; outside there won't be much to do. I will enjoy being with her."

"Thanks. Oh, look." Rex nodded toward the house. "Here we are." Rex pulled through the gates of the ranch. Cows were lined up by the fences.

"My heart is pounding out of my chest. I never thought I'd feel this way about returning." Cora gazed into Rex's eyes.

"You know what?"

"What?" Cora inquired.

"I love you." Rex leaned over and placed a gentle kiss on Cora's lips.

"You do? Rex, I love you, too," Cora whispered.

When they pulled up to the house, Cora watched Rex's face break out into a huge smile. He held his shoulders back and his head high. He got out of the truck and helped her out. Hand in hand, they walked onto the front porch and toward the front door. As soon as Cora's feet hit the porch, her heart filled with the assurance she had finally made a right decision. As he opened the door, he held his index finger up to his mouth.

"Hello. I'm home. Is anybody here?" Rex tried to hide Cora behind him.

"Rex? Is that you, honey?" Pearl hollered from the study and came running with Susie behind.

"Daddy!"

"Yes, Mom, it's me. Hey, Susie, look what I brought for you." Rex handed Susie the aquarium with the hermit crab.

"What is it?" Her eyes were as big as quarters, eyeing the clawed creature with the painted shell.

"It's a hermit crab. Now don't reach in without Daddy's help. It will pinch you."

"Okay, Daddy."

"I'm glad you made it back safely. How did it go?"

"Pretty good." Rex smiled. "And look who followed me home." Rex stepped aside so Pearl could see Cora.

"Oh, Cora. You're back!" Pearl grabbed Cora and squeezed her.

"Cora!" Susie immediately set the hermit crab cage on the ground. She jumped up and down and wrapped her arms around Cora's legs.

Cora bent down and picked her up. "Hey, baby, how are you?"

"What about me, Mom?" Rex pouted jokingly.

"Oh, come here, you big boy. Oh, my, look at your face. You're so handsome. When did you shave that hairy old beard off? I'd forgotten what you looked like," Pearl teased.

"Thanks, Mom. I never knew I was so undesirable to look at before. I shaved it off before I got to Cora's parents' house."

"You look great." Pearl rubbed her hand across her oldest son's face.

"He didn't look that bad before, if you ask me. But I truly love seeing his baby soft skin." Cora rubbed Rex's other cheek.

"I must say, Cora, whatever you're doing is working. He looks great."

"Stop! You two are embarrassin' me."

"Oh, look at him turn red. I'd never have imagined you were bashful." Cora pinched his cheek.

"Where's everyone else?" Rex pulled away from his two favorite women and hugged his little girl, still clasped around Cora's legs.

"They're out back in the kitchen. They were watching the rain. Come on." Pearl led them to the back of the house.

Shouts came from the kitchen when they entered. "Cora, I'm so glad you returned to the ranch, and surprised, especially after the way this rascal of a cowboy treated you when you left."

"Oh, don't be so hard on him, R.L. Rex was only running from his feelings. I knew he'd eventually come to his senses."

Everyone hooted at Cora's remark.

While Jimmy prepared the evening meal, everyone sat in the den around a blazing fire. "I want to hear what's been going on while I was away. I know I was away only a month, but I bet there are plenty of stories to hear. Were there any developments on the kidnappings?" Cora sipped her hot cider while everyone filled her in on the previous month.

140

Then Rex announced, "You guys, Susie and I will be movin' back home. It's time."

"Good for you, Rex." Pearl patted Rex on the back.

"Cora, we'd love for you to stay with us. You could have the pool house all to yourself for some privacy. You're welcome to stay as long as you like," R.L. offered.

"Thank you, R.L. That would be great. I may eventually get a place of my own, but I accept the invitation to stay in the pool house for a while. If okay with you, I'll go there tomorrow and get it ready."

Susie studied Cora. "Why do you have to leave Gramma's house?"

"Cora needs to stay by herself some," Rex swiftly explained. "And I want to be home with my little girl."

"Okay, Daddy."

Cora noticed the pout on the girl's face. But what she noticed, as well, was that Rex did not give in to Susie's wishes and stood firm in his decision, unlike how R.L. usually was with Clarice.

After dinner, Cora excused herself to her old room upstairs. She yawned all throughout dinner, wanting nothing more than to take a shower and go straight to bed. Susie and Rex also planned to stay at the main house for the night since it was rainy still, and Rex didn't have the energy to pack Susie's things.

Rex walked Cora to her room, carrying her luggage for her. He tried to get her to sit in the den by the fire for a little while longer, but Cora gently turned down his offer. Then Rex took Susie to her room to read her a bedtime story and put her to bed. Cora's heart swelled at the sight of the father and daughter together in a way they were not before.

Cora turned on the lamp by the bed and climbed in, sighing at the coolness of the sheets. She picked up her cell phone and hit the speed-dial to call Anne.

"Hello?" Anne's voice was like a warm blanket.

Cora grinned. "Hey. Whatcha doin'?"

"Nothing much. Just watching the design channel. I take it you made it safely there?"

"Yes, we did. Sorry I didn't call you earlier. We were visiting and catching up. We finished dinner a little while ago. It was so good. Jimmy cooked roast beef with gravy, mashed potatoes, green beans, biscuits, and peach cobbler. Yum! A good change from all the seafood." She licked her lips, still thinking about the meal.

"Don't rub it in. That sounds really good. Besides, aren't you going to miss the seafood?"

"Sure, but I can get some whenever I come home. You can't find this country cooking in any old restaurant. Maybe you can come for a visit and eat some of it soon." Cora shifted in the bed, pulling the covers up to her chest.

"Okay. So, where are you staying?"

"Tomorrow I'm moving to the pool house to have some space of my own, but for tonight, I'm in the room I stayed in before I left. It's hard having Rex in a room down the hall, though. It was the same way last night, too. He wanted me to stay up with him for a while, but I needed to get away. That ride here with him was so romantic and intense."

"Ooh, sounds exciting."

"To say the least." She yawned. "Anyway, I'm really tired. But I wanted to let you know I made it here safely."

"Wait—what did everybody say when they saw you?"

"They freaked out. Susie wrapped herself around my legs and wouldn't let go. It was good to see everyone. I do miss all of you already, though."

"Don't think about it. Enjoy being there and getting to know Rex."

"I will. Talk to you later."

Cora closed her phone and put it on the nightstand. *How many nightstands have you seen this year?* She picked up her Bible and read for a few minutes. When her eyes wouldn't stay open any longer, she said her prayers, placed her Bible on the nightstand, and turned out her lamp. Instantly she fell asleep. She felt at peace with God and with everyone in her life.

* * *

The following morning, Cora awoke easily with the cows outside mooing and the horses whinnying. Her open bedroom window let in the scent of the late summer air and the rustling of leaves on the patio by the pool. She turned over in her bed and found Susie sleeping soundly next to her. She smiled at the tradition that had started and watched the tiny child as she slept. Her fourth birthday was in a few more weeks, but she was still such a baby. She didn't seem big enough to Cora to send to preschool in the fall. Her cheeks were soft like a Georgia peach and her hair felt silky to her touch, even with the mats from the night of sleep. *I'm so glad she loves me.*

Susie stretched in the bed, slowly opened her eyes, and smiled. "Hey."

"Good morning, sweetheart. Did you sleep well?" Cora brushed the hair out of Susie's face.

"Yes." She snuggled under Cora's blanket. Rubbing her feet together repeatedly, she stretched again.

"When did you come in here?" Cora checked her nightgown to make sure her straps had not slipped off her shoulders, revealing her chest.

"When I was sleeping."

"When you were sleeping? Do you mean in the middle of the night while it was still dark outside?" Cora probed.

"Yes."

"Oh, I see. Why?"

"I missed you." Susie sat up in the bed and hugged Cora. "I love you."

"I love you, too, darling." Cora's eyes filled with tears of joy.

"I'm hungry."

"Me too. Let me get dressed, and we'll go downstairs to see if breakfast is ready. You go to your room, and I'll come help you get ready."

"Okay. Bye." Susie climbed down out of Cora's bed and left the room.

"Nothing changes around here." Cora looked through her suitcase for something to wear.

A couple minutes later Cora emerged from her room dressed and ready for the day in her jeans and new sweater and went down the hall to Susie's room to help her get dressed. When she opened Susie's door, she found Rex there helping Susie instead. She smiled and waved. "I'll see you two at breakfast."

* * *

"Jimmy, you outdid yourself again as always. I didn't think it could get any better than it was last night." Cora wiped her mouth with her linen napkin.

"I'll second that." Rex patted his belly.

"And I'll third. Thank you," R.L. said.

Cora noticed Jimmy's smile and how the O'Reillys' treatment of him had changed.

After breakfast, she went to the pool house to clean and took Susie with her. When she pushed open the door with her elbow, carrying her suitcase in her hand, she gasped at the beauty of the place.

The cozy cottage boasted a white-wicker décor with stripes and miniature checks everywhere in shades of sage and daffodil yellow. Shelving units on the far wall boasted various ranch knickknacks and wicker baskets with enough books to keep Cora's eyes busy all winter. In the corner of the living area sat a big screen television. To Cora's left, was a bedroom with a fluffy bed and a round wicker chair in the corner.

The white kitchen to her right possessed wrought-iron racks on the walls with stainless steel pots and pans hanging from them. The pea-green vintage refrigerator and oven added just the right touch. Through an open doorway on the far side of the kitchen was a laundry area.

While Cora dusted the furniture and cleaned the kitchen and bathroom, she and Susie sang songs and chatted. Then they put their jackets on and headed back to the house to get her other suitcases and boxes. Rex was inside the house, taking a break, and offered to help her with her things.

When they entered the pool house, Rex looked around and inhaled deeply. "Wow, Cora, the place looks and smells so clean. It smells like spring in here, and you're the sunshine."

Cora blushed. "Thank you for the compliment, Mr. O'Reilly."

"My daddy's not Mr. O'Reilly, silly. That's my grandpa." Susie giggled.

"Oh, you're right." Cora goosed Susie.

Rex reached down and scooped Susie into his arms, causing her to giggle even more, and all three headed back to the main house for lunch.

Cora spent most of the day with Susie reading books and putting puzzles together. She picked up where she'd left off teaching her numbers and letters. Her favorite part of the day was when Rex called to ask if she and Susie wanted to go with him across the way to Farmer Smith's farm. He picked them up in the giant, green John Deere tractor. She couldn't tell who squealed the most, herself or Susie, as they bounced and lurched all the way down the unpaved drive, across the highway, and onto Farmer Smith's dirt drive. She coughed and sneezed at the kicked-up dust and hay. This beat city life any day.

When Susie lay down for her nap, Cora went to her new private haven for some time alone. She opened the container of hot cocoa she had taken from the pantry in the main house, prepared a cup, and sat on the couch with a blanket and her book. The cocoa slid down her throat, warming her body to the core.

She still wasn't sure what she would do with her life here in Georgia. She didn't want to sit around, simply waiting for Rex to finish his work each day so they could be together. Helping with the plans for the B&B sounded good to her, but she still wanted to find something more to do. She didn't want to be there only for Rex. It sounded selfish, but she didn't want him to take advantage of her availability.

Cora still wondered when Rex would go to church on Sunday with the family. She hoped and prayed he'd begin going with them soon. He had changed so much in such a short time, and he was now being such a good father to Susie. Cora hoped he'd take the initiative and go with them to church without her having to ask him to go.

The next thing she did was wake up under the warm blanket, her mug still in her hand.

That evening Rex and Cora rode into Lewistown for dinner at Ms. Lottie's. Cora squeezed the tiny woman when they got there because she hadn't had a chance to see her before she left for South Carolina and home.

"Ms. Lottie, it's so good to see you. I was afraid I might not see you again." She surveyed the familiar place—everything still the same. Some potpourri. Same good-smelling food.

"Hey, precious. I sure have missed your help around here." Ms. Lottie hugged her tightly around the waist.

After dinner, Rex took Cora home. He walked her to the pool house door and shuffled his boots on the patio.

"Please come inside for a bit."

"I'm not sure I should." Rex shook his head.

"Why not?" Cora shivered.

"I probably should get back to the house so I can get Susie." Rex shuffled his boots again.

Cora forced eye contact with him. "You're not taking Susie home tonight, are you? I'm sure your mother already has her in bed. Besides, it's too cold to drag her out. Of course, she's your daughter. I shouldn't even offer my opinion."

"I love to hear your opinions, Cora. I guess I should leave her there. I'm going to go home, though."

Noticing Rex's temper no longer flared by her suggestions, she smiled. "Please come in and have some coffee." She fluttered her eyelashes playfully.

"Cora." Rex widened his eyes and stared into hers.

"Why not?" She pulled on his arm, like a child.

"It's too difficult for me to be alone with you." He focused on his boots.

"We've been alone before." She put her hands on her hips.

"I know, but that was before we actually admitted we had feelings for each other." Rex looked up at her. His dark eyes melted like chocolate.

"You're coming in. You can trust me. I promise." Cora grabbed Rex by the coat sleeve and yanked him into the house.

"Okay, I'm puttin' my trust in you. You better behave."

In the kitchen, Cora poured them each a cup of coffee, returned to the living area, and sat next to Rex on the couch. She took her boots off and pulled her feet up onto the couch, tucking them under Rex's leg.

"Your feet are cold."

"I know, but they won't be for long," Cora grinned mischievously.

"You're a troublemaker, you know that? You're tryin' to drive me crazy." Rex tapped her on the nose with his forefinger.

Cora broke into a throaty laugh. "So, tell me about your plans to save the ranch. How can I help?"

They sipped their coffee slowly and enjoyed spending time together. Cora knew her life at the ranch was going to be extraordinary. When Rex left Cora that evening, he kissed her very gently. Cora watched him walk back to the main house through the window in her door. *He is definitely the man I hope to spend the rest of my life with, no doubt.*

After Cora climbed into bed, she remembered she'd forgotten to lock the door. Slinging the covers back, she hopped out of the bed. When she walked into the dark living room, fear shot down her spine. She reached for the light switch on the wall and quickly turned on the overhead light. This was the first night she'd been alone in a long time—maybe ever.

Cora ran across the room and locked the door. She switched on the porch light, then scurried off to the kitchen to check the back door in the laundry room. Everything appeared to be secure. She ran back to the bedroom, turning the lamp on by the couch, before switching off the overhead light. She took one last look at the living room and then climbed back into bed.

Cora picked up her cell phone and dialed Rex's number.

"Hello?" Rex cleared his throat sleepily.

"Rex?" Cora bit her bottom lip, feeling instantly like a little girl.

"Yeah? Is everything okay?"

"I'm scared." She laughed nervously, scratching her head.

"You're scared? Why?"

"I just am. I'm out here alone and realized the kidnapper is still out there somewhere. I had forgotten to lock the door when you left, and I got creeped out." She peered through the sheers at the dark outside.

"Do you want me to come back and get you?"

"No. I need to be able to stay here by myself. But I've never been by myself at night since Clark left me, and I moved in with his parents right after he disappeared."

"I'll come over, check the perimeter, and let you know everything's fine. Turn on the TV; watch something funny. It'll be mornin' before you know it."

"Okay." She let out a sigh of relief, the tension in her neck relaxing.

"And don't worry about the kidnapper. It was a random attack. You'll be fine."

"Thanks, Rex."

16

Cora unpacked some of the boxes that had been sitting in her car since her trip from South Carolina. Besides her clothes, a few trinkets, and her scrapbooks, she possessed very little. She unpacked the last of her clothes from her suitcase. In between two of her pairs of jeans, she found a flat scrapbook. She put her jeans on the bed and sat down with the scrapbook in her hand. Cora rubbed the gold-foiled embossed letters of the pink cover. *"Precious Memories.* What is this?"

Cora carefully opened the book and, on the first page, saw a picture of a baby cradled in the arms of a nurse. Tears welled in her eyes at the sight of the familiar photo. She let out a tearful laugh. Glued on the page were a pink hair ribbon and the hospital bracelet that had been on her ankle. She read the words written in calligraphy below the picture. "Cora Amelia Sinclair. Six pounds, ten ounces. Twenty inches long. January 16, 1987."

Cora flipped the page. She pushed her hair behind her ear and scooted back to rest on the pillow at the head of the bed. The next page had a clipping of hair tied in a white ribbon and a picture of her sitting on the bathroom counter in front of the mirror. "Baby's first haircut. Aww."

She turned the page again and saw more photographs of herself. Crawling. Walking. Playing dress-up. Dancing. Eighth-grade dance. Piano recital. Prom. "She did keep mementos of me," she said out loud, awed. "They might not have been on the wall in picture frames or marked on the door facing, but she kept memories of me just the same."

After Cora flipped through the rest of the pages that ended right before her marriage to Clark, she noticed a 9x12 manila envelope taped to the inside back cover of the scrapbook. "What's this?" She pulled it off, her heart pounding. When she opened the envelope and slid out the contents, her world as she knew it changed forever.

She saw a photograph of a dark-haired pregnant woman. Her eyes sparkled like emeralds in the afternoon sunlight of the beach. Her smile was so wide and welcoming, Cora could not help but smile back at it. She shook her head in protest at the eighties' clothes and permed hair, though. Flipping the photograph over, she read: *Your mother, Amelia Marie Peoples.*

Cora burst into tears. "This is my mother." She flipped through the stack of pictures, one after the other of the same woman. A few of them had her dad in them—thinner and smiling. The papers included were her mother's birth certificate and a family tree. "Everything I would have wanted to know is here." The included note from her dad explained what he knew about her birth mother. After she read the letter, she placed it and everything else back in the envelope. She wiped her nose with her hand. "Thank you, Dad."

* * *

"Hey, Anne." Cora sat on the couch looking out the back window at the cows in the pasture. Even after a month, the sight never grew old. She propped her feet on the coffee table and pulled the fleece throw up over her shoulders and stretched it across her legs.

"Hey. How are things going back at the ranch? Sorry I haven't checked in with you before now. I had that big job in Houston."

"Oh, that's okay. Things are going so great. My parents sent a scrapbook home with me by surprise and it was full of stuff of my mother...my real mother!"

"Awesome!"

"I know! She was so pretty. I'm staying in the pool house, which is the coolest place ever. It's got the best wood-burning stove. There's a hot tub out by the pool, and I sit in it all the time. I've been doing lots of reading and helping Rex start the B&B. Matt still wants to do a dude ranch, but Rex is holding out. You should see his face every time it gets brought up. He says he'd end up babysitting a bunch of cowboy wannabes." She grinned as she pushed her hair behind her ear.

"That's hilarious. With everything you've said about Matt, it surprises me he'd want the dude ranch. He sounds more like the B&B type since he's in the city all the time."

Cora threw her hands up. "I know. I think he thinks the dude ranch will be more of a moneymaker. That's what he thinks of most...money. He expects Rex to run it, though, and Rex says he's got enough going on with the hired hands to have to worry about guests getting injured on the ranch."

"Good point. What else have you been doing?"

"Besides getting used to cows being everywhere I turn? Not much." She picked up the remote and turned on the television. "Just going to church and helping Ms. Lottie some. Susie was so happy to see me come back. I keep her with me during the day most of the time. At night, she's with Rex, which means she's with me because we spend time together practically every night."

Cora giggled.

"Speaking of Rex, how is that going?"

Cora smiled. "He's really a neat guy. He's moody and bossy and stubborn and opinionated, but that's nothing more than a hard shell. When it comes to Susie, his mom, or Clarice, Ms. Lottie, and…well…me, he's a softie. He's a marshmallow."

"Are you glad you went back with him?"

"Definitely." Cora gazed out her window at the green grass and blue sky as they merged. Opposites, yet part of each other—belonging together.

"So what's your status?"

"We're definitely a couple. We spend most weekday evenings here at the ranch. But on the weekends, we go into town and eat at Ms. Lottie's or somewhere else. Sometimes we go on into Columbus and go to the movies or to the bowling alley."

"So it's pretty slow-paced?"

"A lot more than at the beach. And it's slower than when I was in South Carolina, working for the law firm."

"So are you guys staying together?"

"No way. Are you crazy?" She bristled at the thought.

"Well, you never know."

"No. In fact, I can hardly get him to come to the pool house. If he does, he usually has Susie with him. I did get him to get in the hot tub once or twice, and that was funny. Quite a switch from when he practically mauled me this summer in the pool when he was acting like a horse's—you get my drift." She turned off the television and put the remote on the cushion beside her.

"Sure do. Men!"

"Gotta love 'em."

"So you're getting serious or what?"

"I mean, we're not seeing anyone else. We're going to church together every Sunday now. We go out. We spend time with Susie. He hasn't specifically asked me to go steady with him."

"Ha, ha. You're funny. But I'm glad it's all working out for you. What about the sister?"

"She's a real prize."

"What do you mean?"

"I haven't had much interaction with her. But when I came back, she confronted me and wanted to know why I was back."

"What?"

"Yeah. She basically wanted to know what my motives were. At first, she acted as if she was concerned for me, like she didn't want me to get hurt if Rex rejected me. But then it really boiled down to her marking her territory."

"Do you think that's because you didn't stick up for her?"

"I'm sure. But I can't worry about it."

"You're right. What about the kidnapper?"

"It's your turn to talk. Tell me about Houston and how your love life is."

* * *

"Rex, I've had it with your pitiful plans and your avoidance of the inevitable," Matt said, crashing through the back door and into the kitchen. Cora sat at the kitchen table as Susie colored and watched the birds peck at the seeds on the birdfeeder outside. When Matt came through the door, the birds scattered. Cora looked at him crossly. Rex followed close behind.

"What are you talking about, Matt? Just because I'm not acting as quickly as you'd like doesn't mean I'm avoiding something. The inevitable? What is that supposed to mean anyway?"

"Never mind." Matt waved his hand to dismiss Rex.

"And besides, I'm working on some great plans. Cora's been helping me." Rex grabbed a coffee mug off a hook under the kitchen cabinet and poured a cup of coffee. The steam coming from the cup matched the steam coming from his ears.

Cora noticed the beads of sweat on his upper lip and the damp curls surrounding his ears. She glanced at Matt in time to see him give her an annoyed look.

"Rex, you're driving me insane. You don't realize how vital it is we get something up and running very soon. When winter sets in, we're gonna be in deep. The drought this summer killed us, and we've got to find a way to recover. The war in Iraq has cost us because so many of the guys stationed in Columbus are gone and so we're losing sales. The economy's going downhill fast. By the election, I hate to see how things are in this country."

"Matt —"

"No!" He pointed his finger in Rex's face. "Listen, Rex. We either need to open the dude ranch or the B&B. If we open the dude ranch, we can renovate the old bunkhouse. That would be the easiest approach. If we go with the B&B idea, we need to start building."

"I know, Matt. That's what I was gonna tell you. Cora and I talked about adding a two-story, four-suite wing right out here on the other side of the kitchen. The kitchen and dining hall will be right out here and the gathering hall can be in the front." Rex pointed out the kitchen window. "Right out here on the other end, past the dining hall, will be a separate mini-wing where we hope to have Ms. Lottie's quarters, if she'll agree to come on board. The upstairs will have a common area and the four suites."

Matt rubbed his face with his hands in exasperation. "Rex, you're such a simple man."

"What does that mean?" Rex walked closer to Matt.

"You're scared to branch out and try something new like the dude ranch." He crossed his arms.

"First of all, that has nothing to do with it. A B&B would be quite new for me. But I've got a little girl to raise, Matt. I can't be playing host to a bunch of fake cowboys—businessmen who come to the country for a weekend to strut around like peacocks in their high-dollar snakeskin boots with no idea how to ride a horse or shovel manure." Rex cut his eyes over to Matt. "We've got to go with what's most advantageous for us. It's not exactly what I want, but I know we have to do something. People are into B&Bs these days. Ms. Lottie's business has seen a slump, and she can't keep up with the repairs on that old home. It would be in her best interest to do this."

"Who cares about her? I'm looking at keeping my pocketbook from getting empty. You're just selfish."

"Me? Selfish? Can you believe this guy?" Rex cocked his head toward Cora. "Who wants to do things his own way? If you want a dude ranch so bad, why don't you run it?"

Cora held her breath and squeezed her eyes shut as the two stood chest-to-chest, blowing verbal smoke in each other's faces. Rex's fists were balled up, and Matt's arms were swinging. Jimmy stayed in the pantry, pretending to inventory the contents.

"Boys! What are you fighting about?" Pearl entered the kitchen.

"Stupid Rex and his failure to move into this century." Matt backed away from the brother who stood a head taller.

"I don't know how much more of this I can take." Pearl grabbed her forehead.

"Pearl, here, sit down. Let me get you some coffee." Cora headed to the counter, regarding both brothers in disdain.

"Okay. Decaf, please."

"Rex? Matt? I want to know what all this yelling is about. I've had about enough of it. I was on the phone with a client, and I could barely hear him." R.L. stood in the doorway glaring from one son to the next.

"Dad, Rex is a pain in the rear."

Rex let out a groan and walked to the window. Susie ran into the living room singing a song she learned in Sunday school. Rex scratched his head.

"Rex? You're not saying anything."

"Dad, I want to do what's best for the ranch, whatever that is. I'm not leaning toward the dude ranch because I don't have time to manage guests out there. There's enough work to do with the ranch hands to manage. I don't think we can afford the liability insurance we'd have to have either. Do you know how much it would cost to protect us against lawsuits?"

"Lawsuits?"

"Yes, Matt. Lawsuits." There was nothing but dead silence except for the sound of the ice dropping into the bucket from the icemaker.

"Good research, Rex. We do have to prepare for such things. What about the B&B? Sit down here and tell me what you've come up with."

Matt stomped out the back door, slamming it behind him. Cora jumped. Jimmy poked his head out of the pantry and then went back in.

"Dad, here's what Cora and I have put together…"

* * *

Cora pulled into Millburn's Station on fumes. The double bell sounded as she drove up to the pump. She turned off the ignition, zipped her jacket, and got out of the car. She opened the gas cover and swiped her debit card at the pump. She fixed the handle so it would pump until her tank was full, then glanced down at the dented side panel.

"Hey, Cora."

Cora jumped at the voice that sounded like a character from Mayberry, turning to find Bobby standing right behind her. "Oh, hey, Bobby. You startled me."

"Sorry." He grinned a crooked grin. "So, what finds you this far from the ranch?"

"Oh, I had errands to run and I wanted to stop in and check on Ms. Lottie." She put her hands in her back pockets.

"How's she doin'?"

"I don't know. I haven't made it over there yet. I'm on my way now."

"Oh. Well…"

The gas continued to pump into the tank. *How many gallons does this car take?* "So." She watched the numbers slowly tick on the old gas pump. She picked up the squeegee and washed her windshield.

"So."

"Are you getting ready for the holidays, Bobby?"

"I suppose. There's not much to the holidays for me. Not much family." He looked down at the ground.

"Oh, I hate to hear that." She put the squeegee back in the holder and tapped on the roof of the car with her left hand.

"Yeah." Bobby bent down and picked up a disposable coffee cup lid. "I hate when people litter. People are so ungrateful these days for the things we do for them."

"I guess you're right, Bobby." The tank finally reached full. Cora returned the handle to the pump, tightened the cap on the tank, and pushed the button for a receipt, all while Bobby watched her.

"You want me to check your oil?"

"No, I think it's okay today. You changed it when you worked on the car. Thanks, though." Cora grabbed her receipt and reached for the car door handle.

"What are ya doin' later tonight?" He shoved his hands in his back pockets.

"I'm not really sure. It depends on what time I get back to the ranch."

"Do ya want to go to a movie with me?"

Cora swallowed hard. *So that's what that was all about. He wasn't being creepy. He wanted to ask me out.* "Oh, thanks for asking, Bobby. I'm going out with Rex right now."

"Oh, figures."

"Sorry. But thanks again for asking."

"Sure thing. Let me know if that doesn't work out." He tipped his ball cap.

"Okay." Cora climbed in the car and pulled out of the gas station as quickly as she could. "That was weird." She shuddered.

* * *

"Ms. Lottie, the strangest thing just happened." Cora gave Ms. Lottie a hug and a kiss on her cheek in the lobby of the B&B.

"What?" Ms. Lottie sat down with her hot tea in the living room.

Cora sat down and then stirred sugar into her tea, testing it for sweetness. "I stopped to get gas at Bobby's station and he really creeped me out."

"Why?" Ms. Lottie looked her directly in the eye, concern pouring out.

"I felt like he was stalking me or hovering or something."

"What did he do?" Ms. Lottie's kind eyes never left Cora's.

"He popped up behind me while I was pumping my gas like some kind of clown at the circus. It scared me half to death." Cora shivered.

"Then what?"

"Then he asked me out."

"Doesn't he know you and Rex are together?"

"He acted like he didn't know." Cora shrugged.

"Well, everyone knows. I don't know how he couldn't. You might want to steer clear of him for a while."

"Why?"

"I don't mean to talk bad about him, but that boy has always been a little odd."

* * *

On the way home, Cora almost took the back roads that Bobby recommended, but after the last fiasco, she kept her car on the main road. A pain shot through her chest at the thought of seeing where she had broken down and the shack where she was held captive. A chill ran up her spine. She rubbed her right wrist as she drove. That one hurt worse than the left one.

"Lord, I guess these scars aren't going to go away for a long time. The nerves around them are so sensitive." Cora drove on for about five minutes in silence, with no radio playing. "Lord, did your wrists hurt like this when you hung on the cross? I'm sure they hurt more than mine do." A logging truck whizzed by, snapping Cora out of her prayer. "Lord, would you have me use my experience to help others? What can I do?"

* * *

After a few days of pondering how she could use her kidnapping to help others, it was as though a door opened inside Cora's brain, revealing an idea that curled her toes. She threw on her jeans and a sweater, her boots and coat, and ran from the pool house to the main house. "Hey, Pearl. Do you know where Rex is?"

Pearl sat in the living room floor with Susie playing with puzzles. "The last time I saw him, he was headed out to the stables to take Rusty his paycheck."

"Do you think he'll be back soon?" Cora rested her hand on her hip.

"He should be. He said he was coming back to eat lunch."

"Okay. Goodie."

"You want to call him?"

"No, I'll wait." Cora sat on the floor and began helping Susie with her puzzles.

"What's up?" Pearl peered into Cora's olive green eyes.

"I had the greatest idea for the B&B." Cora squeezed Pearl's hand.

"I can't wait to hear what it is."

The front door opened. "Hello. Where is everybody?"

"We're in here, Rex."

Rex appeared in the living room doorway with Clarice by his side. Her skin looked a shade darker than earlier in the summer, her teeth whiter, and her cup size larger. "Hey, Cora."

"Rex." Cora stood just in time to receive his hug. "Hi, Clarice."

"Hey." Clarice looked her up and down, chewing her gum like a cow chewing its cud.

"Rex, I had a great idea for the B&B and I can't wait to tell you about it."

"Okay, tell me."

"Why don't we go ahead into the dining room for lunch? Cora, you can share your idea with all of us, if you don't mind."

"Okay, Pearl."

"Are you sure you don't mind telling everyone?" Rex placed his arm around her back.

"No, I don't mind."

"I'm not gonna be home for lunch. I'm meeting some friends in town. I'll have to miss all the excitement." Clarice threw her Liz Claiborne bag over her shoulder.

Cora looked at Clarice sadly. *There's nothing I can do about her feelings toward me. I can't help it if she's carrying a grudge against me for not taking her side the morning after Wild Bill's. Hopefully she'll come around.*

At the table, Cora felt like a child waiting for Santa to come.

"So, Cora, I hear you have some ideas for the B&B." R.L. cut his meatloaf in half and spooned sauce on top of it.

"I sure do. You know, I've been through a lot this past year or so. Losing Clark, hearing of his death, moving, coming here, getting kidnapped, reconciling with my parents."

Everyone affirmed her comments between bites of food and sips of drink.

"I've tried to piece everything together to figure out why all of these things happened to me. I know both good and bad things happen for a reason. The reason for these bad events has escaped me. Until the other day, that is."

"What do you mean?" Rex asked.

"What happened?" Pearl asked.

"I was coming home from Ms. Lottie's and almost took the back roads. I changed my mind, but not before I remembered my scars and the pain they've caused me—emotionally and physically. I started asking God to reveal the purpose and how I could use it to help people."

"Okay, Cora. The mystery is getting to me. What's your idea?" Rex shoveled mashed potatoes into his mouth.

"What would you think about using the B&B as a retreat for women and men who are suffering from post-traumatic stress disorder or who are grieving? They could come on scholarships from churches. We could let counselors come. How about Apple Springs @ the Southern Hope?"

Everyone remained silent and stared at Cora. Rex put his fork down with a clink on his plate. R.L. wiped his mouth with his napkin and then placed the napkin on the table. Pearl looked back and forth from Rex to R.L. and then to Cora. *Oh, they hate the idea.*

"Cora! You're a genius. I love it. That's the best idea."

"I agree with Pearl, Cora."

Cora turned to Rex and waited for his response. He turned in his seat, scooted closer to Cora, took her face in his hands, and planted a firm kiss on her lips. "You're wonderful. You're the most terrific woman in this world, except for Mom." He turned and gave Pearl a wink, then looked at Cora again. "You're the breath of life this old place needed. God has been good to us to send you here."

Matt came into the dining room and took a seat next to Pearl.

"Matt, Cora has come up with a great plan for the B&B." Pearl sprinkled salt on her mashed potatoes.

"Please, Mom. I don't need anything else to turn my stomach today."

"Matt! That's uncalled for," Pearl defended.

"Matt, apologize to Cora," Rex commanded.

"Shut up, Rex!"

Cora pushed her chair back and left the dining room crying, Susie following closely behind.

17

Cora sat on the sofa in the pool house and flipped through her Bible. These days, reading Scripture meant more to her than it had in years. But today, reading did not come easy. Matt's attack on her idea left a wound that would not heal easily.

Lord, I know I'm supposed to turn the other cheek and forgive and all that, but Matt's anger toward Rex keeps getting directed at me and it hurts. I don't know why he's so angry, but it doesn't give him excuse to lash out at me. It makes me feel like leaving. Just when I get things worked out with Mom and Dad, and with Rex, I have another person to settle matters with. Lord, please help me.

* * *

"I'm gonna talk to Matt when he comes in from the office this evening about your idea."

"You are?" Cora squeezed her face together in a pucker.

"Yes. I'm gonna make him hear me out. I've tried and tried to get him to listen." Rex crossed his legs at the ankles, stacking one boot on top of the other.

"I know. I've been hearing you guys go round and round all week. It's been a little unnerving." Cora played with her dark hair.

"Sorry about that. That's just the way two bull-headed country boys hash things out. I'm gonna make him listen to me if it's the last thing I do. Will you be there with me?"

"If you want me to. You need me for moral support?"

"Yeah, something like that."

"I'm not sure how much help I will be. I think Matt hates me." She frowned at Rex.

"No, he doesn't. But he does think I'm a pansy for choosing the B&B over the dude ranch. Once he finds out we want to use it as a ministry, he'll think I've lost my mind."

"Poor Matt. He's searching for peace and doesn't even know it. He sees you turning your life around and getting a second chance. I think he's jealous of you."

"Maybe."

"He is. And I think it puts pressure on him, too. If you straighten up, he knows your parents will expect him to do the same."

"You may be right there."

"We can keep praying for him and hoping he looks up to his big brother one day." She patted his forearm.

"I've made lots of mistakes, Cora, so I don't know how good of an example I would be to him. But I have learned from my mistakes and hopefully I won't make them again. I can't imagine him saying I helped him figure his life out." He rubbed his weary eyes.

"I'm sure one day he will. I think he's got a long road ahead before he's ready to surrender, though. He seems to be having too much fun to change his ways right now. And he's got so much going on in his heart, it makes him angry when it comes to business. That's why he needs you."

"What do you mean?" Rex crinkled his brow.

"He needs you to think responsibly, like you're doing by insisting on the B&B instead of the dude ranch."

"Maybe you're right."

"I am right. He's out of control by trying to be in control of his life. Any decision he makes right now without you to be objective could be detrimental to the ranch."

"I'm really more worried about his private life than his business life. The partying and the girls…"

"Did you go through that?" Cora searched Rex's dark eyes until her own began to sting.

"You mean, did I sleep around?"

"Well…"

"No. I met Patty pretty early on, and we behaved for the most part. What about you?"

"No. Only Clark. I have been thinking about being tested, though, because I don't know how faithful he was to me. I'd like to think he was, but with the circles he traveled in, who knows."

"I know what you mean. I was tested after Patty died. I know she was unfaithful to me."

"I'm so sorry, Rex. She was a foolish woman. I would never cheat on you." Cora smiled and kissed him on the cheek.

"I'll remember that." Rex smiled back.

* * *

"Matt, Cora and I would like to talk to you about some ideas we've got for the B&B." Rex caught Matt in the foyer before he climbed the stairs. Cora stood quietly behind him.

"Can it wait? I'm going out tonight, and I need to get a shower." Matt looked at Rex, then Cora, and turned to head up the stairs.

"It won't take long." Rex motioned toward the living room.

Matt sighed and checked his watch. "All right. But let's go in Dad's office." They went into R.L.'s office and shut the door. "I wonder where Dad's at."

"They went to the hospital to visit someone from church who had surgery." Rex flipped on the office light.

Matt laughed, mockingly. "They kill me. They're like Mr. and Mrs. Preacher these days." He flipped through the papers on R.L.'s desk.

"They're trying to get involved with people their age and get away from the ranch more often." Rex watched Matt closely.

"Yeah, I can see that. But I can think of more exciting things to do." Matt sat in R.L.'s leather desk chair and lifted an eyebrow at Cora. Rex stood by the window and looked out at the north pasture. "So what's your idea?"

Cora remained silent and sat on the leather couch under the window. She stared at the Oriental rug in the center of the room. "Well..."

"Hang on a minute. Do you guys want something to drink? I'm thirsty."

"No."

"No, I'm fine. Thanks, though," Cora answered.

Matt pressed the intercom button on R.L.'s desk. "Cook, can you bring me a glass of tea in here in the office—Dad's office?" He took his finger off the intercom button and waited.

Cora flinched. *I hate when he degrades Jimmy that way.*

"Yes, sir. Hot or cold?" Jimmy answered over the speaker.

"Hot."

"I'll be right in."

"So, you were saying?"

"Cora has offered to stay here at the ranch and help us see the place into the next century. She's had great input toward what we could do. She had the idea of making the B&B more than just a place for people to come on vacation."

Jimmy knocked at the office door, entered, and placed the mug of tea on the coaster on the walnut desk. He turned and smiled at Cora as he left the office. She winked.

"Back to the B&B idea." Matt groaned. "Okay, I'm listening."

"Cora has been through a lot of trauma this year, much of it since arriving at the ranch—the kidnapping, her husband's death. The ranch has been a big part in her healing. Right, Cora?"

Cora looked up at Rex, then Matt. "Definitely. This place is wonderful."

"Okay…"

"We thought—Cora thought and I agreed—this place, the new B&B, would be a great place for people to come on retreats. The possibilities are limitless. Couples could come who need renewal. Women or men suffering from post trauma or grief could come. We could even arrange for counselors to be available." Rex stood, his hands shoved in his front pockets, waiting for Matt's opinion.

"That's a pretty good idea, Cora." Matt winked at her, the first sign of civility out of him in weeks.

Her eyes widened. This was the Matt she knew from the night out at Wild Bill's. "Thanks. I thought people could even be sponsored by their church or organizations if they could not afford to come."

"That's great. I like it." Matt laced his fingers together and twiddled his thumbs.

Rex smiled, looking from Matt to Cora. "You do?"

"Yeah, I really do." He smiled.

"Man, that's great. And listen, I'm sorry about the blowouts lately. I have been selfish, like you said."

"No, man, I'm the one that's been out of line. I've been focused on the money and that's all. Honestly, I'm kind of sick of it all. I hate working in the city. I miss being on the ranch every day." He ruffled his fingers through his perfect hair.

"You do?"

"Yeah. You know, I'm a cowboy first and a businessman second." He smiled like a little boy.

"Why don't you talk to Dad about it? There might be a way to bring the office home."

"Maybe. To be perfectly honest, it's more than that. I'm envious of you getting to work the ranch. I want to be more hands-on. The cattle byproduct isn't where my heart is." He swiveled back and forth in R.L.'s chair.

"What do you want to do, Matt?" Cora shifted her position on the couch and relaxed her shoulders.

"I want to run the dude ranch."

"Run it?" They all burst out laughing. Rex walked over to Matt and slapped him on the back. "Brother, you should go for it. You start the dude ranch. Cora and I will do the B&B. Dad can run the office in the city or move it home."

"But what about the liability?"

"We'll work that out. Don't worry." Rex acted as the big brother for the first time in years.

* * *

Cora sat down at her new laptop and pulled up her email account. "Thirty-five messages? Who from?" She scanned the screen, filtering through the junk, looking for mail from friends. Most messages were from the library notifying her of books ready for pick up, the Department of Drivers Services about her Georgia Drivers License, and the bank about her new checking and savings accounts. She clicked on the one from the bank. She smiled after reading it. "It's amazing how they act when you deposit a chunk of money." A dark cloud floated over her head when she thought of the source of her money, but she pushed it away. She cleared her throat. She clicked on the email from Anne.

Hey, Cora. How is it going? Haven't heard from you this week. I figure you're busy getting the B&B off the ground. I had a date last night with Tim Jacobs from school. I ran into him at the mall and we ended up eating in the food court, going to a movie, and getting coffee. Call me when you get the chance, and I'll fill you in.

"Well, good for her. Tim, huh?" Cora opened the next email.

Cora, Dad and I miss you. I hope everything is going well with you and Rex. Keep us posted. Dad and I are thinking about coming your way for Thanksgiving or Christmas. Not sure which yet. I've attached some pictures I took when you were home. I just now uploaded them from my camera. Okay, I had better get off this computer and get dinner ready. Love you, Mom.

Cora clicked on the attached pictures and burst out laughing. The pictures of she and Rex warmed her soul. "I'll have to have some prints made of those."

An email from the Buchanans waited in her inbox, as well. She decided to read it later when Susie called her name from the living room.

"What are you doing, little one?"

"Getting ready for dinner." She twisted her hair with her finger.

"Is it that time already?" Cora closed her laptop.

"Yes, ma'am. And I'm hungry."

"Me, too." Cora took Susie in her arms. "Let's go see if we can help Jimmy in the kitchen with setting the table."

"Okay."

* * *

Cora and Susie finished setting the table as R.L. and Pearl came into the dining room. Rex came in from the back porch. "There's my favorite girls." He kissed Susie on the top of the head and Cora on the cheek. He winked at Pearl. "Dad, did Matt talk to you before he headed out?"

"He actually called me from the road. He told me the ideas y'all have come up with. I like everything I've heard so far."

"What exactly did he tell you?"

"He also told me he wants to make a go of the dude ranch in addition to the B&B. When you told him you didn't want to deal with a bunch of cowboy wannabes, he realized he was the perfect person to deal with them. He's a cowboy in a suit wanting to be a cowboy."

"He said that? Wow." Rex chuckled and Cora echoed his laughter.

"Yes, he did. You had some impact on him there, Son. You know, the service industry is where it's at these days. I think it's all sounding great. I say let's get moving immediately on all of it."

"Really, Dad?"

"Sure thing. The sooner, the better. We can start to get the word out while we begin construction on the wing you want to add and get the old bunkhouse renovated. Maybe people will be here by the first of the year."

"Great."

"R.L., I've been looking at website development on my new computer. There are a lot of easy ways to get a website up and going without even having to have a webmaster. Domain names are cheap and web hosting is about $200.00 a year. There are so many social networks out there too. It won't take long to spread the word."

"Let's get going on that too, then. Cora, I'm glad we have you here."

* * *

"Cora?"

"Yes, ma'am?" Cora put down the book she was reading while Susie napped.

162

"Have you seen or talked to Clarice since before lunch?" Pearl wrung her hands.

"No, I sure haven't. She said she was having lunch with friends in town. Have you called her?" Cora pushed her hair behind her ears. *When is Clarice going to stop causing her mother so much worry?*

"No, I didn't want to make her think I'm checking up on her. But..." Pearl let out the kind of sigh that could blow out the candles on a birthday cake.

"You're checking up on her."

Pearl smiled guiltily. "Yes, I suppose I am. I don't mean to pry."

"I know, Pearl. You're just concerned for her." Pearl's concern was different from Cora's mother's concern. Brenda only wanted to control Cora. Pearl wanted to keep Clarice from ruining her life.

"She's not very careful." Pearl massaged her right shoulder where it stayed tight from worrying about Clarice. "You know—her choice in friends and where she goes."

"I know. Maybe you should call her. Ask her if she'll be home for dinner." Cora patted Pearl's hand.

"Maybe I will."

* * *

Cora busied herself with helping Jimmy and getting Susie ready for dinner. Pictures of the missing women she had seen on the news flashed in her mind. *Lord, please protect Clarice from herself.*

"Hey, what's got you looking so puzzled?" Rex came up behind Cora and rubbed her shoulders.

"Your mom hasn't heard from Clarice and is worried about her."

"Mom's always worried about her. You know that." Rex sat next to Cora at the table.

"No, I think it's more than that this time. I think she's worried because all of the women who have been kidnapped except for me have been found dead. She knows Clarice meets up with people and shows very little discernment."

"She's not going to get kidnapped. Anyone who tried to take Clarice by force would be sorry. That girl may seem like a city girl, but underneath that façade is a homegrown country girl who can fend for herself."

"But what about the morning after Wild Bill's? She was obviously beaten up."

"Those places on Clarice were not from an attacker, Cora." Rex's look into Cora's eyes lingered for effect. "She likes to be rough when..."

Cora held up her hands. "Enough. I don't need to hear anymore. Yuck. She needs to stop this carelessness. She's going to be the death of your mom."

"I know. Don't worry about her. She'll be fine. If we don't see her or hear from her in a couple of hours, I'll call around and see if anyone knows where she is."

"Okay, that makes me feel better."

* * *

"Rex, this has been the best day ever," Cora said as she and Rex soaked in the hot tub.

"Why?" He wiped sweat from his upper lip.

"We've gotten a lot of details worked out for the B&B. Your parents approve. Matt approves. Matt showed his heart today, which is a first. To see him let his guard down was awesome."

"Yeah, I suppose you're right." He nodded in agreement.

"Then, on top of that, it's cold out and I'm sitting in a hot tub with a very handsome man." She grinned.

"Your boyfriend."

"My boyfriend?"

"Aren't I your boyfriend?"

"I suppose you are." She winked at him and leaned across the hot tub to give him a peck on the cheek, lingering a few seconds.

"Hey, now, watch it."

"What?" She fluttered her eyelashes in false naïveté.

"We're alone out here. You keep your distance."

"Why?" Cora grinned.

"You know why, Cora."

She stuck out her bottom lip.

Rex chortled, tapping her lip with his index finger. "I've been wondering about something lately."

"What?"

"When did you decide to leave South Carolina?"

"What do you mean?"

"How did you know it was time?"

"Why? Are you planning to leave?"

"No. Just curious."

"I'd been waiting for Clark to come home for a year. I felt like I was spinning my wheels there living with his parents. My relationship with my own parents was practically dead. I knew I couldn't live the rest of my life with that hanging over my head. It was time. Why do you ask?"

"I've always been resistant to change and when I think about the steps you took to get your life going again, I really admire you."

"I just did what I felt God was leading me to do."

"Maybe, but it sure took lots of guts to do it."

"I don't know about guts. I was trying to be obedient. Don't make me out to be a heroine. You've made some pretty big steps and changes lately. You're heading your life and Susie's in a new direction."

"Yeah, I suppose. I'm still scared, though."

"Scared?"

"Yeah, I don't want to mess things up."

"What do you mean?"

"I don't want to be a bad dad. I want to be a good man."

"You are. You will be. Rex, have faith."

The back porch light from the house turned on. "Rex? Are you out there?"

"Yeah, Dad. I'm in the hot tub."

Cora sat back in the hot tub, resting her head on the headrest. She closed her eyes and let the jets beat the cares of the day away. R.L. walked across the patio toward them.

"He'll probably just be a minute." Rex smiled apologetically at Cora.

"That's fine, Rex. I don't mind." *If there is one thing I'm used to around here, it's family.*

"Son, have you talked to Clarice?"

"No, Dad, I haven't. I talked to her before lunch."

"Have you seen her or talked to her, Cora?"

Cora leaned up and looked up at R.L. "No, sir, I sure haven't. I saw her when Rex did."

"Are you worried about her?"

"Yeah. Your mom has called her cell phone several times, but there is no answer. I don't know who she was going out with but we've called everyone we can think of, and no one has seen her all day."

Rex lifted himself out of the hot tub and wrapped his towel around him. "She didn't say who she was going to be with. Did she, Cora?"

"No, I don't think so. She didn't say much when she was here." Cora lifted herself out of the hot tub and grabbed her towel.

"Dad, Clarice could have told her friends not to tell you guys who she was with if you asked. She's pretty secretive with her social life."

R.L. threw his hands up in the air. "I know, Son. I know. I don't know where we went wrong with that girl. I hate to ask you, but do you think you could go look for her? We'll put Susie to bed here."

"Where's Matt?"

"He's in town and he's been looking for her. He went to Wild Bill's and some other places."

"Did he check with Ms. Lottie?"

R.L. laughed. "Rex, you know she wouldn't have gone there."

"I know."

Cora noticed the look exchanged between them.

"Would you mind going to look for her?"

"I don't mind, Dad, but I can't think of any other places she'd be. She said something about meeting a guy stationed over at the base, but I don't remember what his name was."

"What about calling the cell phone company? Maybe they can try to locate her cell phone." Cora looked from R.L. to Rex.

"That's an idea."

"Have you called the police?" Cora shivered in the night air.

"No, not yet. I was hoping it wouldn't come to that. Do either of you remember what she was wearing?"

"No." Rex rumpled his hair and sighed. "This is ridiculous."

Cora turned to R.L. "She was wearing jeans and a blouse when she came in earlier, but she went upstairs to change. We weren't in the hall when she left, so I didn't see what she had on. What about her car? Isn't there some kind of tracker on it?"

"Yes, I think there is. I guess I should call the police. Rex, your mother is worried sick. It's been noon since she was seen."

"Dad, Cora and I will go looking for her. If I find her and she's okay, I'm going to put her over my knee and wear her out!"

16

By 2:00 a.m., Cora could barely move. She and Rex had walked the streets of Southern Hope, had driven into Lewistown, and walked the streets there, too. Clarice was nowhere.

"I'm gonna call Matt and see if he's heard anything; then we're gonna go to the police station."

"Okay." Cora watched the car lights flicker in the window. She sat in the middle next to Rex, her head on his shoulder. She yawned. "Rex, do you think she's left home? Or do you think something has happened to her?"

"Nothing is missing from her room. She promised me she would never do what she did that night at Wild Bill's. She said she'd never stay out all night and she would never make Mom worry about her."

"Do you believe her?" She raised her head and looked up at him.

"Yeah, I do."

"Then she's in trouble?"

"I think so."

"Then let's call Matt and head to the police."

* * *

Cora and Rex pulled up outside the police department. Rex let out a groan. "Here we go." He pulled the keys out of the ignition and got out of the truck.

Cora watched him walk around the front, putting his cowboy hat on top of his head. He came around to Cora's side. She slid over, watching the sadness in his eyes. It gripped her heart in a vise. "It's going to be okay, Rex."

"I hope so. I'm so tired of this junk with Clarice. She's on a fast track to destruction and for no reason." He helped Cora climb down from the truck, closed her door, and took her hand.

"I know." She squeezed his hand. "But she's no different than we were, Rex. She's young and she's living life wild and crazy."

"I know. Her wildness involves the opposite sex, though. She has no idea what kind of damage she's doin' to her body and to her future. Not to mention to Mom and Dad."

"Let's go get this over with and go home. Maybe she's already made it there."

When Cora and Rex entered the police station, Cora's eyes immediately went to a crying mother in the corner with a female officer. Then she saw a drunk in overalls singing. She squeezed Rex's hand tightly. They walked to the clerk's desk.

"Can I help you?"

"Yes, I want to report a missing person."

"Okay. Let me see if we've got a detective on duty. Have a seat over there, and I'll call you when we have someone available."

Cora and Rex sat on the bench against the wall. She shivered. Rex leaned forward. "Are you cold?"

"No. I have a tendency to shake when I'm tired. My body always gets the chills."

"Hi, can I help you?"

Cora and Rex stood to greet the detective in the black suit. Rex held out his hand.

"Detective Ikeson?"

"Yes?"

"We met a few months ago at the hospital. I was kidnapped."

"Ms. Buchanan?" His blue eyes widened in recognition. He offered his hand.

"Yes, sir. How are you?" Cora reached for his hand.

"I'm doing well. And you?"

"Much better. Rex, this is the detective that handled my kidnapping case."

"Hey, Ike. Good to see you." Then Rex turned to Cora. "We go to church together."

"Oh, I didn't realize it. When I met you in the hospital, you didn't seem to know the O'Reillys. I would have never guessed."

"Yes, I know them, formally. I know Rex better, though."

"What a small world. I didn't know you went to the church. I've never seen you there."

"I haven't been much lately. The missing girls' cases have been dominating my time." He ran his hand across the back of his neck.

"I hate that." Cora looked into his tired eyes and almost hated to tell him about Clarice.

"Me, too. So what can I do for you? Let's head back to my office."

They walked down the pale blue hall, decorated with awards and tributes, towards the back of the station. Their feet clacked on the tile floor. Rex talked as they walked. They entered Detective Ikeson's office and he offered them the two seats across from his desk as he opened a drawer and pulled out a three-part form. "How long has she been missing?" He rolled up his dress shirtsleeves.

"Just since this afternoon. I know that's hardly long enough to be considered missing, but no one has seen her. She's not with friends and no one knows where she might be."

"I see. Did she have an argument with your parents?" He took notes as they talked.

"Not today. Not that I know of. I mean, they're always fightin' or disagreein' about something, but that's normal with her age." Rex looked at Cora.

"I know your parents have been worried about her. Let's write down all the places you looked for her and a list of her friends. They might tell us things they won't tell you guys. Is there anything else you can think of that would help us find her?"

"She had recently met someone from the base, but I didn't catch his name."

"What about you, Cora?" He turned his eyes to her.

She shook her head. "She and I weren't that close. She's been a little mad at me for a while because I didn't bail her out of trouble with the O'Reillys. I actually went home for a while and came back recently. I haven't seen her much since my return."

"Okay." Ikeson continuously wrote as he listened. "We've had a total of seven missing girls since your kidnapping. None of them has been recovered yet. But we're very close. Very close." He leaned back in his chair.

"Anything you can share with us that might help us find my sister? Is it someone connected to Wild Bill's?"

"A lot of the info I can't really share yet. We're trying to keep the details away from the public. We don't want to compromise the investigation and we don't want a lot of false confessions or copycats."

"You're right." Cora let her head rest against the wall. Her bones ached to the core. Her feet throbbed. Her mind drifted back to the shack she had been held captive in and the terrifying escape. She rubbed her wrists. "Do you know if the others fit my description?"

"Some did. Some didn't."

"What's the common denominator then?" Rex's dark eyes stayed glued on the detective.

"I'm not sure. The missing women are not all from out of town. They aren't all dark-headed. They didn't drive cars like yours. They didn't stay at the inns or at the ranch. I don't have any way of knowing if they all went to Wild

Bill's, but I suppose it's highly likely. That's the main gathering place around here. Have you felt like you were being watched?"

"No. I mean, I haven't even thought of it…much. I guess I did think about it when I first came back, but I've tried not to worry. Should I be worried?"

"I don't think so. If this person was after you specifically, then he or she would have already come after you again." He looked back and forth from Rex to Cora.

"Ike, help me find my sister."

"I'll do all I can. Are you sure she didn't just leave home?"

"Nothing's missing from her room."

"Are you sure she isn't home now?"

"I called Matt. He said she's not there."

"Okay. What about the usual roads she travels?"

"I don't know. We never know where she is half the time."

"Does she have a credit card or debit card she uses?"

"I'm sure she uses Dad's card. The girl has never earned a dollar of her own."

"Okay. I'll need that card info so we can run a check on any purchases she may have made."

"Okay. I can call home and get Matt to look for it. I don't want to wake Mom and Dad."

"Rex." Cora put her hand on his arm. "I'm sure they're still awake."

"You're probably right."

While Rex got the card information and talked for a minute with Matt, Cora discussed the cases with Ikeson. "Cora, are there any other details you can think of that might help us find Clarice?"

"No. Seriously, I wasn't close to her. She really likes going out. I'm a homebody."

"Ike, I got that card number for you and Clarice's tag number. Her car has a tracker on it."

"Okay. I'll go get a deputy to start tracing her purchases and we'll see if we can locate her vehicle with the GPS. You guys sit here and think. There's coffee in the break room down the hall." Ikeson walked out of the office calling a deputy's name.

"Thanks."

"Do you want some coffee, Rex?"

"Yeah. I'll go get us some."

Cora put her hand on Rex's arm. "No, you sit here. I'll go."

"Thanks."

Cora left Ikeson's office and headed to the break room. The fluorescent lights made her eyes burn. Or was it the fact that the clock on the wall over the microwave read 3:00 a.m.? *3:00 a.m.—dead in the middle of the night. If she's out there somewhere, Lord, please keep her warm...and safe.* As Cora walked back to the detective's office, she saw him huddled up with a deputy. The look in his eyes as they talked sent a shiver down her spine. She went into the office and handed Rex the coffee and some sugar and creamer packets.

"Thanks."

"Any news while I was gone?"

"No. Any while you were out there?"

"No."

Ikeson came back into the office, buzzing around much like a used car salesman. "Okay, so we may have a lead or two."

Rex sat up in his chair. "What?"

"It looks like she went shopping this afternoon at the outlet mall in Lewistown. So we know she didn't stay in Southern Hope."

"Okay."

"And she got gas at Millburn's Station after eating lunch at the pizza place."

Cora sat quietly, taking it all in.

"What about my sister's car?"

"They're trying to locate it now. With the technology these new cars have nowadays, it won't be hard to find it."

* * *

At 4:30 a.m., Ikeson came into the lounge where Rex and Cora snuggled with each other on the couch. "Rex? Cora?"

"Yes, sir."

"Yeah, Ike."

"We've located Clarice's car."

"Where?"

"Over on Cherry Tree Path back behind town."

"Okay. And Clarice?"

"No. We haven't located her yet. We've got a search party going." Detective Ikeson's brow furrowed, as he stroked the top of his buzzed head.

"Where is that exactly? Cherry Tree?"

"It's near where you we're located, Cora." He looked at her.

"Oh, my gosh! It's the same guy, isn't it?" She stood and began to pace.

"We don't know that for sure, but probably. Yes."

"Ike, I'm goin' out there to find Clarice. I can't sit around and wait anymore. Mom and Dad are gonna want some answers."

"Okay, Rex. But you'll need a walkie-talkie to take with you."

"I'm going too, Rex." Cora straightened to prepare for the argument.

"Okay." He did not argue.

* * *

When they opened the door to the police station, the fall air hit them directly in the face and sucked the breath out of them. "Rex, we may have to stop by the drug store and get some gloves."

"I've got some in the truck. There's an extra pair you can wear."

"Do you want me to drive?" She looked at his tired eyes and stubbly face with concern.

"No. I know how to get us there quickly through some old roads we used to take to go huntin'."

They climbed into the truck. Rex cranked it, put it into reverse, and squealed out of the parking space.

"Rex, please slow down. The last thing you need is a ticket...or a wreck."

"Sorry." He offered a weak smile.

"I wonder if they checked the shack where I was. I can't believe this. It's all so surreal."

"I hope that's the first place they checked. This just makes me so mad. It seems like they would have thought to keep an eye on that place all along." Rex pressed his foot heavier on the pedal.

Cora took in a deep breath and held onto the door handle. "Maybe they have been. I can't imagine how hard it's been for them since the girls don't have anything in common."

"Don't defend them, Cora." He jerked his head in her direction and glared at her.

"I'm not, Rex." Cora's eyes flooded with tears.

"I'm sorry...again. My nerves are shot."

"I know." She turned and looked out the window, her heart in her stomach.

"I'm gonna call Matt while we're on the way." Rex pulled his cell phone out of his shirt pocket and pressed a speed-dial number.

Matt answered on the first ring.

"What's up, Bro?"

* * *

The flashing police lights led the way to the scene. Cora held tightly to the door handle, remembering the last time she had been on this road. Even in the dark, she remembered it. Rex stopped on the shoulder of the road, and they both jumped out of the truck. Ikeson pulled up behind them, the night air sucking their breath away.

"Any luck?"

"Sir, we've got dogs out trying to track her now. We found her purse in her car and the keys still in the ignition. We don't think she left the car of her own will."

"Oh, Rex." Cora let out a cry and covered her mouth with her hands to contain the scream that threatened to escape. Rex grabbed her in a bear hug. "I'm sorry, Rex. I'm trying to be strong."

"It's okay, Cora. I feel the same way." Then he pushed her away from him and placed his hands on her shoulders. "We've got to stay strong for her, though. She's out there, and we have to help the police find her."

"Okay. Okay. Sorry. Where do we start?" Cora turned to Ikeson.

"We're combing the woods over here right now. Take these flashlights and your walkie-talkie and start searching," Ikeson said.

They combed the woods inch by inch to no avail. "Clarice! Clarice! Can you hear me?" Cora called repeatedly. The pine cones crunched under her feet, causing the memories to flood her mind. *Lord, please give me the strength to do this.* She forced the fear back down her throat—choked it down like a big pill. She shivered uncontrollably, the battle between her body temperature and her nerves raging. Her eyes threatened to shut and her feet barely marched on, but she continued to defy nature. *Lord, please help us find her. She could be anywhere in these woods. Or nowhere near. We can't find her without you pointing the way.*

"Cora?"

The voice startled Cora out of her prayers. "Yes, Detective?"

"I want you to stick close to Rex. I'm not 100 percent sure you're safe out here."

"What do you mean?" Her eyes widened in the dark.

"Truthfully, you're the only escapee we know of. The guy could still be out to get you. Stay close to Rex. It will make me feel better."

"Yes, sir."

The detective walked away, and Rex joined Cora. "Cora?"

"Yeah?"

"I don't have a good feeling about this."

"Rex, don't doubt. God is going to help us find her. He is our shepherd, and he'll lead us."

"Oh, I know he's gonna help us find her. But I don't think she's gonna be alive."

"Don't, Rex. Don't." Cora shook her head back and forth.

"Cora, I'm not being negative. I'm being realistic."

"But God..."

"I know, Cora. But Clarice has been puttin' herself in harmful situations when she's known there was a kidnapper out there. You even warned her."

"I don't want to talk about it with you. I'm not giving up hope. Clarice! Clarice! Can you hear me? It's Cora!"

"Over here!" a woman's voice called in the distance.

Rex and Cora turned immediately toward the voice, along with the rest of the search team. They followed the flashlights to the source of the call.

"I found these shoes," the woman said, regret heavy in her voice.

Cora shined her flashlight on the shoes. "Those are Clarice's. I saw her with those on one day last week." The weight of a thousand pounds rested on her chest.

"Are you sure?" Rex studied her in the glow of his flashlight.

Cora nodded.

"Okay, let's keep looking. Let's don't slow down. The dogs are leading us this way." Ikeson pointed and everyone followed.

In the distance, a single light glowed in a window of a small cabin. The dogs began to howl and bark out of control and pull at their leashes.

"Silence these dogs! Get them out of here! We may have found what we're looking for," Ikeson commanded.

Immediately the task force team led the dogs away. "Whose cabin is that? Does anybody know?"

"I don't know. According to our map, no one lives out here this far. Maybe a few hunting cabins, but no year-round residents that I know of," a deputy answered.

"Let's go! My sister could be in there." Rex charged off.

"Rex! Come back. This could be a hostage situation. You don't want to jeopardize Clarice's safety or her life."

Rex's shoulders slumped and Cora ran over to him. "Rex, we've got to follow his lead. Listen to him."

"Okay." He held up his hands in surrender. "You're right." His breath puffed repeatedly from his mouth in a fog.

"I want all civilians to stay right here. You do not go any further. Do I make myself clear?" A chorus of yeses rang out. "Rex?"

"You have my word."

"Okay. Good. I'm going to hold you to it. I'll call for you when it's clear for you to come closer. Cora, keep an eye on this guy."

"I will." She smiled weakly.

19

At 5:37 a.m., loud shots rang in the distance coming from the cabin. Rex bolted as fast as he could and Cora trailed behind him, trying to find her way through the thicket. She tried to call for Rex, but her breath refused to come from her frozen lungs. *Now I know what a deer feels like when it's being stalked by a hunter.* Cora followed Rex onto the dark unfamiliar porch of the cabin. This was not the place she had been held captive.

Ikeson came out of the door in time to stop Rex from entering. "Wait, Rex." He held his hand to Rex's chest.

"No, Ike, let me in." Rex pushed.

"No! And don't think I won't arrest you."

"Please?"

Ikeson kept his hand to Rex's chest. "Wait. Come with me over here first. Then I'll let you go in."

Rex and Cora followed Ikeson to the corner of the porch. Cora tried to look in through the door but could not see into the darkness. Rex removed his cowboy hat and wiped his brow. Cora began to catch her breath finally. Hard pellets of rain started to hit the tin roof of the porch.

"Rex, Clarice is in there."

"Okay."

"But she's dead." The words tumbled out of Ikeson's mouth like boulders off a cliff.

Rex let out a wail. Cora's hair stood on end. Rex collapsed on the porch floor in a mound. Cora squatted and put her arm across his back. Tears flowed from her olive green eyes. Her chest grew tighter by the minute. "Rex, I'm so sorry."

"I should have been there. I should have been able to see this coming. I should have..." He slammed his fist repeatedly against the railing.

"Rex, listen to me. There is nothing you could have done. Nothing. This guy has made himself undetectable. He fits in to the area, and no one has been able to catch him."

"Rex, you were just with Clarice today. Things were fine with her. You can't blame yourself for something some creep has done. I wish I had been able to help more in the investigation to stop this guy."

"Y'all listen to me. There is nothing either of you could have done any differently."

Cora sat in silence, replaying the last half hour in her mind. "Detective, what were the gunshots all about?"

Rex looked up at the detective. "Ike?"

"We busted down the door and found the guy in the main room with a knife to a woman's throat."

A siren squealed as an ambulance approached the shack.

"A woman? Clarice?"

"No, Rex. It was another woman."

Rex stood. "I'm goin' in there, Ike!"

"Wait, Rex. Please. The woman is not dead, and we've got to let the paramedics get her out of here. She's lost a lot of blood already."

"Okay." He held up his hands in surrender.

"Detective? Who is it?"

"I don't know yet. We couldn't get her name."

The door opened and the paramedics rushed out, pushing the stretcher. Cora ran over to it. "May I talk to her?"

"Just for a minute."

Cora looked into the eyes of the young woman and immediately recognized her. "It's Mindy, Clarice's best friend! She works at the hair salon. Mindy, it's Cora. They're going to take you to the hospital now. You're safe. You're going to be okay." Tears streamed down Cora's face as the paramedics loaded the stretcher into the ambulance. She turned to find Rex entering the cabin, as the sun lightened the sky. The rain came down lighter than before.

"Rex, wait for me." Cora followed him into the cabin. The smell of blood instantly turned her stomach. Bile rose from her stomach to her throat.

"Rex, I want you to stay as close to the walls as possible. I really shouldn't even let you in here. I don't want any forensic evidence compromised."

"Okay."

"Clarice is in the other room. I'll let you see her, but you cannot touch her or anything else."

"Okay." Rex reached for Cora's hand, and they followed the detective.

Clarice was on the bed covered in a sheet. Ikeson pulled back the sheet to reveal Clarice's bruised and bloodstained face. Rex buried his head in his hands and cried.

"Ike, was she..."

"We won't know any details until the coroner does the autopsy."

"And the cause of death?"

"Stabbing."

"Who was this son of a—"

"Rex! Please. Try to…"

"Try to what, Ike? My sister just got brutally murdered. Who was it?"

"We're waiting on a positive I.D." Ike looked at Cora.

"Oh, no. I can't. Please don't make me look. I didn't even see the kidnapper."

"But we believe you know the killer."

"You're calling him a killer. Do you think he's killed all the others?"

"Yes, Cora."

Cora swallowed hard and let out a heavy sigh. She walked out of the bedroom where Clarice's body lay and went back to the main room. In the faint light of the morning, she saw the body still on the floor where it must have been when they first entered. Heavy boots stuck out from under the sheet. She walked over to the body and looked down at it. The deputy pulled back the sheet to reveal the face of the killer. "Bobby!" Cora let out a scream.

"Get her out of here!"

* * *

Rex, then Cora, climbed out of the truck on the passenger side. The deputy put the truck in park and turned off the ignition. The fog hovered low on the ground, blanketing the ranch in doom. The deputy in the sheriff's car behind the truck got out and joined the others. Rex led the way up to the porch. He reached for the door handle with his right hand and for Cora's hand with his other. He opened the door and stepped in, Cora following. The deputies stepped up behind them. He stopped and turned his face toward Cora. A tear slid down his cheek to his shirt collar. When they entered the hallway, the rush of family flooding in to meet them nearly knocked them down.

"Mom, Dad, let's go into the living room."

"Rex, where's Clarice?"

"Mom, let's go in here, please?"

Rex and Cora sat on the sofa across from R.L. and Pearl. Matt sat in the wingback chair. The deputies stood in the doorway.

"Son, I know there's bad news. You would have called us had there been any word. We knew when you didn't call last night. Just tell us."

Rex broke the troublesome news to his parents and Matt. Matt sat in silence, his fists balled up. R.L. and Pearl wept. As the morning fog lifted and the sun cast its glow, the O'Reilly home settled into a time of deep mourning.

"Hey, Anne."

"Hey, Cora. What's going on?"

"Oh, you won't believe what's happened here at the ranch."

"What?"

"Clarice is dead." Cora began to weep.

"She's dead? How?"

"She was murdered. The guy that kidnapped me kidnapped her. He kidnapped about seven or eight other women, too. The police think he killed them all."

"Do they know who it is?"

"Yeah, it's that guy, Bobby, who runs the gas station in town. He's the one who fixed my car when I first came here. I told you how he creeped me out."

"Oh, yeah. Well, why did he do it? Do they know?"

"No. The police said they're investigating his past. And they would've asked him, but with twenty or so holes in him, I don't think they got to it."

"How did he kill Clarice?"

"He stabbed her. They don't know yet if he raped her or not. What's weird is how Bobby kept asking about my wrists. Isn't that strange?"

"Yeah, that's pretty strange."

"I never thought much of it. I thought he was being nice. And when he asked me out, he acted strange, but I just thought he was awkward."

"I can't believe he didn't try to kill you."

"I think that's why he asked me out. I think if I had gone, he would have killed me."

* * *

Cora sat at the kitchen table drinking coffee with Rex. Susie colored quietly. Jimmy heated up rolls in the oven to go with the ham and turkey and side dishes the church friends provided. Ms. Lottie washed the pots and pans and hummed while she worked. The house buzzed with talking and subdued laughter; people trying to retain a sense of normalcy. Clarice's friends sat in the dining room sharing stories about her.

"The funeral was nice, although the burial was chilly," Pearl said.

"Yes, ma'am." Cora sighed.

"I thought the pastor did a great job, considering," R.L. added.

"Yes, he did." Cora forced a weak smile.

"I still remember the day she was saved and baptized. Don't you, Rex?" Pearl continued.

"Yes, Mama." He walked to the window.

"Cora, she was the sweetest thing."

"Tell me about it, Pearl."

"Well, we had had Vacation Bible School and all week I had watched her take in those Bible stories. She loved the one about Esther getting all the beauty treatments in preparation for meeting the King."

Cora nodded. "That sounds like Clarice."

"Yeah. Anyway, at the end of the week she said she wanted to be special and go to heaven when she died. She was saved right then and baptized in the creek behind the church. I never knew she'd be taken from us so soon." Pearl began to cry.

"I hate she took a wrong turn these last six months or so," R.L. said.

"You both can rest in the fact that she's safe in the arms of God now." *Thank you, Lord, that you saved her as a child.*

"Are you sure, Cora?" Matt asked from the doorway, still handsome despite the worry etched into his brow.

"What do you mean?" Cora tilted her head in question.

"I mean she's become quite the partier lately."

Jimmy took the rolls out of the oven and set them on the trivet on the counter. He began to unwrap the casserole dishes. A lady Cora did not recognize put ice in the glasses.

"Matt, from what I know about God, he would never reject a child of his. True, Clarice was going through a phase in her life, testing the waters and such, but she was secure in the promise she belonged to the Lord."

He lifted his eyebrows and smiled. "I've never really thought about it that way."

Rex turned and looked at Cora. He smiled for the first time in three days. She smiled back.

"Mr. and Mrs. O'Reilly, lunch is ready. Come on and get you something to eat. I'm gonna let the guests know the food is ready." Jimmy put the potholders down and walked into the hallway.

"Thank you, Cook—I mean, *Jimmy*," Matt said.

Cora smiled at the progress he was making.

"Jimmy is right, folks. Let's get ya somethin' to eat. And soon." Ms. Lottie picked up a plate and handed it to R.L.

"Yes, ma'am."

* * *

After the meal, and after the guests left, Rex and Cora put on their jackets and sat on the porch watching the sun move lower in the sky and the fog roll in.

"Do you want to take a walk?" Rex glanced at Cora from underneath the brim of his cowboy hat.

"Sure, if you do." She put her hands in her coat pockets.

"I want to get away from the house for a bit. How about we get a horse and go ridin' for a while?" He winked at her and nudged her with his shoulder.

"Ooh, I don't know." She shook her head. "You know my history with horses."

"Cora, I'm a cowboy. A cowboy without a horse is a sad thing. If I can't protect you on a horse, then I'm even sadder than I thought." He took her hand and led her toward the stables.

* * *

"I'm glad I'm wearing dress pants and not a skirt today. I really would not have let you talk me into this." Cora sat atop the stallion, her arms wrapped around Rex's waist.

"I never would have asked you if you were."

Cora drew closer to the warmth of Rex.

"Next week, we need to get back to our plans for the B&B."

"Rex? This soon?"

"Yes. If we don't get busy with our plans, it's gonna be months before we get everything going. We need something to get us through the winter and through the grief. Matt's dude ranch is gonna take longer to get off the ground so he'll have a pretty good diversion for a while."

"Well, I'm ready to get going on it. Building the extra wing shouldn't cost too much and it should only take six weeks or so. I can get Anne to come up here and help me decorate. She's wanted to come for a visit anyway. She and I can hit the outlet mall and pick out the décor for the bedrooms and the living area. We can let Ms. Lottie help us with the kitchen and dining décor. She can move her own stuff over from her place for her wing."

"You've really put a lot of thought into this, haven't you?"

"The last few days I've had to keep my mind pretty busy."

"I'm glad you're here. Have I told you that lately?"

"Yeah, but I love hearing it anyway."

"Ms. Lottie?" Cora came into the dining hall of the inn, putting her keys in her front jeans pocket and taking off her gloves.

"Hello, Cora. Good to see ya today." Ms. Lottie put a serving tray full of dirty dishes on the counter. "How are ya doin'?"

Cora hugged Ms. Lottie. "I'm fine. How are you?"

"I'm enjoyin' the slow-down after the lunch crowd. Coffee?" Ms. Lottie poured Cora a cup of coffee without waiting for her reply.

"Thank you. So business is still pretty good?"

"Oh, yeah. I'm always goin' to have a lunch crowd. I haven't had too many overnight guests lately but that's normal for this time of year. Not too many people wantin' to stay in middle Georgia around the holidays."

"I guess so. But I'm an exception." She grinned. "So, did Rex talk to you about moving out to the ranch, Ms. Lottie?"

"Yeah, he said something about it." Ms. Lottie walked around wiping off tables with a rag and putting menus back in the holders on the tables.

"Well, what do you say?" Cora sipped her coffee.

"Rex thinks it would be good for me. He's always lookin' out for me. I'm willin' to hear more about it."

"Oh, goodie." Cora smiled and squeezed Ms. Lottie's arm.

"Come over here in the sittin' room by the fireplace and let's talk."

Cora followed Ms. Lottie as she stiffly walked into the room, red and flowery in décor. The fire blazed so hot, Cora removed her jacket. She sipped on her coffee but hardly wanted it still.

"Before we get to talkin' about Rex's plans for me, I want to know how you're handlin' Clarice's death and the fact that Bobby was the one responsible for it and the other women disappearin' and your own kidnappin'."

Cora shivered in spite of the warmth of the room. "To be honest, I knew something was strange about Bobby. You said so yourself. At first, I thought he was just shy and a little odd. Then he kept asking me how my wrists were. I didn't even remember there being anything in the news about my wrists being cut. So how would he have known about that?"

"You're right." She folded her hands across her lap.

"Then he asked me out and you told me to be wary of him. So I stayed away from his gas station as much as possible. But when we found Clarice and I identified Bobby, it's as if a floodgate opened in my mind. I remembered him being the one to tell me which back roads to take that day I picked up my car. I remembered something in the voice of the person who came in the cabin sounding like Bobby. And his eyes—they were so creepy. Kind of like a snake or something."

"Okay, well, we don't need to dredge all that up. The important thing is: you're safe now."

"Yes, ma'am."

"Safe in the arms of my little Rex." Ms. Lottie smiled.

"Why did you warn me about Bobby?"

She sighed. "He's been in this town for years. He's always been the town misfit, but I'd never have thought he could do somethin' like this. I had suspected him of somethin' strange for a while, but it certainly wasn't murder. He seemed to lurk around here a lot, watchin' women who were passin' through. It wouldn't surprise me if they didn't find a whole trail of missin' women leadin' back to him. Consider yourself blessed your life was spared."

"Oh, I do. I do." Cora took another sip of her coffee. "Ms. Lottie, when Clarice was missing, Rex asked R.L. if he thought Clarice would have come to your place. R.L. said she would never have come here. What did he mean by that?"

"Last year, she got herself in some big trouble with a fella she went out with. She got drunk and then wanted to get a room here to have a romantic fling with him. I refused to let her use my place for somethin' like that. She got really angry with me and cussed me out. She actually tried to make me feel bad and tried to blame it on me that she would end up in a sleazy motel with her friend. I not only refused her, I called her daddy and told him what she was up to. He called Rex, and he picked her up. He was in the area and got to her before she could make a mistake with that young man. Of course, they soon discovered she had already been livin' that way and did not stop after that." She shook her head back forth.

Cora squeezed her forehead with her fingers. "Wow. I knew Clarice was into partying and all, but I didn't know she was so open with it."

"She never came around here after that. She didn't really come much before that, but she vowed never to see me again. It would have been tough livin' at the ranch when the B&B opens if she was still alive." She sighed.

"I don't even know what to say to that, Ms. Lottie. I'm sad Clarice is gone, especially before she had the chance to get her life together. But I'm glad you're going to be able to come live with us."

20

The smell of hay, mixed with funnel cake, cotton candy, and corn dogs, filled Cora's nostrils as she walked through the fairgrounds with Rex and Susie. Susie held hands with both of them. Cora could not stop looking at Rex in his cowboy hat with his full beard, which had come in rather quickly. The way he walked in his tight jeans and boots reminded her of Clint Eastwood in one of his westerns. He knew his way around the fairgrounds like she knew her way around the beach.

"What do you think about the fair?"

The evening sky and the bright lights lit Rex's face up in a way Cora had never seen. It was like he was a little boy at the fair for the first time. "I love it. I want to eat everything, though. It all smells so good."

"Yep! That's the thrill of the fair."

"But I'm not hungry."

"So what?" He winked at her. "The fair comes only one time a year. You gotta eat a corndog, then a turkey leg and a fried onion. After that, you get a caramel apple and a funnel cake."

"Don't forget the cotton candy." Susie added.

"You know it." Rex patted Susie on the head. "Then wash it all down with a lemon ice."

Cora stuck her tongue out in disgust. "Oh, Rex, I'd be so sick tomorrow if I ate all that."

"Yep! You sure would." He tripped over someone's soda cup and reached down and picked it up, tossing it into a nearby can.

As they walked toward the north end of the fairgrounds, screams bellowed out from the pink and red spinning ride, swinging like a pendulum over their heads. They passed the guy who made sculptures out of logs with a chainsaw and the 4H displays in the barn. The thing that made Cora laugh the most was the potbelly pig race.

"Yay, Daddy! Look, the giant cow!" Susie pointed to the statue of the dairy cow at the entrance to the barn. She dropped Rex's hand and ran over to the cow.

When they entered the barn, Cora covered her nose with her hand. "Shew-wee, it stinks in here."

"What?" Rex nudged her arm. "Ain't you ever smelled this many animals mixed together before?"

"I don't believe so. I can handle the animal smells. It's the mixture of cow, horse, sheep, goat, llama, chicken, and pig all together with their waste."

"This ain't nothin', love. Wait till you get to the elephants."

"Elephants?"

"Yep."

"Elephants at the county fair?"

"For some reason they have them. I know—it doesn't make sense." Rex let out a rowdy laugh.

"No, it doesn't." Cora looked at every animal as they stomped through the hay on the barn floor. She wanted to touch the baby chicks under the heat lamps, but the sign on the cage said not to. Their fuzzy feathers and little peeps made her giggle. When she got to the Jersey cow and saw the blue ribbon by its sign, she asked, "Rex, what's the deal with the blue ribbon?"

"Oh, this is Mr. Peterson's prize Jersey. It wins every year."

"Do you mean they have competitions?"

"Sure do. Every year. People enter their cows and pigs and chickens and sheep. They have sheep shearing contests and everything."

"Oh, I want a cow."

"We have cows." Rex looked at her quizzically as he put a quarter into the feed machine. He handed the food to Susie and she fed the pygmy goats.

"I mean, I want to have my own cow for the competition."

"You do?" He quirked a brow.

"Yeah, she's pretty. I love her eyes."

"Well, if you want one, you can pick a calf out and have her."

"I can?"

"Anything for my lady."

"Thank you, Rex. Next year, I'll enter her in the competition and win!"

* * *

Anne arrived a few days before Thanksgiving. She called when she was turning into the long drive at the ranch and Cora immediately grabbed Susie up, threw their coats on, and ran out to the front porch. She could hear the Expedition coming down the drive and her heart threatened to leap from her chest.

"Who is it, Cora?" Susie looked up at her in question.

"My best friend, Anne. She's coming to stay for a week or so and help me and your daddy get the new business started."

"Oh." Susie leaped off the steps and started kicking her ball.

"Stay over here in the grass. Anne will be pulling up in a minute, and I don't want you to dart out in front of her."

"Okay."

Anne pulled up beside the house in the parking spot for guests. Cora ran over to her. She opened the truck door and practically yanked her out. "Hey!"

"Hey!" She received Cora's embrace, grunting to emphasize her merriment. "You look great! Life on the ranch has done wonders for you."

"Ya think so? Thanks. You look pretty fabulous yourself. I think you get prettier and prettier each time I see you."

"I wish you could convince some great guy of that."

"You're so funny. You won't find one here. After all, you don't like country boys or cowboys." She elbowed Anne. Anne stuck out her tongue at Cora. "Besides, what about Tim?"

"Don't even go there. That turned out to be nothing."

"Well, did you have an okay drive?"

"Yes, it was fine. The road up from the coast isn't too bad. Eufaula is so pretty. I love the old houses." She stretched her back, cracking her vertebrae.

"I know. They're gorgeous."

Anne shut her truck door and opened the back door to retrieve her duffle bag. She shut the door and looked over at Susie. "So, is that her?"

"Yep. Isn't she a doll?"

"A doll!"

* * *

After leaving Susie with Pearl, Cora and Anne went out back to the pool house. The two almost-sisters contrasted in every way. Cora's dark shoulder-length hair and olive green eyes contrasted Anne's glowing, golden mid-back-length locks and brilliant blue eyes. Cora's skin no longer boasted a tan, while Anne looked fresh from the beach. Anne dressed like a soap opera star while Cora sported her jeans and sweater from the outlet mall. "Great pool. Too bad it's not summer. I'd like to soak in that hot tub, for sure."

"We'll get in the hot tub, and if I'm still here this summer, I give you an open invitation to come back and stay awhile and swim all you'd like."

"Great. But what do you mean when you say, *if* you're still here?"

"I mean, I hope I am, but that's five or six months away." Cora opened the door to the pool house and led the way inside.

"Oh, please. You think Rex is going to let you leave?" They both laughed.

"Wow! This is a great place. Thanks for letting me come for a visit. I really needed the break away from work."

"Thanks for coming. I knew you'd be the person to help decorate, seeing as you're like a design expert and everything."

"Oh, sure I am."

"Well, you are. Plus, I missed you and I wanted you to meet Rex. I still can't believe there was no time for introducing y'all when we were home."

"I know. So where do you want me to put my things?"

"Right in here in the bedroom." She walked across the living room to the bedroom. "You don't mind sharing a bed with me, do you?"

"No way. We've done it for years. No need to change now." Anne nudged Cora.

Cora's cell phone rang. She looked at the caller I.D. "It's Rex." She smiled. "Hello?"

"Hey. Is your friend there yet?"

"Yep, she's here." She smiled in Anne's direction.

"Can I come meet her?"

"Sure, come on over." Cora closed the phone. "He's coming over."

"Oh, goodie. I can't wait to meet him." Anne clapped her hands together.

"He's probably dirty from working on the ranch, so you'll have to look past that."

"Okay, I'm going to go to the bathroom real quick before he gets here."

Cora put a few dishes into the dishwasher and then went into her laundry area. Humming while she worked, she pulled the towels out of the washer with a grunt and tossed them into the dryer, turning it on.

"Knock, knock."

"Come on in. I'm in the laundry room."

"Hey." Rex came in and greeted Cora with a tender tone.

When she turned to see him standing there in his jeans and flannel shirt with his Stetson on top of his head, she held onto the door facing. "Hey." She barely exhaled.

"Can I have a hug?"

"Of course." Cora stretched out her arms.

Rex enveloped her in his arms. He pulled away just long enough to bring his face close to hers. "You're so warm."

"I am?"

"Yes, ma'am, you are. I could stand here all day huggin' you."

"Me, too." Cora pulled away when she heard Anne let out a quiet giggle. She turned and eyed her friend. They exchanged a knowing glance.

"You must be Rex." Anne came toward them with her hand held out.

"And you must be Anne." Rex shook her hand gently and tipped his hat. "Excuse my appearance. Cora tells me you're a decorating master, and you're gonna help us get Apple Springs off to a great start."

"I don't know where she gets the idea that I'm a master, but I'll sure try. I think it's really an excuse to get me up here to meet you."

"I hope you're not disappointed." Rex gave himself a look from the boots up, using his hands to demonstrate the extent of who he was.

"So far, so good. Are there any more of you around here?"

"As a matter-of-fact, I—"

"Let's go sit on the couch and chat for a little while." Cora gently interrupted, not so sure Matt was Anne's type. As she sat with her best friend and her favorite man, her two worlds melded together like sugar in hot tea. The soothing feeling that overtook her at the sound of Anne's lilting voice and Rex's low rumble caused her to relax like she did when she sat by the seashore.

* * *

"So, what do ya think of the family?" Cora rubbed lotion into her dry hands.

"I love them. Susie is precious, just like you said. You've done a great job teaching her the alphabet and her numbers." Anne finished brushing her blonde locks from the tangles of the day.

"She's very smart."

"And you're teaching her here instead of sending her to preschool?"

"Yep. I met some ladies at the park one day and they all homeschool. They told me that kids don't have to be registered with the Board of Education at four. So I asked Rex if I could teach her here."

"That's so great. I love Pearl and R.L. And Jimmy is so nice and such a great cook." Anne put the brush on the nightstand.

"I know. A funny story about Jimmy. When I first started working here, everyone called him Cook." Cora snuggled into the bed and turned the lamp off on her side of the bed.

"What?" Anne snuggled in as well and turned off her lamp.

"Yep. It's as if he was a slave or something. I started calling him Jimmy and eventually they all did."

"So when will I get to meet the infamous Matt?"

Cora shrugged. "Who knows? He comes and goes so much, I never know when he'll be home. He has been here more lately, though, because of the plans to open the dude ranch."

"Are you avoiding me meeting him?"

"Not at all." Cora averted her eyes in the dark, feeling the guilt of the lie creep up to her face.

"Maybe we'll get to meet before I leave."

"Maybe."

"I hate that Clarice isn't here."

"Yep, me, too." Cora stepped around the topic of Matt the same as she would a cow-pie in the pasture. Anne started giggling. "What are you laughing at?"

"I just realized something really funny. I didn't mean to break the mood from talking about Clarice, though."

"What is it?"

"You keep saying y'all and ya and yep. It cracks me up."

"I do?"

"Yep!" Anne teased.

"No, I don't." Cora buried her head in her hands and kicked Anne playfully under the covers.

"Yes, you do. Oh, boy, the Georgia people have already rubbed off on you."

The black night outside the windows slowly began to lighten as the friends fell asleep with words still drifting sporadically out of their mouths. Cora slept like a newborn baby, dreaming of laughter and romance until morning.

* * *

Cora and Anne helped Jimmy set the table, while Rex read a story out of the Children's Bible to Susie. Susie sat on his lap and held onto his thumbs with her little hands. Her pigtails brushed against his chin.

"Read it again, Daddy."

"Again?"

"Yep!" She looked up at him and smiled.

Rex groaned good-humoredly and began the story again. Pearl and R.L. came into the dining room and took their places at the table. "Did you ladies have a good night catchin' up?"

"Besides staying up too late talking? We sure did." Cora yawned.

"Yes, we did. I slept so great. There's something about this ranch," Anne said.

Rex came into the dining room carrying Susie. He sat her down in the chair next to Cora where she always sat and then went to the other side of the table to take his seat.

"Sit by me, Daddy."

Cora's eyes filled with tears. Rex smiled a huge smile and took his place next to Susie. The previous months had fused the father and daughter together.

Matt came in; finishing a call on his cell phone. He poured a cup of coffee from the carafé and added cream. He said good-bye and closed his phone, while stirring his coffee. He looked up, saw Anne, and froze. "Hi." No other words escaped his mouth. He cocked his head toward Cora and then Rex.

"Hi. I'm Anne, Cora's friend from Florida." She smiled.

"Hi." He stared, star-struck, back at Anne. Despite his professional appearance, Matt resembled an adolescent boy viewing a pretty girl for the first time in his life.

"This is my brother, Matt, Anne. Forgive his dumbfounded demeanor. He probably hasn't seen such a fine lady in—well, since Cora came."

Matt smiled, but said nothing. Cora exchanged a wide-eyed look with Rex.

* * *

"So what was Matt's deal at breakfast? I thought you said he was this suave lady's man."

Susie napped on the couch in the pool house while Cora and Anne sat on Cora's bed. "He is! I've never seen him act that way. When I first came to the ranch, he practically undressed me with his eyes. And when we went dancing that night, same thing. That's why I've been reserved about you meeting him. I know how he is. So I'm a little bit puzzled by his behavior." She shrugged.

"Maybe he thinks I'm disgusting." Anne looked at Cora sincerely.

"No way. That's what I thought when I first met Rex, and I was totally wrong. I actually intimidated Rex. My guess is Matt finds you beautiful beyond his league and he didn't know what to say."

"If you say so." Anne lay back on the bed and closed her eyes.

"It's definitely a first for him." Cora reached into her nightstand drawer and pulled out her nail file. She filed a snag that had been catching on things all day. "Hey, when Susie wakes up, let's go over to the main house and I'll show you the floor plans. We'll bundle up, and I'll show you where the wing is going to be added."

"Sounds like a plan."

* * *

Cora and Anne perused the floor plans of the new wing, spread out on the kitchen table. Jimmy made out a grocery list and checked in the refrigerator for needed items.

"Let's go out here and I'll show you where everything's supposed to be laid out." They went outside, the cold wind hitting them in their faces.

"Ooh, it's so much colder here than at the beach." Anne shivered and drew her coat closed.

"I know. But it's supposed to warm up tomorrow. In the high fifties."

"Good."

The two walked around while Cora explained to Anne where the new wing would be.

"Hey, Cora?"

"Yeah?" She turned toward Jimmy, whose head was stuck out of the cracked open kitchen door.

"I'm going in to town. Do you ladies want to ride in with me? You could catch some lunch while I do errands."

Cora looked at Anne. Anne nodded. "Sure, that sounds great." They went back inside and grabbed their things.

* * *

Cora showed Anne around town, telling her about the 4th of July parade, the barbecue, the friendly people. Anne took pictures with her digital camera, using Cora as her model. They ended their walk on Ms. Lottie's doorstep. "Come on, I want you to meet Ms. Lottie. We can eat lunch in here if you want to."

"Sounds good to me. I'm starving."

Cora and Anne walked into the inn and across the foyer to the dining area. Ms. Lottie buzzed around, smacking her chewing gum—apron around her waist and order pad in her hand. She saw Cora and waved, pointing to a table in the corner. Cora smiled and waved back, then headed to the table, stopping to say hello to church friends along the way. When Cora looked up to find her way to the table in the corner, she burst out laughing. Rex and Matt sat at the table, unaware that the two women headed their way. *Ms. Lottie must have thought we were meeting them here.*

"Good afternoon, gentlemen. Fancy meeting you here."

Rex and Matt both stood, Matt's chair nearly tipping over. His face turned red at the sight of Anne. Rex smirked at Cora, vividly showing the laugh lines in the corners of his eyes. "Please join us, ladies."

"Yes, pl-please." Matt straightened his shirt collar and made sure the shirt was tucked in properly.

"Okay, sure. If you don't mind." Cora sat next to Rex.

"Hi, Anne. Nice to see you again." Matt pulled the chair out beside him for Anne.

"Hey, kids. How are all of you doin' today?" Ms. Lottie patted Cora on the arm and winked at Rex.

Everyone answered in a chorus of greats and fines.

"Ms. Lottie, do you need help today? It seems pretty busy in here." Cora scanned the dining room.

"Thanks, baby. No, I'm taken care of today. Two of the college kids home on holiday break are helpin' me out. Not as good as you did, of course." She pinched Cora's cheek.

"Okay. Just checking. This is my friend Anne from home." Cora held out her hand in Anne's direction.

"It's nice to meet ya."

"Nice to meet you, too. I've heard so much about you." Anne smiled.

"Oh, I hope it was all good. What can I get for ya?"

"Cheddar potato soup." Anne closed the menu.

"Me, too." Cora grinned at Ms. Lottie.

"I'll have your meatloaf, Ms. Lottie."

"Okay, honey. Matt, what do you want?"

"I'm gonna have the fried chicken."

"Okay, I'll be right back."

* * *

As the four of them ate their lunches, they discussed the plans for the B&B. Matt shared his ideas for the dude ranch between bites of fried chicken. Rex occasionally pressed his knee against Cora's at the boyish grin on Matt's face.

"Hey, Anne, are you gonna be here for Thanksgiving?" Matt fidgeted with his napkin.

"I guess that depends on whether or not Cora is going home for a visit and if she still wants my help around here." Anne boldly directed her blue eyes at Matt.

"I could sure use your input on the bunkhouse, if you can spare the time." Matt's face reddened.

"I'd love to help." Anne patted Matt's forearm, lingering there a moment. "Cora, are you going home?"

"No, I'm staying here. I wouldn't have invited you here so close to the holidays if I was going home. Mom and Dad are coming up for Christmas so I'll be here."

"Well, you have to stay for Thanksgiving. We're havin' Rex's turkeys." Matt gave Rex a whack on the back.

"Rex, did you hunt them?" Anne sipped a spoonful of soup and directed her gaze to Rex.

"No, I raised them."

"Then I guess I'll have to stay."

"Can you take time off work?" Matt spread butter on his biscuit, glancing at her.

"I'm self-employed, so, yes." Anne looked quickly in Cora's direction.

"Good. That will be fun." Matt blushed again.

"All of our aunts, uncles, and cousins come, and we have a big family gathering." Rex salted his green beans.

"It takes more than one of Rex's turkeys, that's for sure."

Cora ate her soup and watched the casual, complimentary exchange between the brothers. Her heart swelled with joy at the changes since she'd first arrived at the Southern Hope.

* * *

"So, what's up with Matt?"

"I think he's been bit by a love-bug."

"Seriously! I've never seen him like this."

"You've never seen him like this? I've known him his entire life and never have seen him like this."

Cora and Rex sat in her living room whispering while Anne took a shower and got ready for bed. "I've seen a lot of change in him since I got back from Florida."

"Me, too. He's changed a lot since Clarice died. I think he saw that living life in the fast lane is dangerous."

"I hope so. Do you know much about his past with women?"

"No. I know what he wanted us to think, but I don't know if he acted upon most of it. Why?"

"I don't want Anne to get involved with him if he's just playing with her or trying to have a fling while she's here. She'll likely come back again, and I don't want any weirdness between them to mess up what we've got going."

"I'll talk to him and make sure he stays away from Anne if he's just messin' with her."

"Thanks." Cora placed a sweet kiss on Rex's cheek.

Rex put his arm around Cora's shoulder and leaned his head against hers. Cora snuggled closer. "Do you want to go out to the cabin with me to put Susie to bed? We can have some hot chocolate by the fire."

"I'd love to. But I don't want to leave Anne alone."

"Go ask her if she cares. I really want to spend some one-on-one time with you." Rex stared into Cora's eyes deeply, as he did when he came to get her in Florida.

Cora stared back, hesitantly. Her body began to tremble at the thought of being alone with Rex, really alone. "I'm not so sure that's such a good idea."

"Cora, please?" He rubbed his finger along her wrist.

"Okay. Let me go check with Anne."

* * *

Cora came out of her room from talking with Anne with freshly brushed hair and changed clothes. She grabbed her keys. "Come on. Let's go before I change my mind."

Rex looked at her keys in her hand. "You drivin'?"

"Yep. If we're putting Susie to bed, you won't want to leave her to bring me back."

"Good thinkin'." Rex tapped his finger on his forehead. "Let's stop in at the house and get Susie."

"Sounds good."

* * *

"This place looks so homey now."

"That's right. You haven't been back out here, have you?"

"No, you haven't invited me until now."

"For good reason." His eyes widened.

"So what makes tonight any different?"

"I need to spend some time with you...alone. I want to talk about things that don't involve the B&B or Clarice or the dude ranch or anything else. I want to have a little Rex and Cora time."

"Okay. I'm up for it."

"Susie, go get a book and I'll read you a story."

"Okay, Cora."

"But, first, go pick out a clean nightgown from your top drawer and get dressed for bed. Then bring a book in here."

"Yes, sir." Susie scampered off to her room down the hall.

"And go ahead and brush your teeth, too."

"Yes, sir."

"Rex, you're doing such a great job with her."

"Thanks. I hope so. I'm determined to be her daddy and not a big daddy like dad was to Clarice. I want Susie to learn to be responsible and unspoiled."

"It looks like you're off to a great start."

Rex started a fire in the fireplace and then went to the kitchen to heat milk for the hot chocolate. Cora watched him walk to the kitchen and listened to his boots hit the hardwood floor with force. *A tender man in a rough man's body.*

Susie ran into the living room from the hallway and pounced onto Cora's lap. "Yay! A fire!"

"Yes, ma'am, but you're only in here for one story. So you'll get to enjoy the fire for a bit."

"I want to roast marshmallows, Daddy."

"Not tonight."

"But Daddy…" Susie puckered her mouth.

"Susie, I said not tonight. Do you want to lose story time?"

"No, sir."

"Okay then."

* * *

After Susie's story, filled with Rex's deep villain voices and soothing princely expressions, along with Cora's pleasant princess impersonations, Cora and Rex said good night to Susie.

In the kitchen, Cora spooned three heaping spoonfuls of hot chocolate mix into her mug and added the steaming milk. Rex stood beside her doing the same. He opened a bag of mini marshmallows and offered them to Cora. She looked at the bag, then up at him, reaching in to grab a handful of the sweet treats. She sprinkled the marshmallows on top of her hot chocolate and stirred again. She followed Rex into the living room.

Rex pulled the cushions off the couch and laid them on the floor in front of the fire. He took the cushions off the loveseat and leaned them against the coffee table. He turned on the CD player and music softly played. They sat down in front of the fire and drank their hot chocolate. Cora let out a sigh as she relaxed in front of the fire. The popping and crackling soothed them. Cora took another sip of her hot chocolate and then gazed up at Rex.

"Come here."

"What?"

"Come here." Rex leaned toward Cora as she leaned toward him. He kissed her softly, and then moved away.

"What was that for?" She smiled.

"You had marshmallow cream on your lip." He winked at her.

"Well, thank you for aiding me with that."

Rex put his mug on the floor beside him and removed his boots. The reached over to slip off Cora's shoes. He rubbed his socked feet against hers. A sound escaped Cora's throat that she was sure had never done so before.

"I love you, Cora."

"I love you, too, Rex."

"It's so hard for me to believe that half a year ago my life was goin' down the drain and now I have you and things are the best they've ever been."

"Well, I didn't do anything. Just showed up here with a bunch of baggage of my own and wanted a place to fit in. I never intended to change anyone's world. I selfishly wanted my own world changed."

"I think we both got a lot of prayers answered."

"You're right about that."

Rex got up and poked the fire. Cora went to the kitchen and fixed another mug of hot chocolate for each of them. When she came back in, Rex was coming from the hallway. She tilted her head in question.

"I went to check on Susie."

"She's doing okay?"

"Sound asleep."

"Good."

Rex sat back down next to Cora, the smell of his cologne wafting in front of her nose. He sipped on his hot drink. The thoughts that ran around in his head remained a mystery to Cora, but she knew they were there just the same. "What's on your mind, Rex?"

"What do you think you're gonna do with your money from the life insurance?"

"What?" She raised the corner of her upper lip.

"I mean, I know it's none of my business, but I'm curious about what you plan to do with it all."

"I want to buy a new car—something that will hold more passengers and something more practical."

"That will take about $25,000.00," he figured.

"I bought a computer and some clothes and gave some money to the church. I put some of it in securities for my retirement."

"You're not plannin' on takin' any big trips or anything?"

"Not by myself." She smiled at him. "I've been thinking about finishing my degree online."

"That would be good. I've thought about gettin' my degree, but I don't know what this old cowboy would study."

"You make yourself sound so old. I don't really know what I want to major in either. But up until this point, my life's been one left turn after another in a busy intersection. I've spun my wheels like your tractors out there in a muddy field. I want my life to have real purpose."

Rex cleared his throat. "Deep. What else do you plan to do?"

"I don't really have any other plans right now. I love being here, and I'd like to stay and get the B&B off the ground."

"And then?"

"Then? Well, that depends on if you decide to kick me off your property. He he." Cora finished the last sip of her cocoa and put her mug on the coffee table behind her.

Rex got up and stoked the fire. Cora watched the muscles in his strong shoulders. When he sat back down next to Cora, he asked, "Will you stay six more months?"

"Sure."

"Nine?" He placed a kiss on her mouth.

"If you want me to."

"Twelve? Will you be here next Christmas?" He placed another kiss on her lips and lingered there.

She answered while his lips still touched hers. "Yes, if you want me."

"I want you." Rex pulled her close to him and they kissed until Cora was sure she heard the violins she always heard in movies. They kissed and hugged until they were exhausted.

* * *

Cora felt a chill spread through her body all the way to her toes. She stretched and opened her eyes. She looked around at the unfamiliar room and rubbed her eyes, while wincing at the pain in her hip. She sat up and gasped at her surroundings. Next to her on the cushions on the floor was Rex, sound asleep. She looked down at her body and let out a sigh of relief to see she still had her clothes on. The extinguished fire and lack of a blanket caused the cold she felt.

She reached to get her shoes quietly and planned to sneak home without waking Rex or Susie when her cell phone buzzed. She grabbed it off the coffee table and ran into the kitchen as quickly and quietly as she could. She opened the phone and read the name of the caller. Anne. "Hello?" she whispered.

"Cora? Where are you?"

"I'm at Rex's." Cora pulled back the curtain and looked out the kitchen window to see if anyone was outside.

"Cora!"

"I know. I just woke up on the floor in front of the fireplace."

"Well, breakfast is in forty-five minutes."

"It's 7:15 a.m.?"

"Yes."

"Okay, okay. Oh, my gosh! Rex missed feeding. I can't believe this." She ran her fingers through her hair frantically.

"Did you guys—"

"No! We fell asleep in front of the fire. I'll be right there." Cora closed her phone and tiptoed out of the kitchen, reaching for her coat on the back of the couch.

Rex rolled over and sat up with a jolt. He looked around, as confused as Cora had been a few minutes before. Cora let out a quiet giggle. He turned and saw her standing by the door and jumped up, wiping sleep from his eyes. "What happened?"

"My guess is we fell asleep making out last night."

"Boy, I must be a *real* good kisser." He straightened his shirt.

"*You?* The same goes for me. I bored you to sleep."

"It's probably a good thing we fell asleep, huh?" He shoved his hands in his front pockets.

Cora put her hair behind her ears. "Yeah, I suppose so. Anyway, Anne called. It's 7:15 a.m. I was trying to sneak home."

"Why didn't you wake me up?" His hair was tousled.

"I don't know. You were cute sleeping."

"Well, now I'm behind for the day." He crossed his arms across his chest.

"Sorry." Cora focused on the floor.

"No, it's okay. I didn't mean to sound like I was blamin' you. I'm a grouch in the morning."

"That's okay. I have a feeling Matt or someone else has already spotted my car out here."

"No, I doubt it. No one is ever out here by my house in the winter."

"Are you sure?" She wiggled her brows.

"Yeah."

"That's a relief." She threw her hand to her chest.

"But someone will see you drivin' home." He snorted.

"Great. Caught red-handed and I'm not even guilty."

"Ain't that the way it always is?"

"I guess."

"Well, you go on home and change. I'll get Susie up and dressed. I'll see you at the house at 8:00 a.m."

Cora turned to open the front door, but Rex bolted across the room and grabbed her in a bear hug before she could. "I love you, Cora."

"I love you, too, Rex."

"I had fun spendin' the night with you." He let out a deep chuckle, laced with a slight rumble of nervousness.

"Me, too. But this sleepover can't happen again. Okay?"

"I know. I don't want to do anything to damage your reputation."

"I'm worried about more than my reputation."

* * *

Cora pulled her Camaro up to the pool house, quickly turned off the engine, and jumped out. She ran into the pool house and out of sight at the speed of a spring bunny running from a coyote. When she opened the door, Anne greeted her with a cup of hot coffee, a blanket wrapped around her shoulders.

"Thanks." Cora accepted the mug. Anne burst into laughter. "I promise nothing happened, and I've never spent the night with him before."

"I believe you. What did you do over there?"

"It was the most romantic night I've ever had in my life."

21

Christmas Day

"Merry Christmas, Cora."

"Merry Christmas, Pearl." Cora came through the kitchen door with gifts in hand. She leaned in to receive a hug from Pearl. Ms. Lottie hummed a Christmas carol and blew a kiss in her direction.

"Let me help ya with those."

"Thank you, Jimmy."

Jimmy took some of the packages from Cora and followed her into the hall and to the living room.

"How are you today, Jimmy? And why aren't you with your family?"

"I'm doin' great. I'm stayin' here for lunch, and then I'm goin' in to Columbus for dinner with my family."

"That sounds like fun." They placed the gifts around the tree and then Jimmy headed back to the kitchen. Cora removed her coat and hung it on the hall tree by the front door. She checked her hair to make sure it still looked okay. She turned to go to the kitchen and saw Rex coming down the staircase. Her breath caught in her throat. "Hey."

"Hey."

"Whatcha doin'?"

"We spent the night here last night because Susie was convinced our chimney was too small for Santa." Cora laughed while Rex crossed his eyes. "She's upstairs playin' with her tea set and her new doll."

"Oh, did she like her?"

"Like her? She loves her."

"Good. One day you'll have to tell her how many stores we had to stop in to find her," Cora whispered.

"One day maybe you can tell her." He winked and leaned in for a quick kiss.

She cut her eyes at him. "If you say so." *What does he mean by that? One day?*

"Before we go back into the kitchen with everyone, come sit with me in the living room for a few minutes."

"Okay." Cora heart began to pound in her chest.

Rex took Cora's hand in his, lacing their fingers. His hand warmed Cora's hand like a piece of fresh bread from the oven. In the den, he drew her to sit beside him on the couch. The fire blazed and heated the room to a toasty mid-seventy. Cora's heart warmed as she sat with Rex, holding his hand and watching the fire. Several days without seeing each other had left Cora lonely for him. Time away from Clark could not compare to time without Rex.

"I've missed you the last few days."

"Me, too. Did you get everything done you needed to so your guys could take the holidays off?"

"Yep. We had to really bust it for long hours, but now we can kick back."

"Good."

"So how's the new car doin'?"

"Great! It's got so many features I didn't know about. I love that it's a seven passenger. I can take the kids in my Sunday school class places without having to have other drivers. Plus, the seat in the back lies down and I can haul things. It's great." She wiggled her leg in excitement.

"Is your class the high school girls?"

"It sure is. They're so adorable. I'm really looking forward to working with them. Maybe I can help them not to make the same mistakes I made."

"I was thinkin' about askin' the pastor if they need help with the guys that age. It would be fun to take the kids and do activities together."

"Oh, Rex, that would be awesome." She smiled at the man who had changed so much. Although it was winter, Rex was in the summer of his life.

"I know I should have been more of a big brother to Clarice and Matt. I'd like to have a good and lastin' effect on some kids."

"You already do. Look at Susie."

"What I mean is: teenaged kids. I want to help them solidify their faith before they leave home. So many of these kids grow up in church and are forced to believe what their parents believe. I want to help them embrace God as their own God."

A tear slid down Cora's face and her lips quivered.

* * *

Before lunch, Rex and Cora walked through the new wing. The tiled kitchen boasted commercial-sized stainless steel appliances and a sink deep enough to pile dishes two feet high. The dining hall invited even the weariest of guests to stay awhile and enjoy the hospitality Ms. Lottie provided.

"I'm glad we chose the bright red for the back wall. Aren't you?"

"Oh, yes, I think it really accents the blue curtains, Rex. What does Matt think about it?"

"Why don't you ask Matt?" Matt called out from the doorway.

"Hey, Matt." Cora turned to see the younger O'Reilly.

"Hey, brother. Good to have you home. Did you enjoy your trip away from the ranch for a few days?"

Matt let out a deep sigh. "Like you can't even imagine. Gettin' this dude ranch up and runnin' has about beat me to death. I needed that break."

"Where did you go? I've been so busy and so has Rex. I haven't been here at the house for a few days. I didn't even realize you were gone."

"I went to the beach. I've never been. It was unbelievable." He took off his hat and boasted his warm glow.

Cora noticed the tight jeans and casual shirt he wore. His chin was covered in stubble and his hair had no gel in it. "The beach?" She ran her finger across one of the new tables in the dining hall. The wood felt smooth against her skin.

"Yep." Matt grinned as if he was hiding something.

"Where?" She looked at him again and lifted her brow.

"Panama City."

"You went to P.C.? What?" She eyed Rex and he shrugged.

"Yep."

Cora's mouth hung open and her brain filled with confusion. As she processed the reality of what was going on, she heard a familiar voice.

"Tah-dah!" Out jumped Anne from behind Matt.

"Anne! What are you doing here?" Cora ran over to her.

"It seems I take after my big brother when it comes to goin' after what I want. I couldn't have Christmas without Anne."

Cora let out a squeal. "I wondered why you hadn't emailed or called."

"Sorry." She giggled. "He really surprised me. We spent a few days together, and he asked me to come stay for the holidays." Anne's blue eyes sparkled. "Hey, the place looks great, by the way. Who's your decorator?"

"You goof! I can't believe you're here." Cora grabbed Anne and squeezed her, squealing. She grinned over Anne's shoulder at Matt. "Thank you, Matt." He winked at her.

* * *

"This year has been such an eventful one. I can't believe I've ended up where I am." Cora and Anne sat on the couch in the sitting room by the fire. "I find it hard to fathom that I'm as happy as I am."

"I know. I'm starting to feel a bit the same way." Anne patted Cora's hand.

"God is so good. I still can't believe Matt came after you."

"I know."

Cora stared at the fire, feeling its warmth. She smiled and sighed. Not only was she with the man she loved, and his entire family, but also her best friend sat beside her and her parents were joining them at the ranch for the holidays.

"I can't wait until this evening."

"Why?"

"After dinner, we'll gather around the Christmas tree and open our gifts. I bought special gifts for everyone since I had the money to. But I sent yours in the mail."

"That's okay. I'll get it when I go back."

"And the gifts aren't the most important things anyway. I'm so excited everyone is healthy and happy."

"Except for Clarice."

"Well, she's in heaven, so I think she's pretty happy, too."

"Oh, yeah. You're right."

* * *

"Cora! Come in here!" Rex called from the den.

"What?" Cora yelled, coming from the kitchen with Susie close behind.

"A motor home just pulled up outside. Is it your parents?" Rex pointed out the window at the front yard.

"Let me see." Cora peered out through the fogged up window. "It is! It is! They're finally here!" Cora closed the curtain and ran out into the foyer.

"Wait till they knock, Cora. Don't go out without your coat." Pearl grabbed Cora's coat off the hall tree.

Cora turned and grinned at her and opened the front door anyway. Just as she did, her parents walked up the steps to the front porch. "Mom! Dad! You're here."

"Yes. We made it. I thought we'd never get here." Brenda entered the O'Reilly home.

"This place is beautiful. I had no idea it would be this massive." Walt followed behind his wife, looking all throughout the foyer.

"Mom, Dad, I'd like you to meet Pearl and R.L. O'Reilly. And Rex, you remember." Cora nervously twiddled her thumbs.

"Yes, how could we forget this handsome face," Brenda said.

"It's our pleasure to meet you both." Walt reached to shake R.L.'s hand.

"Meet Ms. Lottie and Matt. And Anne's here. Can you believe it?"

They went into the den to sit by the fire and talk. Jimmy, as the entire family called him now, served coffee, which was a welcome sight to the Sinclairs. Cora smiled at the exchange of pleasantries between her two families.

Susie twirled around singing and playing with her new doll. Brenda beamed when Susie crawled into her lap and started singing Christmas songs to her. Cora noticed Rex watching Brenda with Susie and when he glanced her way, they smiled at each other.

Cora gasped when she saw the table in the dining room at dinnertime, covered in a shimmering red tablecloth and sparkling candles lit as a centerpiece. She ran her fingers across the tablecloth and smiled. The holly and berry Christmas china, trimmed in gold and sitting atop gold chargers, was of the finest from England, as was the silverware and the crystal glassware. Cora sighed happily, knowing the O'Reilly dinner would impress her parents. She could tell by their expressions that they already were amazed.

The meal Jimmy and Ms. Lottie prepared melted in Cora's mouth. Even though honey ham graced the menu, one of Rex's turkeys was the star. The sauces and gravies, side dishes, and desserts disappeared quickly.

After dinner, they all retired to the den to open the Christmas presents.

"Susie, you go first," R.L. said.

"Okay, Papa." She ran to the tree and searched for a package with her name on the tag.

Cora took pictures of everyone as they opened their gifts. Her parents had brought gifts for the O'Reillys, as well as for Matt, Rex, and Susie, too. R.L. and Pearl gave Clarice's gifts to Cora and Anne. Cora's heart threatened to burst from her chest with happiness. In all of her years of life, she could not remember a happier Christmas.

"Now that everyone is through opening gifts, I do have one last gift that needs to be given." Rex got out of his chair near the fireplace.

"Who is it for, Son?" R.L. asked.

"It's for Cora." Rex moved to where Cora stood by the doorway, behind the chair Walt sat in. He took her hand in his.

"For me? You already gave me my gifts, Rex. Nothing more is necessary. Actually, you overdid it." Cora felt the sweatiness of Rex's hand.

"No, I still have one more. Come on over here with me, please, ma'am." Rex tugged Cora toward the fireplace.

"You're arousing my curiosity. What is it?" Cora looked from Rex to everyone else in the room. "Do any of you know what it is?"

204

Cora eyed Anne to see if she knew. Anne shrugged. Everyone else sat still in their seats and smiled. No one admitted to knowing anything.

Rex drew Cora down on the hearth in front of the fire and then sat next to her. "I had a few things to say to you, and I did not want to write them down. I wanted them to come straight from my heart and to be heard by everyone here tonight."

"So you didn't buy me anything else? Good. You didn't need to spend any more money on me." Cora shook her leg involuntarily because everyone stared at her.

"This is my gift. I want you to know I love you. I know you already do know that, but I had to say it so everyone else would know. You mean everything to me. Since I've known you, there has been a joy in my heart I never knew before." Rex shuffled his feet against the brick flooring in front of the fireplace. The fire popped and crackled.

"Thank you. I knew that already because you make me feel so special."

"I also want you to know you have changed my whole family. I think everyone will agree." Rex glanced around, and his family nodded in agreement. "Our lives would not be the same without you. Susie has grown to love you so much. You've helped us all through a terrible tragedy." Susie sat on the floor by Rex, looking up at them and smiling.

"I haven't done all that you say, Rex," Cora murmured. "I've just been myself. Your family has been the one to help me through rough times. If I hadn't had Susie to look after I'd have been lost. And you, well, you're everything to me." Cora felt her face heat up but didn't mind the full room. "And we have Ms. Lottie to thank. She's the one who led me here."

"That's right, I did. And a good thing I did. You've been such an angel to everyone."

Rex took Cora's hands in his, slid off the hearth, and went down on one knee. Cora's eyes flew wide open when she saw what he had done. She fidgeted in her seat. A log rolled in the fireplace and a spark shot out. Rex smothered it with his boot.

"Cora, I want you to always be a part of my life, and the life of my daughter. I want you to remain here with us at the ranch and to be a part of the B&B. That's why I saved this gift for last." Rex released Cora's hands and reached into his pocket. He pulled out a tiny black velvet box.

He opened it and Cora's face paled when she saw what was inside. All of the blood rushed from her head and she steadied herself. There, before her eyes, was a diamond solitaire ring, heart-shaped and set in gold.

"Cora, I would be honored if you would wear this ring and become my wife." Rex took the ring out of the box and offered it to her. His hands trembled.

Cora's eyes filled with tears. She looked around the room to see everyone else. She let out a laugh at the tears. "Oh, Rex, I had no idea you would ask me this. Especially tonight. I have hoped for this for so long. You haven't even mentioned to me that you wanted us to be married since we were in Florida. I had almost given up hope," Cora sobbed.

"Well? What's your answer? I don't have much, but I give you what I have."

"Yeah, answer the poor goof. His legs are goin' numb." Matt winced when Anne playfully smacked him on the arm while she wiped tears from her face.

"Shhh!" R.L. interrupted.

Cora wiped her running nose. "I'd be honored to be your wife. You've shown me you're a wonderful father and a believer in God, and I could ask for no more. You have been so wonderful to me. I love you, and I can't wait to be your wife."

Rex took Cora's left hand in his and slid the engagement ring onto her finger. She grabbed him and hugged him, knocking him to the floor, and crashing down on top of him. Everyone applauded the happy couple. R.L. excused himself for a brief moment. Rex sat up laughing and pulled Cora up as she straightened her hair. When R.L. returned, he carried a silver tray with a champagne bottle and crystal stemware on it.

"Don't worry, everyone. It's sparkling cider. I felt like this called for a toast. I only wish Clarice could be here." R.L. opened the bottle and poured the bubbly, fruity drink. Everyone agreed.

"So you knew?"

R.L. chuckled and winked at her. Everyone took a glass from the tray. Cora and Rex stood with their arms wrapped around each other and Susie stood in front of them. After R.L. made the toast, Susie looked up at Cora.

"Cora, are you goin' to be my mommy now?"

Cora's mouth fell open. She knelt down and gave the child a hug. "Well, I will be your daddy's wife. I will be moving in with you and your daddy as soon as we are married. My official title will be your stepmother."

"Can I call you Mommy?" She blinked her eyes at Cora.

Cora gazed up at Rex and then back at Susie. "Is that what you want to call me?" Cora and Anne's quick glance shared a million unspoken words.

"Yes. I have forever."

"Well, precious, if you want to call Cora Mommy, then you can. She's loved you since she met you. She will be doin' the things your mother used to do but no longer can do because she is in heaven." Rex knelt beside Cora.

"Goodie. I can't wait till you're my mommy." Susie hugged Cora tightly.

Cora walked to her parents. "What do you think? Are you as surprised as I am?"

"Not really. We knew when you left us with this man that you'd marry him. And we also knew that as much as you loved his daughter, she'd love you too," Brenda said.

"Anne, did you know?"

"No, but I expected it." She hugged Cora.

"We also have some news, if anyone would like to hear it," Walt announced.

"What is it, Daddy?" Cora inquired.

"Walt, maybe you shouldn't tell everyone now. It might ruin everyone's evening." Brenda placed her hand on Walt's shoulder.

"Nonsense, you tell us, Mr. Sinclair," Rex said.

"I'm Walt to you, Son."

"Yes, sir, Walt. Please, tell us your news."

"We've decided to retire here in Southern Hope, or at least in Lewistown, to be close to our only daughter. Now that it seems as though she'll be staying for an extended length of time, I believe we have made a wise decision."

"Daddy! Are you serious? Oh, I can't believe it! Mom! Why didn't you tell me sooner? I didn't think I could be any happier than I already was, but I am. You guys are wonderful." Cora jumped up and hugged her parents.

"We wanted it to be a surprise. We sold the house, too," Brenda added.

"You did?"

"Yes. But we kept the beach house. We want everyone to use it for vacationing."

"This is terrific news, Walt," R.L. said. "We've never been to the beach."

Susie climbed into her Uncle Matt's lap and held his thumbs in her hands. Matt kissed the top of her head. Cora and Anne exchanged another knowing look at the preciousness of Matt with the child.

"You let us know if you need any help finding a place to live. You're welcome to stay here for as long as you need to," Pearl offered.

"Thank you so much. You have been so generous," Brenda said.

"I don't mean to change the subject or anything," Anne said. "But when is this wedding going to be? How long will we have to wait?"

"I had an idea of when I wanted to marry Cora, but I thought we should talk about it privately before we definitely set a date. I want to get her full approval first."

"What's the delay?" Matt asked. "Don't you want to get the ball rollin'?"

"Matthew O'Reilly!" Pearl scolded and then winked at him.

"Well, there is a certain musician I would like to sing at our wedding, and he isn't available until spring."

"Spring is fine with me, Rex. I'd marry you tomorrow, but waiting a few more months will give Mom and Dad time to get settled, and we can plan some type of ceremony," Cora agreed.

"Whatever makes you two happy is fine with all of us," Pearl said, and Brenda affirmed.

"And maybe Anne can come and stay for a while."

"I'll second that, Cora," Matt said.

"That won't be a problem. I'm already not wanting to go back home as it is." Anne smiled at Matt.

Cora looked around the room at her family. She already considered Rex's family her own, loving each one of the O'Reillys and her parents more than ever before. She longed to set a date for the wedding and begin their future together. She would be patient, though, for she had grown to know that happiness was worth the wait.

* * *

Cora flipped through her mail as she sat at the kitchen table eating her lunch. Susie sat beside her eating spaghetti rings, an orange ring around her mouth.

"Oh, what is this?"

"What?" Susie took her attention off the bowl full of her favorite lunch.

"It's a letter from some friends I used to live with in South Carolina. They were like my parents."

"Oh. What does it say?"

"Let me see." Cora opened the envelope and pulled out the letter. With the letter was a gift card for the mall. Cora smiled.

Dear Cora,

We love you so much and are so happy for you and Rex. God has been so good to bring new love into your life. We send our best for your blessed day and will keep you in our prayers as you start your new life over. We will not be able to come to the wedding, though, because Ben is taking me on an anniversary trip to Hawaii! We're so excited. Please take this gift card and get you something for your new home. We love you and can't wait to see the pictures. Love, Judy

A tear slid down Cora's cheek. As she put the letter back into the envelope, her cell phone rang. She put the letter on the table and reached into her pocket for her phone. "Hello?"

"Hey."

She smiled. "Hey. What are you doing?"

"Just takin' a break to cool off." Rex let out a heavy sigh.

"From what?" Cora watched Susie climb down from her seat at the table. She snapped her fingers at her and motioned for her to wipe her mouth with her napkin.

"Veronica."

"Veronica?" Cora stood quickly.

"Yep. She just drove out here to see me."

"What did *she* want?" Cora put her hand on her hip.

"Me."

"You? You've got to be kidding." She reached for Susie's bowl and carried it to the sink.

"No, and she was firin' mad that you and I are gettin' married."

"Really? Well, I don't blame her. I'd be mad if another woman stole you from me, too. What did you say to her?"

"I told her I had banished her from my property and that banishment still stood. I told her I was in love with you, and I didn't want to see her again."

"Did you hurt her feelings?" She wiped her hands on the hand towel, while looking out the window at the cows walking by.

"No, way. I don't think that woman has feelings. She's just a sore loser. She already knew we were gettin' married. That's why she drove all the way out here. She just can't stand for someone to have something she wants."

"And she wants you still."

"She wants the O'Reilly name and money."

"I'm glad you chose to stay with me."

"I love you, Cora. I would never go back to that woman. I love you and always will."

"I love you, too, Rex."

22

Today was the day Cora would become Rex O'Reilly's wife. The previous few months had mimicked the long wait for garden crops to come in after the planting season. Cora found the long nights dreaming about her future man almost unbearable.

Over the winter, in preparation for their marriage, Rex completely redecorated the cabin with the help of Anne over the phone and Internet. He and Cora chose furniture, colors, and patterns that would suit them both.

Walt and Brenda purchased twenty-five acres near the city and built a retirement home. Although not completely furnished, they lived there nevertheless. Cora breathed a sigh of relief knowing her parents were close by if she needed them, but not too close, in case she needed space from them.

Matt and Anne's relationship blossomed over the winter. She was very sweet and patient with Matt and his arrogant ways. Cora had given her some insight into how the O'Reilly men ticked. Living on the ranch with all three men had turned Cora into an expert on the topic.

Susie helped Cora with wedding details, looking through wedding magazines with her, and helping her decide on what type of dress to wear for the wedding. Susie also chose her own dress, complete with a wreath of flowers for her head. She had also been very sweet about letting Cora spend time with Rex alone without trying to break them apart. Cora could not have asked for a more loving child. Now if Cora's allergies would clear up from the Bradford pear trees on the ranch, making her scratchy throat and runny nose disappear, she would be completely ready for the wedding.

Rex still kept the identity of the musician a secret. Cora had begged him to tell her repeatedly, but he would not.

* * *

The afternoon sun sank over the mountains as the crisp spring air settled in for the evening. The guests began to arrive—one hundred, including all of Cora's close friends from Panama City. A huge tent in the left pasture housed chairs for guests to sit in and a small platform, where Rex, Cora, and the minister would stand, along with R.L., the best man, and Brenda, the matron of honor.

As car after car arrived at the Southern Hope, Cora got dressed in her bedroom in the pool house. She fidgeted with her veil and the bodice. "Anne, does this look all right?"

"Yes, Cora. It's beautiful."

"Okay." She smiled at her reflection in the mirror. "Hey, are you okay with the fact I asked Mom to be my matron of honor?" She whispered so that Brenda would not hear.

"Of course. Besides, I was your maid of honor before…"

Cora smoothed out the skirt of her long shell-pink wedding dress, and fingered the sequins and pink pearls. The dress, tight against her figure and flaring out like a mermaid's fin at the bottom, fit her perfectly. She turned around several times in front of the mirror to inspect the fit. She wore her long dark hair pulled up in a bun, with a wreath of baby's breath cradling her head. Her bouquet consisted of delicate pink roses, tied together with a ribbon of white lace. Her lavender eyeshadow lit up her olive green eyes.

"Rex won't tell me what he's wearing. Have either of you seen him?"

"Maybe."

"Anne!"

Anne smiled widely. "No, I haven't." She adjusted her bra strap.

"No, Honey. It's a surprise for us all." Brenda, dressed in lavender, said. "Come here, Susie. Let me fix your wreath." Susie twirled around Brenda's legs.

"I wonder if he re-shaved his beard or not. I can't wait to see him. I can't wait till the honeymoon, wherever we're going."

"It won't be long now." Anne rubbed her shoulders.

When the knock came on the pool house door, Cora jumped.

"Cora, calm down, Sweetie. It is only Dad," Brenda said. "I'll let him in."

"Oh, my, you are so beautiful." Walt's eyes lit up. "Cora, you make me so proud. I am so pleased with the man you are marrying. He is truly sent from heaven for you." Susie ran over to Walt and jumped into his arms. "Hey, there, Susie." He kissed her on top of the head and turned his attention back to Cora.

"I know, Daddy." Cora walked over to him and hugged him, enclosing Susie in her embrace.

"Well, are you ready? They want us to head that way now. I brought the car around so you wouldn't have to walk."

"Thank you. I appreciate that." Cora squeezed his arm. "Let's go."

Once outside, Walt opened the car door and Cora, Susie, and Anne climbed in the back seat. He walked around to the passenger's side of the vehicle and let Brenda in. When he got back into the car, he cranked it and slowly drove around the back of the house to the tent. He pulled up at the place designated specifically for the bridal car.

As the ceremony began, the afternoon sun completely disappeared and the moon shone bright and full. Tiki lights and citronella candles glowed all around the tent. A piano and an acoustic guitar played soft music as Matt escorted Pearl to her seat in front, and sat down beside her. From the back of the tent came R.L. and Brenda. They walked slowly up the center isle to the platform. R.L. took his place next to Rex, while Brenda waited for Cora to join her.

The piano began to play the wedding march, and Cora took her first step with her father toward the front of the tent. When she saw Rex, she nearly fainted—dressed all in black, with black boots and a black Stetson on top of his head. She saw the sparkle in his eyes immediately, and knew he found pleasure in her choice of wedding dresses. His freshly shaven face uncovered the strong jaw she loved to touch. When she reached her groom, she bit her lip to keep from kissing him. She grinned at the little drop of sweat on his lip. He winked at her and her heart fluttered.

Before she could think about kissing him further, the minister began the ceremony. The piano continued to play softly. "There's a special bond called love that many of us are blessed to find once in our lives. Rex and Cora have been fortunate to find it for a second time. If anyone here has any doubts about them marrying again, he should wipe them from his mind. Since they've both lost their previous mates to death, they're free in God's eyes to marry again. Their love is as pure as first love—and maybe more. And now, we will have the exchanging of the vows."

Cora and Rex said their vows to each other, exchanged rings, and then the minister turned to Rex. "Rex has a word he would like to say." He signaled for Rex to begin.

"Cora, I know I told you at Christmas I wanted to wait to get married until spring. I said there was a special singer that I wanted to be here."

"Yes, you did." Cora inquired.

Turning to the guests briefly, then back to Cora, Rex began again, "If everyone would try to remain as quiet as possible, and if the musicians would stop playing, you'll be able to hear the song I planned for Cora."

Cora crinkled her nose and eyebrows in confusion. She listened with her ears and with her heart, and heard the song of which Rex had been speaking. Tears came to her eyes as she heard the song of the meadowlark singing from a tree nearby. She knew no one else would understand the significance of this bird, but she did. The song of this bird had first brought Cora and Rex to common ground. She looked deeply into Rex's eyes and squeezed his hand; a tear slid down his cheek.

"Thank you, Rex. I know you had no idea whether or not that bird would sing for you tonight, but you had faith, and it did. I will never forget the beautiful song of the meadowlark, because it has been with us since the beginning—since before we had a beginning."

"I love you, Cora. I hope there is always a song in your heart for me." Rex then turned to the minister.

"Rex, you may kiss your bride."

Rex obeyed the minister without hesitation. The guests applauded as he sealed their wedding vows with the kiss. Matt put his fingers to his mouth and whistled. When Rex finally released Cora, they turned toward their guests.

"It is my pleasure to present to you Mr. and Mrs. Rex O'Reilly."

* * *

Everyone crowded around the blissful couple to say their congratulations at the reception. Cora's eyes sparkled in the glow of the tiki lights as her childhood friends surrounded her, filling her ears with nothing but compliments about her new husband.

"Cora?"

"Ike! How are you? Thanks so much for coming." Cora hugged the detective around the neck. "Rex, Ike is here."

"Howdy, Ike. Thanks so much for comin' today."

"I wouldn't have missed it for the world. I'm so happy for you guys. And a little jealous of you, Rex. You've got the prettiest wife I've ever seen." He winked at Cora.

"Yep. I sure do. And she's all mine." Rex grabbed Cora around the waist and squeezed her.

Once everyone had partaken in the feast, Rex took Cora's hand in his, and moved her to the center of the tent where the two danced the slow two-step to a tune played by the band. The fiddle and steel guitar floated out into the spring night air and the guests joined in the celebration. Rex danced with Susie in his arms and then with Pearl and next Brenda. After over an hour of dancing, guests began to say their good-byes.

"Before everyone leaves, I have a gift for Cora." Rex drew her close to him.

"Another gift? I'm not so sure about this. Every time you surprise me with something, it always knocks me off my feet. Should I sit down?"

"No, no. You stand right here beside me, young lady. Here, open this." Rex handed Cora an envelope, tied with a gold ribbon.

Cora untied the ribbon and opened the envelope, revealing two plane tickets to New York and tickets for a cruise to Bermuda. "Rex! What are these?"

"This is your—I mean, *our* honeymoon tickets. I've never been to New York or to Bermuda. I thought this would be a perfect opportunity."

"Oh, Rex. You're so precious. I can't believe it." She threw her arms around his neck and he spun her around. "I could not have asked for a better gift." Rex gently sat her back down. "I finally have the man of my dreams, and I'm going on the most exquisite honeymoon ever. You have made me so happy." Cora grabbed Rex and kissed him with all her might.

"We leave in two days. I hope that's okay," Rex said.

"It's wonderful. That will give us time to recuperate from the wedding and have a little honeymoon here at home." Cora wiggled her brows at her groom. The guests laughed at Cora's boldness and at Rex's blushing face. "But what about the B&B and everything around the ranch and Susie and—"

Rex placed his index finger over Cora's lips. "Everything here at home will be just fine. Mom and Dad have Susie covered. Anne has agreed to stay and help out with the B&B, and Matt is handlin' the ranch. I mean, after all, a cowboy deserves a break every now and then."

"Thank you, Anne, for staying." Cora hugged her best friend.

"No problem." She grinned at Matt.

Matt smirked at Anne. "Yeah, we'll keep her busy. She'll never even know you're gone. In fact—"

"Matt, wait." Anne held up her hand to stop his words.

"Oh, okay. I get the drift."

"What? What's going on?" Cora looked back and forth from Anne to Matt. She stared at Rex, who seemed just as confused.

"Well…," Anne started.

"What? Tell me!" By this point, all of the remaining guests, plus the family, encircled the two couples.

"Matt asked me to marry him last night!" Anne squealed.

Cora's mouth flew open and she grabbed Anne. The two jumped up and down like schoolgirls. "Oh, Anne! Oh, Matt!"

"Put her here, big guy." Rex held out his hand to Matt.

Matt placed his hand in Rex's, and Rex grabbed him in a bear hug.

The cheers from the family and the guests drowned out the music and the cows mooing in the pasture. Walt and Brenda hugged R.L. and Pearl; Susie grabbed onto the back of Rex's legs. He bent and scooped her up into his arms. Susie reached for Cora and the three shared their first family hug. When the excitement died, the faint song of the meadowlark in the distance filled the ears and hearts of Cora and Rex, promising a bright future.

214

SHERRI WILSON JOHNSON

**All Lydia wants is to travel the world
before she has to settle down with a husband.
But she may not have that choice anymore.**

April 1886

Debutante Lydia Jane Barrington lives a carefree, protected existence on Live Oaks Plantation in Florida. But while her sisters happily learn the traditional tasks of women and talk of courting, Lydia dreams of adventure and independence. Even her friendship with handsome Hamilton Scarbrough isn't enough to hold her back.

Then one day Hamilton opens Lydia's eyes and her heart to love. But before they can receive permission to court, Lydia overhears a secret conversation about an unscrupulous business deal. Worse, it has everything to do with her and her future. Now she's faced with the biggest decision of her life—to concede or to fight. Either choice will require great sacrifice…and, perhaps, countless rewards.

*Passion. Friendship. A bitter enemy. A life-changing decision.
Set in Victorian-era Florida.*

About the Author

Sherri Wilson Johnson: Where Faith and Fiction Collide

SHERRI WILSON JOHNSON has enjoyed creative writing since she was a young girl and strives to bring others closer to God through her work. She loves to write stories that challenge her readers while entertaining them at the same time. She marvels at the beauty of horses from a distance but is afraid of them up close, which makes the fact that this story is on a ranch a bit humorous. She always wanted a candy-apple red 1968 Camaro but never got one, so her main character drives one.

Sherri has been married since 1988 and homeschooled her children from 1997 to 2010. She, her family, and their dogs live in Georgia. A graduate of the Christian Writers Guild *Writing for the Soul* course, Sherri has been published in multiple homeschool publications. She is also the author of two other inspirational romances, including *To Dance Once More* (OakTara), three Bible studyguides, and various other resources for homeschoolers and churches, and leads workshops on homeschooling and various other topics. Look for her next inspirational romance, *To Laugh Once More* (OakTara) soon!

www.sherriwilsonjohnson.com
www.sherrijohnsonministries.com
www.sherrijinga.wordpress.com
www.sherriwilsonjohnson.blogspot.com
twitter.com/#!/swj_thewriter
nicoleodell.com/sherri-wilson-johnson-on-inspiring-purity/
www.goodreads.com/author/show5233294.Sherri_Wilson_Johnson
www.oaktara.com

CPSIA information can be obtained at www.ICGtesting.com
Printed in the USA
LVOW101117251112

308683LV00002B/604/P